Just Right For Him

A FABLE NOTCH NOVEL
BOOK SEVEN

ELENA MARKEM

JGP
Jersey
Girl
Press

Books by Elena Markem

Fable Notch Series

Once More With You
Meant To Be His
This Time For Us
Can't Let You Go
Bring Back Her Heart
What You Wish For
Just Right For Him

Edited by: DogStar Creative Co.

Cover by: 100Covers.com

First edition

Dedication

For Alyssa Montasersky

Who first brought joy and love
to my brother and then to all of us – and Hank.
I'm so very glad you are a part of our family.

Chapter One

As happy as he was for his three brothers, Ryan Sinclair was going to be happier when their weddings were over. But that was still five months away.

He had been more than a little horrified when he'd received the group email months before from Devon Tremont, the woman the brides hired as a wedding planner, asking for his availability so these "Attendants" Zoom calls could be scheduled. It was a way to get everyone involved in the weddings together to make certain efforts weren't being duplicated, people were available for pre-event happenings, and where they needed to be when they needed to be there. Ryan found them ridiculous, but if it made his future sisters-in-law happy, he'd do it.

Can't I show up, smile, and take pictures, Ryan suggested when he messaged his brothers after hearing about the calls. They'd started a group text conversation years before to make communication easier after his father's heart attack. *Tell me what to wear and where to be, and I'm set.*

Sorry, little brother, Cole had texted back. *From everything I'm hearing, there is too much going on, and we all need to participate.*

Ryan was glad none of his brothers could see the scowl on his face when he read the reply. Fortunately, these calls would be done for a while after tonight because the first wedding event was less than two weeks away.

He was thrilled his brothers had found love — or re-found it. Somehow they'd all ended up with their first loves — but he knew the celebrations were going to come with uncomfortable moments. And more than a few of those would be courtesy of his mother.

When they'd asked him to be their photographer, he'd said yes instantly. He'd gotten his first digital camera when he was nine and continued to spend as much time as possible with one, both professionally and personally. After graduating from community college — and leaving Fable Notch — and especially since getting his agent two years ago, he'd been able to make a very comfortable living as a freelance photographer. The more time he could be behind the lens while he was in town, the better.

But first, he had to get through one last Zoom call.

Ryan sat in front of his laptop, staring at the familiar faces from his childhood and the most important people in his life. They didn't always have all three grooms on the call, but tonight, with Theo and Eden's May wedding less than two weeks away, everyone was here. And two days from now, Ryan would arrive in Fable Notch for the first time in over three years.

He tried to stay focused on the call, but his mind kept wandering. The weddings themselves would be fun, and he was looking forward to seeing friends and family, especially some he hadn't seen in decades, like Dani's brother. On the flip side, as soon as he arrived, he'd be directly in the path of his mother's meddling. Once Theo moved back to Fable Notch — followed soon after by Nick and Cole — she'd been dropping less than subtle hints about his settling down and moving home. Ryan had no interest in either.

If he had his way, he would fly in, take pictures, party a bit, and leave. A few months earlier, he'd been on a video call with Cole, Theo, and Nick, who told him he would have to be the best man for all of them so they wouldn't have to choose between one another. He'd thought they were serious and was genuinely panicked until they burst out laughing.

"Oh man, I wish I'd taken a picture of your face," Nick said. "You looked horrified."

"Fuck you," he'd responded, relieved. Oh, the joys of older brothers. He considered the Hansons as his brothers, and they were in every way, except biologically.

Ryan would never forget the day his father, Martin, Fable Notch's fire chief, came home with three local boys. They'd accidentally set fire to the shed in their yard. At the time, Ryan was eight and too young to understand what was going on with the Hanson family, only that their father was gone and their mother wasn't around the way his was. As the months passed, they came around more often. It didn't take long before they were family.

Ryan would do anything for his brothers. Even go back to Fable Notch three times in the space of five months. Fortunately, he was his own boss, and he could manage his schedule so the extra travel wasn't a problem. Taking photos was his gift to them, although for two of the weddings he would turn the camera over to Devon during the ceremony, since he'd be standing at the altar with the bride and groom. He made a mental note to take time with her to explain angles and sunlight, so she'd get the shots he wanted.

"I think everyone has what they need for the next week, right?" Devon asked, and there were murmurs of agreement.

He wouldn't admit it to anyone, but these calls hadn't been as terrible as he'd originally feared. As much as he'd been dreading them, they had given him the opportunity to reconnect.

"Can't believe I get to see you in person again," Xander Vaughn said at the beginning of tonight's call. Xander was Dani's brother, and he and Ryan had been summer friends when Xander and Dani came to town to spend two months with their aunts. "Gotta be what, close to fifteen years?"

"Sounds right," Ryan said, marveling at how much time had passed. Xander, who was two years older, stopped coming yearly when Ryan was sixteen. "Seriously, I'm not convinced all of you have legs."

"Some of us have better legs than others," said Janelle. As Eden's best friend from high school, she was someone Ryan had known tangentially, but he'd come to appreciate her humor and candor. She was good at keeping them on task and cutting through the bullshit. He heard she'd recently gotten engaged, too, to the man she'd been partnered with for a reality show. He had to remember not to drink the water when he got home. There had to be something in it. "Sheridan's are particularly lovely."

As he watched, the woman with curly blonde hair blushed. He couldn't help picturing her legs. Would they be as lovely as her smile?

She was one of the only people he didn't know before the calls started. A bridesmaid for Dani, she'd moved to Fable Notch five years earlier to help Laurel Stewart get her brewery running. She'd liked the town so much she'd stayed to open her own café, which was going to be the site for Theo and Eden's rehearsal dinner. He'd been hearing about her cinnamon rolls for ages, but now that they'd "met," he was more interested in the woman behind the baked goods.

"I don't think any of us can compete with Eden in the leg department," Sheridan said, her soft Southern accent making everything sound lyrical as she deflected the compliment.

Ryan had noticed over the last few months that Sheridan did that regularly. She didn't chime in unless it was in response to a direct question, and he got the sense she was as unsure about these calls and the coming weddings as he was.

Even without her accent and unruly hair, Sheridan stood out to him. Maybe it was the way she always seemed to be listening, regardless of whether she said much. Or maybe it was the way she smiled and laughed. There was something immediately likable about her. He'd caught himself staring at her square during the calls, quickly looking away when he realized what he was doing, glad no one could tell.

There had been one call when they were the first ones on, both of them having missed the message saying things were starting a half-hour later. Fortunately, Devon had opened the Zoom room at the regular time because they hadn't responded to the update message. He was eating dinner, something leftover and tasteless, and Sheridan had just gotten out of the shower, her wet curls framing her face.

She fiddled with them, clearly self-conscious. He couldn't stop himself from thinking of her wet and soapy a few minutes before. "I almost forgot the call. Thank goodness for phone alerts."

He swallowed the bite he'd taken. "Except we both missed the time change."

"Probably a good thing for me, since it's my bedtime an hour from now. I might have skipped coming all together and had Laurel or Dani fill me in later. I am plumb worn out."

Ryan knew Sheridan had early mornings, but it hadn't occurred to him that meant ending her nights early, too. "If you want to pop off, I'll let everyone know. Wouldn't want you to be grumpy in the morning."

"Believe it or not, I typically get grumpy now. Mornings are my best time. I like waking up early." He could tell from her smile that she meant it.

"Guess you're in the right business," he said. He'd looked up the Just Right Café website after the first of these calls. "You open at seven, if I remember correctly."

"Officially, yes," she said, "but locals know I unlock the door at six-thirty in case anyone needs their caffeine hit extra early. Not all the baked goods are ready by that time, but coffee is."

He tried to do the math in his head and gave up. "So, what time do you wake up?"

"Do you really want to know?" He nodded. "Five. I'm at the cafe by five thirty. On Sundays, I sleep in until six."

He groaned. He'd had his share of jobs that started early, but they had an end date. "That's an ungodly hour to be up and going. It's got to be dark half the year."

"And cold. That's what took the most getting used to after being out of the area for several years." From asking, he knew she was from Alabama and had gone to college with Laurel in Rhode Island. "But things warm up pretty quickly once I'm in my kitchen."

It might be fun to warm *her* up. They'd continued talking until the others arrived. He hadn't had any one-on-one time with her since, but he hoped that might change when he was in town. Seeing Sheridan in person was one thing he was looking forward to.

"Ryan, are you with us?" Theo's voice broke through his thoughts, and Ryan realized he'd missed something.

"Sorry, I zoned out. Still trying to figure out what I need to do before I fly out. Should I say yes to whatever you said and hope for the best?"

"He's trying to figure out how many hearts he'll have time to break while he's in town," Nick said, adding a wink to show he was teasing.

"Very funny," Ryan said, shaking his head. Sometimes it wasn't fun being with people who knew your past. Not that Nick was wrong.

Where each of his brothers had given his heart completely — and early — Ryan was more a 'play the field' kind of guy. In high school, if a girl started wanting something serious — and they all seemed to — it was an immediate sign to stop dating them. And while he'd had longer relationships over the years, mostly he kept his heart safe so he could be free to do whatever he wanted for work. Sure, he believed in love and marriage. His parents had been together for almost forty years. Some day he hoped to have what they had, but he didn't see any reason to rush it. He was barely thirty.

"I wanted to make sure you'll be there for the dance lesson with everyone on Friday," Eden said with a smile. Ryan wasn't surprised that as a former professional dancer and now an instructor, she had something specific planned for the reception and everyone in her wedding party had to join in.

He was fairly certain he kept the eye roll off his face and out of his tone when he said, "Wouldn't miss it. Have you decided who the unlucky person is who will be my partner?" There were four men and three women in Eden's wedding party. He'd offered to sit it out to make the numbers even, but was vetoed. "Or am I dancing with Theo's dog?"

Sheridan raised her hand. "That would be me."

Okay, things were looking up. He couldn't tell how she felt, so he kept his response light. "You pulled the short straw, huh? Sorry. I promise to do my best not to make us both look ridiculous."

"Well, I appreciate that, but how do you know I'm not the one who's going to make us look ridiculous?" Sheridan said. More deflection.

"No one is looking ridiculous," said Eden. "Unless you're suggesting I can't teach a group of adults a basic dance."

Ryan and Sheridan mumbled apologies and reassurances. The things he was willing to do for family, Ryan thought, amused by the situation but sorry that his face-to-face introduction with Sheridan was potentially going to be uncomfortable. At least, as far as he could tell, Sheridan was feeling equally challenged by the prospect.

After they reviewed details, the call wound down. Ryan said his goodbyes and closed his laptop, then leaned back in his chair and rubbed his hands over his face. He couldn't believe he was heading to New Hampshire in two days, with plans to stay for over a week. The last time he'd spent that long in Fable Notch was after his father's heart attack. There hadn't been much to do for the nearly four weeks, but he'd come so close to losing Martin he'd needed to be sure everything was fine. He'd stayed in his old room and did as much as he could to help.

And still his mother tried to fix him up with everyone, from his dad's cardiology nurse to the single mother of one of her students. He could not go through that again.

Fortunately, for the wedding trips, Nick had offered him Dani's old house for all three events. He had no idea what to expect, but he knew one thing for sure — his mother was going to be a handful. He wasn't looking forward to the inevitable conversations regarding his love life, or lack thereof. If he were living under her roof, she'd invite women over daily for dinner so he could meet them. He shuddered.

He was pulled from his concerns when his phone buzzed. Turning it over, he saw a text from Theo in their group chat: *Hey man, we're excited to see you. Don't worry about Ma. She's so happy to have all her boys home, even if you don't plan to stay. We'll protect you as best we can.*

Yeah, his brothers understood what he was likely walking into. Ryan appreciated the understanding and responded with a simple, *Thanks*. But as much as his brothers might want to help, they each had lives of their own and wouldn't be available to run interference. Not to mention the fact they were all so in love, they would likely agree with Millie that settling down was the right thing to do.

When Theo had gone home to help Martin with an arson case two years ago, Ryan expected to hear Theo had been successful, but not that he had fallen back in love with Eden and was relocating permanently to Fable Notch. Then, a few months later, Nick had gone home when he had job issues and also reconnected with his first love, Dani, who'd become the town veterinarian. At that point, Ryan joked it was only a matter of time before Cole returned.

He'd been right.

If he hoped his mother would be satisfied having three out of her four sons home, she'd soon proven him wrong. Nearly every call since Cole had returned had included not-so-subtle hints about him moving back.

He sighed. Why couldn't it be *one* of his brothers getting married? If it had been solely Theo, Millie wouldn't be expecting him to change, too. How could he explain to her or his father that as much as he loved them, freedom and flexibility were more important? And he'd had enough experience to know that love and freedom did not go together.

"Give me another ten years, Ma, then I'll settle down," he'd told his mother on their most recent call.

"Ten years?" She'd sounded horrified. He may as well have said a century. He'd always thought that forty would be a good time to scale back the travel — one of his favorite things — and consider having a family, being around more. "I'll never understand how you can always want to move from place to place."

That was true. She couldn't understand. By any account, he had an ideal childhood with parents who showed him nothing but love and support. He knew where home was. Knew he could count on it and his parents being there for him. He could lead what appeared to be a rootless life because he had a base.

He just chose not to live there.

The time for staying put would come and when it did, he couldn't imagine living anywhere but Fable Notch. But not yet. He had no interest in changing his life. It was perfect as it was.

He wondered if there was a way to keep his mother out of his romantic life. Ryan suspected that along with the many other plans Millie was working on for the weddings — including her home being the site for Cole and Mia's ceremony — she was creating a list of eligible women for him to meet.

Too bad he couldn't show up with a girlfriend.

Unbidden, he thought of Sheridan. He liked her humor, her unusual expressions which peppered her speech on occasion, as well as how much she cared for Dani. Whenever Dani appeared overwhelmed, it was Sheridan who was the first to step in to calm her.

He'd also noticed over the last few months that, like him, she generally agreed to ideas that were simpler or required less active involvement from the attendants. And now she'd been roped into being his dance partner at Theo's wedding. He wished he could talk Eden out of including him. Maybe he could convince her he'd be better off only taking pictures.

Still, spending time with Sheridan wouldn't be a hardship. And as he put his laptop away and went to his closet to start packing, a new plan grew.

Chapter Two

The sun was barely up when Sheridan Behr unlocked the back door and entered the Just Right Café. Most people groaned when they heard what time she got up in the morning, but for her, it was perfect. As much as she loved greeting and talking to customers throughout the day, there was something about being here before the world was awake. She'd always been a morning person, which had helped her achieve the goals she wanted, and it was particularly well suited to running a breakfast and lunch restaurant.

She loved having her days start quietly. Turning on the lights in the kitchen, she started the first pot of coffee for herself, then got to work taking out the dough she'd need for her cinnamon rolls, breads, and biscuits, the things she was known for, and which were required for the breakfast crowd. She made the dough in advance, frequently as the last thing she did for the day, so she had what she needed in the mornings. Time management was the second most important thing when running a food business.

The right menu was first, and that was something Sheridan had worked hard on.

When she decided to stay in Fable Notch, she had been very particular choosing the type of restaurant she wanted. It had to be something that fulfilled a need, regardless of overlap between other businesses. The town had a diner everyone adored, including Sheridan. But as she looked around, she noticed they didn't have someone who specialized in baking and that was something she loved doing.

She could get lost in the kneading, mixing, and rising of the baking process, and often did. As she worked the dough, making it even and long across her worktable, she thought over the Attendants call the night before. It was hard to believe after all the planning and talking for the last several months, the first event was coming up. It seemed to Sheridan that everyone in Fable Notch was looking forward to the Hanson brothers' weddings.

Everyone but her.

Okay, that isn't entirely true. There were aspects she expected would be fun, especially the weddings themselves, but she was uneasy. It wasn't that she didn't feel as though she belonged, although there were times she was very aware of being the "newest" of the friends. It was more that social situations focused on love and romance brought out the flirtatious, and sometimes pushy side, in men, and she never felt particularly comfortable in those situations. She'd prefer a girls' night out.

Of the three brides, she was closest to Dani, but since coming to town to help Laurel Stewart when she opened her brewery several years ago, Sheridan had gained a growing circle of friends that now included Eden Barrett who was marrying Theo, and Mia Durant who was marrying former rock star Cole. When she told her Southern friends she was moving to New Hampshire, they had all said she would find the people in the north as cold as their climate, but Sheridan had met Laurel when they were at Johnson and Wales and knew that wasn't true. Sheridan's accent and lingo might be different, but she'd found friends she considered family here. And the distance from her own family was a good thing.

But while she was thrilled for her friends, participating in weddings had never been her thing. Sheridan had been a bridesmaid four times in her life. Once, for a high school friend the summer after they graduated. And three times for her mother.

After Sheridan's father died in a car accident when she was nine, her mother was never able to recapture the true love and good marriage she'd found the first time. Not that she didn't try. Sheridan didn't blame her mother for wanting to find love again but watching her go through marriage after marriage had dampened Sheridan's appreciation for the institution.

Hazel Behr-McLean-Harvey-Robinson believed with every new husband she had found "the one." And to prove it, each time she remarried, she insisted on a lavish ceremony. Sheridan had been a bridesmaid when she was eleven, seventeen, and twenty-four. The first time had been hard because it hadn't felt like long after she and her sister, Paisley, had lost their father. Sheridan couldn't even enjoy the beautiful dress her mother bought her. She and Paisley were happy for their mother, and they liked how engaged she was with them after being in a fog for so long, but they were still feeling their father's loss and not quite ready for the change of a new house, new school, and a stepfather.

That marriage lasted three years. There was an increasing amount of yelling and tension before husband two decided, "I don't need this crap," and left. The only thing Sheridan missed after he was gone was his two children, who spent every other weekend with them.

The third marriage lasted a little longer, and this time, Sheridan and Paisley had three step-siblings in their lives for almost five years, although for much of that Sheridan was at college. Hazel had been in her current and fourth marriage for six years. Any day, Sheridan was expecting to hear that this one was ending, too. Although maybe her mother had gotten lucky and things would work out.

Sheridan didn't hold out much hope. At this point, she had more step-siblings than Laurel had brothers, although she didn't keep in contact with them. She didn't speak with her mother often either. She tried to stay connected with Paisley, but Paisley lived in Oregon and between their busy workdays and the time difference, they rarely spoke. Maybe they should try to have the occasional Zoom call.

The family that mattered to her, who were there for her day in and day out, for the ups, downs, disappointments, tears, and joys, was Laurel, Dani, and the women who hung out together whenever they could. Fable Notch's next generation, so to speak. And if the winters seemed too long, Sheridan had never been happier anywhere. She was grateful for the stability in her life, knowing who she could count on, what her days would hold, and the happiness she'd created for herself.

Shortly before six-thirty, as the smell of cinnamon filled the kitchen, Wesley Howard, her coworker, arrived. That meant it was time to get the first pot of coffee out for customers. "Good morning, Dollface," he said, offering his customary greeting. "You've got flour on your forehead."

She brushed her face with the back of her hand. "Don't I always." She joked she didn't need to use face masks because of the natural ones she gave herself every day.

He gave her a hip bump as he walked past to hang up his coat in their tiny office, then grabbed a mug of coffee and put on an apron. He went to their double refrigerator, took out two dozen eggs, and got to cracking and scrambling them. As soon as those were ready, he prepped the bacon and breakfast sausage while she got icing ready for the cinnamon rolls. When Wesley started working there, the plan was that she would open and he would close, but most days they were both there for at least an hour or two after the last customer left.

Wesley, who'd explained his mother chose the name because she was a huge *Princess Bride* fan, was as much a key to the café's success as her baked goods. When she'd opened, Sheridan tried to do all the food prep along with the baking, using part-time counter help so she could keep things going in the back, but it wasn't sustainable. The café had been immediately popular, and she wasn't able to keep up with demand by working part time in the kitchen, so she ran out of food too often. While it was great not to have leftovers, disappointing customers wasn't a good business plan.

It took a while before she found the right person, but minutes after Wesley arrived for his interview, she'd known he was the one for the job. She liked his sense of humor, his belief that people should live to eat, and his insistence they have the interview in the kitchen while he cooked for her. Proving that he'd reviewed the café's menu and reviews before arriving, he made her a three-cheese grilled cheese sandwich, their most popular lunch offering, and created a delightful side salad from what she had available.

She'd hired him on the spot and hadn't regretted it. In fact, he'd been such an asset, and she was so determined to keep him, that last year for Christmas she'd given him twenty percent ownership in the business. He'd cried, and so had she. He was the big brother she'd never had, and no matter what Laurel said about brothers being a pain, his friendship meant the world to her.

As he continued to prep for their opening, he asked, "Is the menu set for the rehearsal dinner next week?"

Sheridan nodded. "Got the final okay from Eden yesterday." Sheridan had been flattered when Eden asked if she could have the dinner the night before the wedding at the café.

"I know you don't usually cook dinner foods," Eden said, "but I think something simple, like a soup and sandwich buffet, would be perfect. Besides, your café is Theo's favorite place for lunch."

Sheridan had smiled. Theo commuted to Concord four days a week, and most Fridays he came to the café for lunch. Her beef stew was his favorite. "I'd be honored. We can do Italian Wedding Soup and anything else you'd like."

Talking menus and meals was her love language, and she was excited to be a part of Eden's special day in a way that was comfortable for her. It was while they were reviewing the menu that Eden asked Sheridan if she'd partner with Ryan for the group portion of the first dance.

"It's going to start with Theo and me alone, of course," Eden said in a dreamy voice.

Sheridan couldn't help but get caught up in her friend's joy. "Sounds like you have something special planned."

"We do. And it was Theo's idea, which I love." Eden explained she would have been happy to stand there in his arms and sway to "A Thousand Years," but Theo wanted them to really dance together. "When the song changes, we want our wedding party to join us, but we've got an odd number of people, more men than women, so would you dance with Ryan?"

Sheridan had been shocked. She'd known from the Attendants calls Eden had a small wedding party and not many friends from her short time away from Fable Notch, but she hadn't expected to be asked. And Ryan seemed nice enough on the calls, but a dance? While everyone at the reception watched?

She was going to suggest Eden ask someone else — maybe Casey would be up for it even though Casey was involved with Derek Ahern — but Eden looked so hopeful, Sheridan found herself saying, "I'd be honored. Let me know what to do."

Eden had squealed with delight and hugged Sheridan, and Sheridan had been happy she'd said yes. But now tomorrow's dance lesson loomed, and Sheridan was all too aware that she was going to publicly be in the arms of a man she barely knew.

Deciding to keep her focus on what she could control, Sheridan pushed away thoughts of the wedding as she put out the first pots of coffee and unlocked the front door. The sign still said closed, but she had a few early customers who needed their caffeine before commuting, and she was more than happy to help them have a good day. Almost all of them were part of the Just Right Café Coffee Club, which, for a monthly fee, gave them unlimited refills in their JRC travel mugs and one free pastry a month. She wasn't sure if the program would be a financial loss when she started it, but she loved the idea of doing something that connected her customers, so she did it anyway.

It had made money from the first month.

By seven, Sheridan had the first tray of cinnamon rolls in the front display case along with three different muffin choices. She turned the sign to Open, went to the kitchen, switched to a clean apron, and finished the last of her second cup of coffee. With a genuine smile on her face, she was ready to start the rest of her day. And by the time she stepped up to the counter, her first customers were arriving.

The man who walked into the café minutes after it opened looked like a Greek god. He was tall, blond, muscular, and drew appraising looks from women wherever he went. His clothes fit him perfectly, and there was something about him that screamed money. Fortunately, like all men Sheridan met, he didn't do anything for her. Not that she wasn't attracted to men, but that attraction didn't happen until after she'd had the time to get to know someone.

"Is it Wednesday already?" she said, smiling and teasing Ash Royce as she put his still warm cinnamon roll in a box, adding an extra container of icing the way she did for those who wanted to dip the pastry.

He took a deep breath of the sweetly scented air and said, "It is. These are the second best reason to get up early." Sheridan knew the woman he shared a bed with was the first. "I've been craving this since my last one. I swear, Sheridan, if you ever want these to be your exclusive offering and ship them nationwide, you'd make bank."

"If they're so great, why do you only get them once a week?" He did occasionally come by with Janelle for lunch, but he limited himself to the one cinnamon roll. "You had them more often when you were here doing the show."

"Yeah, but then I didn't think I'd be able to have them whenever I wanted." Ash had expected to return to New York City after partnering with Janelle for a reality competition filmed at her thrift store. They hadn't won the competition, but he had won Janelle's heart. And she had his, so he'd moved and started his own design business, Fluid, which specialized in gender neutral clothes. She was a big fan of the oversized sweaters he carried. He turned to leave after paying for his treat, then doubled back. "I almost forgot. Janelle told me to tell you she has two dresses for you which she thinks you'll like for the wedding next week." Sheridan's expression must have shown her surprise because Ash said, "She mentioned you're part of the first dance and might want to wear something longer to better match the women in the wedding party."

"I didn't think of that," Sheridan said. She had a simple blue cocktail dress for Eden's wedding, a longer floral one for Mia's. For Dani's evening event, she and Laurel were wearing elegant black gowns. It was one of the nicest dresses Sheridan had ever owned.

Well, except for one.

"Janelle is good at anticipating. She's saved my ass on more than one occasion. Stop by the store when you can, and she'll have you feeling gorgeous in no time."

Sheridan would settle for cute, but she didn't say that, not only because she didn't put herself down in public, but because there was no way Janelle would never settle. She would want Sheridan to love what she chose. "I'll get there in the next few days," she said with more confidence than she felt. She still wasn't sure about being partnered with Ryan, but she'd wait until after Friday's dance lesson to see if it was going to be a total disaster. She had the feeling Ryan would be more than happy to sit it out if it didn't work.

As the morning went on, Sheridan continued helping customers, most of whom were regulars. She talked with them about jobs and families, and they asked her when their favorite specials might be back on the menu. She loved being known for her cooking. It was everything she dreamed of when she imagined owning and opening her own place. Fable Notch felt like home, a place she belonged.

By nine, the weekday morning rush had ebbed. Sheridan was bringing out a last tray of muffins and saw a man staring into the case. His gaze kept moving from side to side, and he looked concerned. Ah, decision paralysis. It was a good sign. It showed her she was offering what her patrons wanted, and it frequently led to people buying more than they intended. "Good morning," she said. "How can I help you?"

"I heard this was the place to come for cinnamon rolls, but I don't see any," he said, still looking. This was harder. She hated disappointing anyone, but she also preferred to run out than have too much of something.

"No, I'm sorry. You heard right about the cinnamon rolls, but the person should have told you to come earlier. They rarely last beyond nine, even on a weekday. But I have other choices you might like, and a coffee cake muffin that's very popular. Not quite as much cinnamon, but it has the same icing drizzled on the top. We also have delicious breakfast sandwiches on our homemade biscuits."

He glanced from the case to her, and his features changed from concerned to delighted. "I'll try whatever you offer," he said, his voice pitched lower than before.

Her radar went up immediately. She recognized the look. Any moment, he would start to flirt with her, and she was going to have to get out of the conversation without hurting his feelings and, hopefully, without losing the sale. She'd wanted to be in the hospitality industry ever since she learned to cook. But while she was good at chatting with customers and making them feel welcome, on the occasions when someone wanted something more than her cooking, Sheridan was completely out of her element.

More than one friend had tried to teach her basic flirting so she could handle these situations easier, but it never worked. To Sheridan, it was forced and uncomfortable. "We have three different kinds of muffins. The banana-oat is the least sweet and these lemon-raspberry are one of my favorites. I also have peanut-butter and jelly scones and a bacon-cheddar scone that's more savory."

"Savory and sweet. What more could a man ask for?" It wasn't the worst line she'd heard, but it wasn't very inventive. Still, he was a customer, and she could be polite.

"That depends. Some people are happier when they don't have to choose. How about the coffee cake muffin *and* the bacon-cheddar scone?" She offered a smile she hoped was warm without being encouraging, and he nodded.

"Sounds good. I'll take them both." His grin suggested a hunger that had nothing to do with food. Sheridan was glad she'd gotten good at reading the signs, even if she didn't respond to them.

Before she grabbed two pieces of tissue paper, she gave a double knock on the door to the kitchen signaling Wesley, then bagged the order. As she rang him up, she hesitated. She had to ask, but she had a terrible feeling about his answer. "Is there anything else I can get you? Coffee, tea..."

"You?" Yup, there it was. As disappointing as it was expected.

"Sorry, I'm not on the menu," she said, her smile still locked in place but feeling more fake by the minute.

"Can I order off the menu?"

Before she could answer, Wesley came out from the back and stepped behind her. He put his arm around her and kissed the top of her head. "Sorry to interrupt, darlin'," he said. "Needed to tell you we're out of biscuits. Don't offer what we don't have."

At the sight of the other man, the customer's attention visibly cooled. Gone was the flirtatious leer and overeager smile. She'd hired Wesley for his cooking, but his 6'3" tattoo-covered body came with a few helpful advantages. The guest paid for his pastries, put a tip in the jar, and left with a barely mumbled, "Thanks, you too," in response to her "Have a nice day. I hope you'll visit us again."

"Another creep?" Wesley asked as they watched the man leave.

"Not creepy, mostly hopeful."

"Someday, I'm getting you a pin that says, 'Please don't flirt with the staff.'"

"I'm not sure that sends the right message," she said, although there were days when she wouldn't mind having the preemptive help.

The knock on the kitchen door routine had started shortly after Wesley came on board. Things had been going well. She helped customers out front while Wesley took care of things in the kitchen, making their increasingly popular breakfast sandwiches, which she was able to add once he was working with her. One day, she'd called back an order to him and when she didn't come to get it, he came out with it.

And found her trapped in a conversation with a customer who wanted more than what was on the menu. The man was leaning over the counter, and Sheridan was concerned any moment she was going to have to fend him off with a pair of tongs. Wesley stepped up, put an arm around her, and made it clear Sheridan was not available. He never came back, but Sheridan couldn't bring herself to mind.

Later, when there was a lull between the breakfast and lunch crowds, she and Wesley had talked. With his arms crossed in front of him, looking as though he still wanted to rip the guy's arms off, he said, "You do not have to put up with that shit from anyone."

She shrugged, trying to make light of it, though it was something she dreaded. "I know that flirting with customers can be part of — and helpful to — business, but I'm terrible at it and...." She paused for a second and decided she needed to be and could be honest with him. "It makes me uncomfortable when men do that."

"Then we need a system to keep you safe," he said, and she liked that he didn't need more of a reason than that. "I have three younger sisters who relied on me to get rid of unwelcome suitors, and in case you haven't noticed, I can be very intimidating. This is your café, and you should not have to deal with that for any length of time. No woman should. So, what are we going to do?"

They came up with the knocking system. One knock followed by two quick ones told Wesley she needed help. He'd asked if she would be okay with him pretending to show affection as a way of getting rid of any unwanted attention she was receiving, and she said yes. She appreciated his help, as well as his acceptance and understanding. She'd found a gem in Wesley and almost wished she were attracted to him.

Still, he made an awesome big brother, which she needed more than a boyfriend.

Later that afternoon, as they were putting things away and simultaneously prepping for tomorrow, Wesley asked, "You going to be okay at all of the weddings? You won't have a knocking system there."

"Why wouldn't I be okay?" She had a bigger part to play than she expected for the first wedding and was in Dani's wedding party, but she was just a guest.

"There will be lots of strangers there, people from out of town, and you're an attractive, single woman. Weddings put people in odd moods. Depressed, romantic... and more often than they should, drunk. You might want a plan to keep away any unwanted attention."

As Wesley got back to work, Sheridan considered what he said. Laurel would be around, but not a very good wing-woman with Hunter by her side, and Sheridan never wanted to be in her friends' way. Maybe one of Laurel's brothers could be helpful? With seven to choose from and none of them involved with anyone, as far as she knew, they could be a good place to look. She didn't love the idea, but Wesley was right. It would be smart to go in with a plan.

Chapter Three

Ryan arrived in Fable Notch almost six hours later than he expected when his flight was delayed due to the weather in Chicago and his baggage was missing when he arrived. After waiting and searching for over an hour to make sure it wasn't anywhere in the Manchester Airport, he had to go through the red tape of filling out paperwork before he could pick up his rental car and get on the road. Fortunately, after years of travel, he'd packed his carry-on with his cameras and with everything he needed clothing-wise for the first three days. That gave him the weekend to purchase anything he might need.

The only possible problem was his clothes for the wedding.

If his bag didn't arrive by Monday, he would have to figure out where he could buy a new suit. Fortunately, the groomsmen were wearing navy blue suits with vests, so it shouldn't be too hard to find what he needed. Hopefully, Eden wasn't the type to freak out. Women could be funny when it came to weddings. He made a mental note to not check his wedding clothes when he came out for the next two events.

He texted his parents when he hit the road and told them he wasn't going to come by their house until tomorrow morning. After all the delays and unexpected turns, he needed sleep and a quiet night. His mother sent a sad face emoji, then promised him breakfast would be waiting. Her not-so-subtle way of telling him to be there early. He could hardly wait for her other not-so-subtle hints.

The drive from Manchester to Fable Notch was usually beautiful, no matter the season. But because of his late arrival, it was dark before the highway narrowed from two lanes in each direction down to one. He might have been disappointed, except he had a week before the actual wedding, so there would be time to see the more scenic routes of the area.

Just over an hour later, he pulled off at his exit, and shortly after, he could see the lights of the Triangle General Store sign. He was always grateful for the things that didn't change in his hometown, and if it weren't closed, he would have stopped in for a few provisions. Soon, he promised himself, he'd drop by and say hello to Claire Fisher and get a container or two of her famous pickles.

As he drove by the store, he saw the sign for a new garage, Ahern Auto, and the Emporium Souvenir Shop, the place that inspired the name for Cole's band. Nick's directions to Dani's house brought him passed familiar sites including DeMarco's Pizza and Subs and Adam Stewart's Bright Spot Ice Cream store as well as new ones like the Thousand Lives Bookstore and Significant

Paws. Minutes later, his GPS had him pulling up in front of a ranch house with the front lights on. *Thanks, Nick*, he thought. He was indebted to his brother for the use of the house. The idea of staying with his parents wasn't appealing. Not with his mother having wedding and matchmaking fever.

Grabbing his carry on and camera bag from where he'd thrown them in the trunk, he went up to the house, found the key under the mat, and let himself in. He was greeted by the smell of vanilla and a note for him on the dining room table — along with a container of pickles. *Meal from Mom and beer from 7BB in the fridge.* He laughed. His brothers knew him so well.

He sent a text to everyone to say he'd arrived, thanked Nick for the key and the provisions, and his mom for the meal, then unpacked what little he had. That took all of ten minutes. He went to the fridge where he found his mother's roast chicken with all the sides on a plastic wrap covered plate. His second favorite meal. Her lasagna was restaurant worthy, but she was probably saving that for when he could be there — and she could invite someone she wanted him to meet.

He opened up the IPA from the Seven Brothers Brewery and took a swig while his meal heated. Damn, that was good beer. He wouldn't consider himself an expert, but he'd had plenty of microbrews over the years, and this was one of the best. He put the bottle down on the counter, grabbed his camera, and did what he could with the lighting before snapping a few pictures. When he was done, he uploaded the images to his laptop, edited the image a touch, and posted them to his Instagram page, RyanReviews. *First taste of home and it's fabulous.*

Don't miss @sevenbrothersbrewery when you're in Fable Notch. More to come!

For years, he'd posted pictures of places and people on his social media pages. It helped his parents and friends know where he was and what he was doing. Then, a little more than a year ago, he got an incredible response to his series of restaurant and food pictures in a small town outside of Nashville. After, he repurposed his accounts for business and renamed it RyanReviews. He occasionally did sponsored content and was frequently invited to visit businesses who wanted the publicity his posts could generate. It had become a fun and unexpected side-hustle.

Before going to bed, he checked his emails to see if there was any news on his luggage — there wasn't — then sent an invoice to a client he was working with on their product launch. He did have an email from his landlord asking him if he was interested in extending his lease another six months. It was a good question. Southern California had been a lucrative place to live with assignments easy to come by, but after three years, he was getting antsy. It might be time to move again.

But that was a concern for later. For now, he was here and looking forward to celebrating with his brothers and being by their sides as they took the next step in their lives.

Ryan woke early the next morning, which was hellish since he was still on Pacific time, but he couldn't be late for breakfast. He was going to get enough grief from his mother for his other choices. After coffee and a quick shower, he headed to his parents' house.

The red brick colonial hadn't changed much over the years. It was, and always would be, home, a place where love was always waiting for him. And he knew that whatever — whoever — Millie pushed at him, it came from that love. He'd met lots of caring people in his life, but his mother was among the best. She'd created a home for him and his father, and when Cole, Theo, and Nick arrived in their lives, their family felt complete.

Ryan had always wanted siblings. He could remember when he was four, searching under the Christmas tree and not finding what he was looking for.

His mother had asked, "Is there something missing, honey?"

"Kinda," he'd said, sitting on the floor disappointed. "I put something secret in my letter to Santa, and it's not here. I mean, I know it can't be here exactly, but I hoped there would be something about it."

Martin had pulled Ryan onto his lap and said, "I'm sorry. Maybe if you tell us what it is, Mom and I can see if we can fix that."

Ryan had been hesitant to say anything, somehow knowing it was a difficult subject. His parents were waiting for an answer though, so he blurted out, "I want a brother. I mean, a sister would be okay, but I really want a little brother." He didn't understand when his mother's eyes filled with tears. Before they could spill over, she gave his hand a squeeze and left the room. Ryan had been horrified. He'd made his mom angry when he didn't do what he said he was going to, but he'd never made her cry. "What did I say? Is that not something I should want?"

His father wasn't crying, but he looked sad. "No, Ryan. It's a wonderful thing to want, and it's something your mom and I would love to give you, but unfortunately, it hasn't been possible." He kissed the top of Ryan's head and continued. "First, you should know this isn't the kind of request Santa can fulfill. Only Mom and I can. Second, I can't explain all the reasons we haven't been able to have another child. We're going to keep trying, but it might not be possible."

Ryan hadn't fully understood what his father was telling him, but he didn't want to ask more questions. His dad was still holding him when Millie came back and told him she was fine. He didn't believe her, so he climbed from his dad's lap to hers and hugged her tightly. She enveloped him in her arms. Her familiar scent of dryer sheets, floral shampoo, and coffee wrapped around him in comfort. She kissed the top of his head as she continued to hold him, then said, "Thank you for having enough love in your heart to want us to have a bigger family. Maybe someday it will happen."

His mom smiled when he looked at her, but he could see it was forced, and although she said it was okay, he was never going to bring it up again. Four years later, he almost got his wish. Not one brother, but three. Not younger as he expected, but older, which turned out better.

Ryan understood why Millie was so happy to have her boys back. He imagined shortly after the weddings, she'd be dropping hints to all three of them about the grandchildren she wanted next. Although given her own struggles with pregnancies — he'd eventually learned about secondary infertility — she might not push as much.

"Is breakfast ready yet?" he called. It was his old weekend refrain. During the week, everyone handled their own breakfast, but on Saturdays, he'd sleep in and come down to Millie in the kitchen, making enough food to open her own restaurant.

"Just waiting for you," she replied, and it was as if no time at all had passed. He stepped into the kitchen where his mother was at the stove and his father was at the table with his coffee and Kindle. Other than them both being grayer with more wrinkles, nothing had changed, which Ryan appreciated. He could live a somewhat chaotic life knowing that in the mountains of New Hampshire, things would be exactly as he left them.

His dad got up and gave him a big hug as his mom turned down the heat on the food and did the same. "Sorry I'm late," he said as he breathed in the scent of Martin's Old Spice, then the familiar scent of Millie's hairspray. More things that would never change. "It couldn't be helped."

"We understand," Martin said, going back to his place at the table and taking a long drink of his coffee as Millie returned to the stove, moved the bacon to the side of the pan, and dropped in eggs to scramble.

As Ryan helped himself to a cup of coffee, he said, "What's new?" gesturing with his chin to his father's tablet. When Ryan was growing up, his father reading the paper during breakfast had been a staple. Martin would share headlines and highlights with anyone who was in the room. Ryan never realized how much he'd learned until civics class in eighth grade, when he knew more than most of his classmates.

"Locally, the young adult room of the library is open — you know Nick and Dani helped to raise the money for that project. And I read that...." Ryan listened as Martin went on and grabbed a slice of toast as soon as it popped out of the toaster, earning him a swat from Millie.

When Martin paused, Millie jumped in with, "I hear the new youth services librarian is lovely. She used to be a teacher and decided to change careers. We're so lucky to have gotten her." His mother's innocent tone didn't fool Ryan for a second. "What was her name?"

"Clara," Martin said, not looking up.

"Yes, that was it." Ryan waited for Millie to make a pitch for him to meet Clara, but as she plated the finished food and brought it to the table, she switched her focus. "I was thinking of asking Taryn Campbell to join us for dinner this Sunday. She grew up north of here, in Jefferson. Her family's been there for years. She's the massage therapist over at the Castle on the Hill. I treat myself every so often to a spa day. So talented."

Keeping the exasperation out of his tone was not going to be easy. "That's nice. Does she come for dinner often?" Ryan was certain he knew the answer, but his father's sudden cough coupled with Millie's smile changing from hopeful to frozen confirmed it. "Ma, please. I just got here. Couldn't you wait a few minutes before introducing me to every single woman in town?"

Millie harrumphed. "It's hardly every woman."

"Fine every other." He raised a hand to stop her before she could defend her actions.

They ate in silence for a full two minutes before Millie said, "What's wrong with me introducing you to some of the nice younger people who live here now?"

"Nothing, but..." He shouldn't say anything until he spoke to the woman in question, but he needed to get through this meal. "I can't say anything yet, but I've been talking to someone, and I'm hoping she'll be my date for the weddings."

Millie dropped her fork. "Who?"

"Which part of 'I can't say anything yet' wasn't clear?" There was a chance Sheridan would tell him no, although given what he'd learned about her, she'd say it kindly, and possibly with an added "bless your heart" thrown in.

"Well, whoever she is, you better invite her for dinner on Sunday."

He promised he would, and when the rest of the meal passed without additional dating suggestions, Ryan was more committed than ever to getting Sheridan to agree.

At four o'clock, after leisurely driving through the mountains and taking dozens of pictures, Ryan arrived at the Hutchinson Studio for Dance and Physical Therapy. Theo told him Eden named it in honor of her mother, who had died while Eden was in college. The space had been the Elks Lodge when Ryan was growing up, but when membership fell off, the group had merged with others in the area, and the building had been left empty. Not long after Theo had solved the arson investigation and chose to stay in Fable Notch, Eden had taken over the building and opened her own business, combining her first professional passion with her training as a physical therapist.

He grabbed his camera bag and headed in. What he saw when he arrived almost made him envious. No wonder his mother was pushing marriage. Theo and Eden were off to the side talking to one another, and it was as if there wasn't another person in the world. They weren't deliberately shutting anyone out, but the way they looked at each other? Ryan could feel their love as if it was a physical thing.

Quickly, he pulled out his camera and took photos, hoping he'd be able to capture what he saw before anyone noticed him.

Nick, the youngest of the Hanson brothers and a year older than Ryan, was the first to see him and called out, "Look who has finally returned."

Ryan felt like a bug being examined as everyone turned toward him. Eden got to him first. "You're here," she said, giving him a hug. "We heard your flight was delayed. Thank goodness you came in a week early."

As he was passed from person to person for greetings, he said, "Well, I'm here, but not everything I need is." He explained about his suit being lost in transit, and when she looked concerned, he rushed in with his plan to replace it if necessary. "But don't worry, I have my cameras, which are more important. And I promise to look appropriate for your big day. Not that anyone will be looking at me."

She smiled. "What matters is that you're with us. I wouldn't care if you wore jeans and a T-shirt."

"Oh sure, now you tell me," he said with a chuckle. As they waited for the last people to arrive, Ryan went back to taking pictures, happiest and most comfortable behind his camera. Then a laugh he recognized had him turning to the door.

Sheridan was more beautiful in person than on Zoom. Her hair was its usual riot of curls, held away from her face with a thick headband covered with a dusting of rhinestones. She didn't need the extra sparkle. Maybe it was her smile, but there was something that drew him in.

Because of his work, Ryan was always aware of light. Where it was coming from, how it could be created and used. When he realized how important it was, he took courses in lighting design from the theater department at college. It added a dimension and quality to his work that quickly set him apart from his peers, and he attributed his ongoing success to his ability to light things well. One look at Sheridan, and all he could imagine was how easy it would be to make her shine.

The overhead fluorescents of the dance studio weren't flattering, but he didn't care. Quickly, he took a picture of her as she chatted with Dani and Eden. He was looking in the viewfinder, liking what he saw but already seeing how it could be better when his future sister-in-law brought over his dance partner.

"I know you two have sort of met already, but this is your first time face-to-face. Sheridan, this is Ryan Sinclair, who is a world-class, highly sought after photographer, and who never does weddings but is making an exception for all of us. Ryan, this is Sheridan Behr, southern transplant and baker extraordinaire, creator of cinnamon rolls and other desserts and sandwiches so tempting she keeps the local gym memberships and several of my dance classes strong. She never does wedding cakes, but she's making an exception for Mia."

As they shook hands, Ryan thought more than her cooking was tempting. Now that she was closer, his photographer's eye took in her cornflower blue eyes, high cheekbones, and full lips. *So kissable.* He guessed her to be around 5'6", maybe seven. The long shirt she wore over her leggings made it impossible to see what her body looked like, but it didn't matter. He found her compelling, and he hoped more than ever she'd agree to his plan.

Moth meet flame.

"Okay, everyone, you can't put this off forever," Eden said, getting their attention. Her voice was loud but kind, likely the same tone she used with her students and clients. "Theo and I are going to demonstrate the dance, a very basic foxtrot. The first thing to remember is, men, you'll always be starting on your left foot and moving forward. Ladies, right foot and stepping back."

"I have to know my left from my right?" Adam said with a whine that had everyone laughing.

"I could stick you with a pin if that would help you remember which one is which," Janelle offered. "I'm sure I've got one handy." Adam put up his hands in surrender.

"No need to stab anyone," Eden said. "Should you forget, your index finger and thumb on your left hand make an L." Suddenly everyone was looking at their hands to confirm this. Comments of 'that's cool' and 'why didn't I know this years ago' could be heard around the room. "It will be easier if you let one person lead. Traditionally, that's the man, but there are ways for either partner to do it."

"You lead," Sheridan and Ryan said at the same time and laughed. "Jinx. Jinx again."

"You can buy each other beers later," Eden admonished. "The group dance will be to 'Everything' by Michael Bublé. Theo and I will finish our dance, then this song will start. We'll begin, and after a few bars, all of you will join in. This is what it will look like."

Everyone watched as Theo and Eden demonstrated. It didn't look very complicated while the two of them moved together, but Ryan suspected that was due as much to Eden's skill as the steps. When they finished and everyone applauded, Eden took them through it slowly. It didn't take long for Ryan to see why Eden's classes were so successful. She was a good teacher who broke down the dance and made it easy to understand.

Ryan looked at Sheridan. All the joy was gone from her face. Her eyes were like saucers — more like someone watching an autopsy than a dance. Hoping to help her relax, he leaned over and whispered, "Don't worry. We can do this."

"I'd rather cook for a black-tie gala," she said.

Before he could reassure her, Eden asked, "Ready?"

"Not even a little," Dani said. There were echoes of agreement. "But willing to give it a try."

Eden smiled and said, "That's all I ask. We'll practice it without the music, so you won't have to worry about keeping up with the song yet."

Sheridan faced Ryan and gave him a smile. Having seen her earlier one, this one was noticeably forced.

Hoping to help her relax, he said, "May I," before putting his hand on her waist.

"What a gentleman. You may." She offered a genuine smile. "So, who will step on whose feet first?" She did. Three steps in, she landed on his foot. "Right foot. My other left. Sorry," she said, sounding rather miserable, and he found himself wanting to assure her, to get back the smile.

"No problem. We'll get the hang of it."

And sure enough, before the hour was up, he and Sheridan were moving well together. Ryan tried leading, putting pressure on her back so she'd know which way they were going to move. Midway through, Cole and Mia got fancy, adding a spin, and Eden showed them flourishes they could add. Nick and Dani did a small lift, and Ryan dipped Sheridan at the end, which earned him a laugh. Truthfully, they all looked pretty good. Eden was thrilled and appreciative. "Thank you. You did wonderfully, and I know you'll look great at the reception."

"I hope I don't forget everything," Mia said.

Eden's brows drew together. "Do you think we should have a refresher next week, maybe before the rehearsal dinner?"

Everyone looked at each other. Ryan got the feeling no one wanted to do more of this than they had to, but no one wanted to let Eden down, either. Finally, Janelle said, "For you, my dear, we will do anything," and gave her friend a hug before turning to the group and adding, "Won't we?"

There were lots of agreements other than Sheridan, who said, "You'll have to count me out for that one. I'll be getting things set up for the dinner."

"I'm sure everyone will do a great job because you've done a great job," Theo said, taking Eden's hand and giving it a kiss. "And the ladies can practice with you on your night out together."

"That's true. Thank you all so much. This," her voice broke as she addressed them all. "This means a lot to me." She squeezed Theo's hand. "To us both."

Again, the love between them was palpable, and Ryan wished he was holding his camera to capture the moment. He had a feeling that would be happening a lot during these events.

"Are you going to show us your dance?" Janelle asked.

The other women chimed in with 'Yes, show us,' but Eden shook her head. "Nope. We're keeping that under wraps until the big day."

After that, things broke up quickly. Ryan went to talk with Cole and Mia to confirm when he could come over and take the candid photos they wanted. He figured it would be easier and more relaxed if he did them now rather than a few days before their event.

As they talked, out of the corner of his eye, he saw Sheridan walk out, and excused himself. He needed to ask her this as soon as possible, because if she said no, he was going to need another plan.

"Sheridan, wait up," he said. She stopped, and he ran over to where she was standing next to a baby blue Bronco Sport. He couldn't help but smile at her choice. It was perfect for her. It stood out, the way she did, in a fun yet welcoming way. "First, I have to tell you I love your car."

"Thanks. When I moved here, Laurel told me my convertible wouldn't manage through the winters. I hated getting rid of it, so I had to buy something fun as a replacement. Dani calls it my Smurf-mobile."

"It suits you." Trying not to shuffle his feet in embarrassment, he plunged forward. "At the risk of sounding like a bad song, I know we've barely met — although I do feel as though I've gotten to know you thanks to those monthly calls — but I could use your help with something."

"I suppose if my dancing hasn't scared you off, the least I could do is hear your request."

Ryan took a deep breath. He hoped she'd agree to this. It would make his life so much easier. And it wouldn't be a hardship at all. He found her enchanting. "For the next ten days and through the next two weddings, can we please tell my parents and anyone who asks that we're dating?"

Chapter Four

Of all the things Ryan could have suggested, this was the last Sheridan would have guessed. She'd enjoyed getting to know him and Dani's brother — the other members of the wedding parties she'd never met — on the Attendants calls and had been grateful it would mean fewer strangers at the events. She found Ryan to be funny, caring when it came to his family and friends, and passionate about his work, something she understood.

But pretending to be dating? That was a new one. She must have taken too long to answer because he said, "Please?"

"Bless your heart," she said, using the Southern phrase that was good for almost any occasion and especially when she was flustered. His grin got bigger when she said it and she assumed it was because he found the expression cute, as many Northerners did. "I'm flattered. Or I think I am." Truthfully, she had mixed feelings. She didn't mind helping him, because, thinking of Wesley's comments about people getting amorous at weddings, it could help her, too, but dating wasn't something she had much experience with. Not that she was going to tell him. "Before I answer, I'm curious. Why are you asking?" *And why are you asking me?* She thought but didn't say.

"You've probably heard that my mother is beyond thrilled my brothers have moved home and are getting married. Her biggest wish is for me to do the same. I'm hoping if I tell her you and I are seeing each other, she'll back off for the duration of the weddings. Then, after Dani and Nick's ceremony, we can 'break up.' You'll have to suffer through some sympathy and her trying to convince you to take me back but, overall, it should be pretty painless. Unless you don't like me." He put on a puppy dog pout. She imagined the look made most women do whatever he wanted.

She gave his shoulder a swat. "And how are we supposed to say this happened?" One of them should remain practical.

He rubbed a hand on the back of his neck and looked worried. And adorable. "I guess the way it has. We got to know each other on the Zoom calls and once I was here, we decided to see if there was anything to the connection we felt." He sighed. "Does this sound completely ridiculous?"

The part of her that loved taking care of people by feeding them wanted to take care of him, too. "Not completely. I mean, you said she was trying to push women on you while you were here, so she definitely thinks it's a possibility you could meet the right one while you're in for the weddings." She debated with herself for a second before continuing. "And she's brought up your name to me as someone I should consider meeting." His eyebrows shot up. "Yup. You were coming to town for

Thanksgiving one year and she invited me to meet you, but I was going home that year. And, if I remember correctly, she came by the café shortly after Cole returned and suggested I needed to be married off — and I should consider you as a candidate."

Ryan's head fell back, and he groaned. "Guess she wants to see everyone married. I'm sorry. She does like to meddle, although she calls it helping."

With a shrug she said, "It's okay. I didn't mind." Sheridan would have almost liked to have her mother want to interfere in her life instead of being so wrapped up in her own search for love. "She does it because she cares."

"Which makes it bearable," he said, "to a point. But at least you understand what I'm up against. So, if you're not involved with anyone, and don't think it will cause any problems if people think we're together, I would genuinely appreciate the help."

She almost laughed. To say she wasn't involved with anyone was an understatement. And she had no local exes who might be jealous that she'd moved on. There'd been no sexual attraction to any of the men she'd gotten to know, and no chance of wanting to hook up with any of the tourists because they weren't around long enough for her to form a connection. "You're in luck. There's no one in my life who will be bothered by this arrangement."

His face lit up, and a dimple appeared. Who knew he could be cuter? "Does that mean yes?"

She prided herself on living her life in a way that minimized surprises and allowed her to stay in control. Agreeing to this felt like asking for trouble, but having a 'date' for all three weddings could make her life easier as well. She wouldn't have to worry about any of the guests hitting on her if she was already with someone. But before she agreed, her practical side asked, "What do you think this will entail?"

He cocked his head to one side. "Being seen together during the weddings, of course. Maybe the occasional hand holding and laughing like we're sharing a private joke or two. You'll have to look at me like you think I'm wonderful." He added a wink, and she laughed. Truthfully, that wouldn't be too difficult. He was completely charming. "Oh, and it's going to require you to come to Sunday dinner this week. If you're free," he added hastily. She liked that he didn't assume she had nothing on her schedule.

"I've been to your parents' for dinner. That won't be a hardship. Your mom's a great cook." She tried to think if she had any questions or could think of any reason to say no, but nothing came to mind. "Okay, Mr. Sinclair. You have yourself a date."

"Thank you, thank you, thank you." Without warning, he gave her a tight hug and for a second, she wondered if he might pick her up and spin her around.

"Your gratitude is overwhelming," she said.

"You have no idea how much this is going to help me out."

"And it won't cramp your style?" He gave her a puzzled look, so she continued, "Nick's comment on your string of broken hearts."

He winced. "Oh. Yeah. Honestly, that isn't quite true. Don't get me wrong, I did my share of dating when I lived here, and nothing stuck. There's no first love I'm coming home to like my brothers, but I'm not the Casanova they make me out to be. It just seems like it compared to them."

Something in his tone made it sound like it was important she believe him. "Good to know. I'd hate to have an angry mob of women storming my café, thinking I had stolen away the man they pined for."

He shook his head. "Trust me, not gonna happen. There is no one pining for me." He said it with such absolute certainty she wondered about his past relationships. She understood why there was no one in her past who might want her back, but she couldn't imagine Ryan, with his looks and talent, didn't have someone who regretted their relationship ending.

Before she could comment, Cole came out of the studio and called Ryan's name. "Guess I need to go. See you Sunday for dinner. Maybe before. I hear great things about your café. I should stop by."

"Seven to three, eight to three on Sundays."

"Sounds good. And thank you again," he said before running off to talk to his brother.

She watched him for a second longer before getting into her car, then sat there before pulling out, stunned at what had happened, and what she'd agreed to.

Apparently, she had a date for the weddings.

A little more than an hour later, she headed out for her weekly Friday night dinner with Dani, Laurel, and whoever else showed up at the Seven Brothers Brewery. What started as a way to spend time with her friends had become a place where a group of them often hung out, ate, and connected after a long week of work. It was where most of her new friendships had bloomed.

When Dani moved back to Fable Notch over two years ago, she and Laurel had picked up their summer friendship as though they had never been apart. At first, Sheridan had been nervous that her relationship with Laurel would be affected by the new addition. Dani had been nervous, too, wondering if there was a place for her in the friendship Laurel had started with Sheridan when they were in college. Turns out, neither of them needed to worry. Not only did Laurel have space in her life and heart for both of them, but Dani and Sheridan quickly became friends and regularly saw each other without Laurel when the other woman was busy. They'd recently gone to the movies together when Nick was away in New York for a week and Laurel and Hunter were having dinner with his sister, Zoe, and her newborn daughter.

When Sheridan got to the brewery, she gave a nod to the front desk host and went directly to the back booth Laurel held for herself. She'd gotten the idea of an "owner's table" from Rosie at the diner, and Sheridan loved knowing the table would be waiting for them unless the place was particularly busy. Only on Saturday nights was the floor manager allowed to seat people there.

Laurel had suggested Sheridan have a table of her own like that when she opened the Just Right, but her hours were shorter and busier, and her staff smaller, so there was rarely time for her to stop during her workday. And she was more than happy to use the office in the back to do the paperwork required to keep the place going. She also wasn't quite the extrovert Rosie and Laurel were.

Tonight, she was the first to arrive. When a server came over, she ordered the seasonal IPA and a plate of nachos and waited for Dani.

"I'm starving," Dani said, as she dropped onto the bench across from Sheridan a few minutes later. "I had an early lunch because we had a full afternoon of appointments, and I had to go back to the clinic after the dance lesson for one more. Can we order every appetizer?"

"I have no objection," Sheridan said. She caught their server's attention, and when the young man came over, placing a glass of water in front of Dani, she said, "Darlin', we need the poutine, the artichoke dip, and the chicken and pepper flatbread." She looked at her friend who nodded. "For now," Sheridan added.

"You got it, ladies," he said. He looked at Dani. "Anything else for you to drink?"

Dani pointed to Sheridan's drink. "Same as hers."

He made a note and before heading to the kitchen, he said, "And your nachos will be out shortly."

"Please tell me you ordered those with extra guac," Dani said.

Sheridan put a hand to her chest, as if she was offended. "Of course I did."

"Guac and cheese make things better," Dani said with a happy sigh. "And carbs. Carbs are glorious. Although with my wedding in four months, I should lay off of them."

Working in a kitchen and around said carbs all the time, Sheridan had learned how to balance treating herself with staying healthy. Overdoing sugar made her sluggish and impacted her sleep, neither of which supported her success. So while she might not serve a lot of vegetables, she kept them in her refrigerators at all times. She would never be a size two, but she was happy with her weight and her curves. "If you keep your meals balanced for fifteen out of the twenty-one most people have in a week, you'll be fine," Sheridan said.

"Really? I never thought of it like that," Dani said and took a long swallow of her beer, which had arrived. Sheridan knew Dani had grown up with a mother for whom weight was important. It made it hard for her to relax around food choices. "So you're telling me I have six opportunities every week to have whatever I want? That's kind of amazing. And very freeing. Although I have gotten rid of my M&M's stash from my office drawers. Those add up fast."

"Sad, but true."

When the server brought their nachos, both women dug in, and Sheridan was happy to see her friend take a healthy bite. There was something satisfying about the pull of cheese when Dani took out her first loaded chip. And the happy sigh she gave when she filled her mouth. It was what Sheridan loved seeing when people ate at her café.

They'd barely made a dent in the mound when Laurel came over with the poutine and flatbread, their server carrying the artichoke dip. "How did the dance lesson go?" she asked as she joined them.

"Much better than I expected," Sheridan said. "I didn't feel like a complete fool, which is what I expected. Eden's a good teacher. What did you think, Dani?"

"I agree. It took a bit before we all got the hang of it, and there was a lot of bumping into each other at first, but before long it looked good. Maybe Nick and I should ask her to help us with our first dance," Dani said. "You and Ryan looked like you were having a good time."

"We were. We did," Sheridan said. She'd been surprised not only by how they danced together — eventually — but by how comfortable she was with him. "He moves well."

"And he has a cute ass," Dani added. Both women stared at her. "What? I'm getting married, I'm not blind. The last time I saw him, he was sixteen, maybe seventeen. He was cute then. He's hot now."

Objectively, Dani was right, but Sheridan hadn't particularly noticed. Thoughts ping-ponged in her head for a second, and she decided she had to let Dani and Laurel know what Ryan asked and what she said. Besides, this would prevent them from getting caught by surprise when the news spread — because it would. She had no idea what her friends would think of the arrangement, but she trusted them. And she had to tell someone. "Ryan asked me to pretend to be his girlfriend while he's here for the weddings."

Both women looked at her as if she said she was taking baked goods off her menu. Laurel found her voice first. "And you said...."

Wondering how they were going to respond, Sheridan said, "Yes. I said yes." Her answer was met with silence, so she filled it. "According to Ryan, Millie is all over him to settle down and move back. It's not something he's interested in. If anyone understands uncomfortable questions about relationships and people not accepting your choices, it's me. He wants to get through these events without having to argue with his mother at every turn. Or duck the women she wants to throw at him."

"Are you sure you're okay with this?" Dani said. "It's a lot to ask. And Millie is going to be all over you once he tells her. Are you going to be comfortable with that? And with him?"

All reasonable questions and ones she'd been thinking since she'd agreed to his request. "I think so. We've gotten to know each other through the calls. He's a nice guy who needs help. And I get something from it, too. It'll keep guests at the wedding from hitting on me. That makes it a win for us both."

"So it's just two friends helping each other out," Laurel said.

"That's the plan." There was more silence as Laurel and Dani looked at each other. "What?"

"We had plans, too," Dani said. "You're talking to two women who thought their hearts were safe when they got involved with the men they are now in love with."

"And we were wrong," Laurel added.

"Oh so wrong," Dani said with a smile that showed how happy she was to be wrong.

Sheridan understood their concern, but she wasn't worried. Her friends had histories with the men they loved. That wasn't the case for her. "Ryan and I are friends helping each other out of a challenging situation."

"But friendship is how connection starts for you, right?" Laurel asked. Sheridan appreciated her friends understanding the dynamics of being demi.

"It is, but we're safe. The reason Ryan and I are doing this is so neither of us has to worry about unwanted attention through the weddings. It'll also make it easier for him to leave after Dani's wedding."

"Yeah, it's the leaving thing that doesn't seem to happen the way we think it will," Dani said. Nick's plan was to be in town long enough to figure out how to get his New York job back. Hunter had come to sell the family business, then go back to Hollywood. Both had stayed, although only in part because of the fabulous women they were smart enough to love.

"I'm sure it won't be an issue for Ryan. That man loves to travel. He was in hotel rooms for most of our Attendants calls." Neither of her friends looked completely convinced, but time would show them she had things under control. There was, however, one thing she needed. "Dani, please don't tell Nick what Ryan and I are doing. I realize I'm kind of asking you to lie to him and that's not fair, but I don't know if Ryan is going to tell his brothers the truth." How many people could hear about this setup before everyone knew it was for show — and that got back to Millie?

"Well, it's sort of real, at least for the length of the weddings, right? I mean, you two were already friends and you will see each other while he's here, so not letting Nick know the whole truth isn't exactly lying. It's more... not telling everything."

Sheridan hated that she might be causing her friend trouble, but she didn't know what else to do. "You're okay with that?"

"For whatever reason, Ryan asked for your help, and you agreed. As long as Nick doesn't ask me anything directly, I don't think it'll be a problem. And if he does ask, I'll invoke the Girl Code and tell him he should talk to Ryan."

Sheridan relaxed. "Thank you. I guess there are parts of this I didn't think through." Hopefully, there wouldn't be too many more. Sheridan was saved from having to discuss the topic further when Eden and Janelle joined them at the table. They ordered more food and talked weddings and jobs. And when thoughts of Ryan came into her head, Sheridan found herself glad to know that whatever happened between them, it wouldn't last, because she didn't want anything to change what she'd created for herself here.

Chapter Five

On Saturday morning, Ryan let himself sleep in but got up early enough to put him on East coast time for the rest of his visit. The first thing he noticed was a message Sheridan left at five thirty. The woman did get up early. It was handy she had his phone number from the wedding calls, when Devon had insisted on being able to reach the group via text. He was worried at first that she was having second thoughts, but she'd written, *I told L & D about our arrangement. Hope that's okay.*

It took his uncaffeinated brain a second to translate L & D to Laurel and Dani. He was fine with that. He didn't want her lying to her friends. *No problem. I need to tell my brothers,* he texted back. There was no response, so he assumed she was busy at work. He hoped Cole, Theo, and Nick would understand this arrangement, since they knew how their mother worried and meddled. They also needed to keep the truth from Millie.

After coffee and a spoonful of peanut butter, he wasted an hour on the phone with the airlines and got no further in the search for his luggage. He didn't have a good feeling about it being found. Deciding better safe than sorry — and not wanting to do laundry every other day — he ordered clothes and underwear online, paying a ridiculous amount for expedited shipping. He wondered if he should get a few things at Janelle's store. Or maybe go to Ash's place.

He was deciding what he wanted to do for breakfast when his phone buzzed. Turning it over, he was surprised to see a text from his agent, January West. Two words, all caps: *URGENT. CALL.*

Ryan did a quick mental run through of the clients she'd gotten him recently. She was responsible for around half of his bookings, including one waiting for him when he got back for a new art house that was opening. He couldn't think of any problems or concerns previous clients had, but that didn't mean there hadn't been one.

Fortifying himself with more coffee, he called her back.

"What took you so long?" she said by way of a greeting. January was a lot of things. Subtle wasn't one of them.

"I'm great, thanks. The airline lost my luggage, but otherwise, things in New Hampshire are good."

"What are you doing in New Hampshire?" He'd told her his travel schedule, but he wasn't surprised that she'd forgotten. After reminding her, she said, "Right. Weddings. Are you sitting down?"

An interesting directive and one she'd never given him. He sat. "I am now."

"What do you know about the Canillo Group?"

It didn't sound familiar, so he said, "Absolutely nothing. Should I know them?"

"Are you kidding me? They are one of the biggest real estate developers in the world." He could almost hear her eyes rolling with exasperation. He loved the professional connections she had — and how they benefited him — but they'd never clicked personality wise. She went on, telling him about the wealth and size of the company. "Anyway, they are moving into hotels and casinos and plan to open four in the next two to three years. Macau, Malta, the Bahamas, and lastly Las Vegas. They've asked the agency to submit three candidates."

"Terrific. I'd be happy to be considered for any of them." He'd worked in Vegas before, but the others were new, which meant he'd get a chance to add to his online portfolio with new images he'd take on his downtime.

"You're not understanding me." Great, she'd moved to her exasperated voice. "This is a multi year commitment to be part of every project. They want the photos to have a coordinated look. You'd be one of the senior people on their publicity team overseeing the photography on all the sites and hiring any other photographers they might need. You'd have carte blanche, a huge salary and resources you've only dreamed of."

Holy shit. Ryan ran a hand through his hair. As he considered what she described, his heart rate increased. She'd been right to tell him to sit down. This was career altering work. His name as a project lead for a client this size could open doors he'd never had access to. It would also give him career stability years before he thought he'd have it.

Freelance photography wasn't the most financially consistent career. He had some months with almost more work than he could handle, and others that were leaner. When he stopped working for an agency and earning a predictable income — that also came with predictable work — he'd had to learn serious budgeting skills. In the last two years working with January, assignments had been steadier, and he hoped that within the next five, he'd be at the stage when he could be choosier because he had more offers.

This job would move up that timetable significantly. As January shared more details, Ryan found paper and a pen so he could take notes on what she needed and start a list of the photos he wanted to send her from his portfolio once he was back in California.

He'd been silent as she spoke, but his voice was breathless when he said, "January, thank you. I appreciate you recommending me." Something occurred to him. "What made you think of me for this job? I'm sure you've got more experienced photographers you could have suggested."

"Your talent, of course. That comes first. You've got vision and are good at giving the client more than what they ask for. And you come with no strings."

She'd never described him that way before. "No strings?" he asked.

"Nothing holding you down or back. No one you have to check with before agreeing to a job. If it's right for you — you take it. The Canillos need talent *and* availability. That's you."

She wasn't wrong.

After they got off the phone, he spent the next few hours downing coffee and researching the Canillo Group and their holdings. January was right. They were impressive — and wealthy. It was the opportunity of a lifetime.

When Ryan checked the clock again, it was after twelve, and the growl from his stomach reminded him he needed to eat. A quick check of the temperature told him it was getting into the low sixties for the day, so he stuck with jeans and a T-shirt. He grabbed a sub at DeMarcos, eating on one of the benches outside and enjoying the smog-less air, before heading over to Cole and Mia's house to shoot some semi-candid pictures of them, Dean, and Bowie, their dog, which they wanted as part of their wedding photos. The wedding itself was going to be casual, but Mia had asked him for these, and he'd gladly agreed. Because he wasn't going to be in town as long for the next wedding, they arranged to do it while he was here this week.

The next three hours flew by as he did what he loved best. When he was behind his camera, he could see the world the way he wanted to and show others what he experienced. Sometimes he was amazed he got to spend his time doing something he enjoyed so much.

After Ryan had the shots he wanted and showed them to Cole and Mia, who liked what they saw, Dean headed out to a friend's house and Cole asked, "Want to take a ride with me to see the new school? It's only fifteen minutes from here."

"Of course it is," Ryan said as he put his camera away. "Doesn't that make it one of the area's longer commutes?"

"Probably. Especially as I need to drive and not walk. Although that's going to change. Get in," Cole said, motioning to his car with his head.

As they pulled out of Cole's drive and headed to the center of town, Ryan said, "Fifteen minutes hardly gets me out of my neighborhood."

"That was true for me where I was in Colorado," Cole said as he rolled down his window and put his elbow out the door. "I wasn't far from Denver, but everything is so spread out, it took almost twenty minutes to get to the grocery store."

"Nothing like here." Depending on what road you took, you could drive through two more towns in twenty minutes. Before long Cole pulled in front of the Northcott Estate, which now had a sign on the front lawn that said White Mountain Music School. The old Victorian was one of the town's biggest homes, but it had been empty since Ryan was in his teens. The school quietly opened a few months before — because Cole was more than done with the limelight — with teachers for piano, guitar, and violin. As they stepped out, Ryan said, "I can't believe you bought this old place."

"I can't believe we were able to make so many of the rooms soundproof," Cole said. "At least temporarily."

"Okay, what's with all the cryptic comments. 'That's going to change,' 'at least temporarily'? What are you planning?"

Cole gestured to a large area next to the house where a barn previously stood. It had been the first site hit by the arsonist two years before. "In the next few months, that's going to be a state-of-the-art music facility and small recital area. Then Mia and I will be renovating the house for us to live in. Nick's got a list of great ideas." Cole explained how, after he had the idea for the school, he didn't want to wait, so they were changing locations when the new building was completed.

"That's incredible, man," Ryan said, clapping Cole on the back. His brother's face had a glow he could never remember seeing on Cole. "You've really gone all in on this."

"I have. Best thing I've ever done," he said.

"You don't miss it?" Ryan asked. Cole had been a literal rock star. Ryan couldn't imagine what it was like to give up something like that.

"Not at all. Besides, I'm still writing songs, the part I liked most." After Cole made the decision to leave Emporium, the rest of the band decided they were done as well. Ryan didn't know what the other members were doing, but Paxton Jones, their lead singer, used the opportunity to start a solo career. Cole wrote most of the songs on her first album. It was a huge hit and there was already Grammy buzz. "I had to give up love for work once, and I'd do it again to make sure Theo and Nick were taken care of. But I am more than happy to do things differently from here on. Does that sound ridiculous?"

"No," Ryan said. And he meant it. Even with Martin and Millie there to help, Cole had taken on the responsibility for his family, and that had meant hard decisions. Ryan didn't have that problem. "I, however, am happily in my love of work over love of relationships stage. Any time a woman suggests I should travel less or find a company to work for rather than be on my own, I know it's time to end things. If it weren't for that, I wouldn't be up for an amazing new assignment." He told Cole about his earlier call with January.

"Damn, that sounds like a dream job. But I can see where it wouldn't leave you time for a relationship."

"Exactly." And Ryan planned to do whatever it took to show the Canillos he was the best photographer they could hire. "But that doesn't mean I'm not glad for you. For you both." He gave a laugh. "For all six of you."

"Even if it means Mom is after you more than ever to come back and settle down?"

"Don't worry. I've got a plan for that." He explained how Sheridan agreed to act as if they were dating. At Cole's expression — a combination of shock and concern — Ryan said, "I know. It's not a perfect solution, but it will get me through the next several months without Mom throwing every eligible woman at me."

"That doesn't always work the way you think it will," Cole said, sounding every bit the big brother. "Mia and I pretended to be engaged, and now we're getting married."

"Except you two had already been in love. Sheridan and I don't have that kind of history." No history, no future. A completely different situation. "She knows I'm not planning to stay. I'm going to tell Theo and Nick, but don't you dare tell Mom."

"What would I tell her? That you're lying to her, and you're going to break her heart?"

Ryan flinched. Did his brother think he was that much of an asshole? "I told you, I explained everything to Sheridan."

"Not Sheridan. Mom." Ryan didn't like the sound of that. "Seriously, dude. You make a mess, I'm leaving it to you to clean up. And I'm definitely not going to let her know you're making us complicit. I understand why you made the decision, but you get to deal with all the consequences."

"Thanks. I think." Ryan had a feeling there were some consequences he hadn't considered. His mother would be disappointed when he left again in September, and if he got the Canillo job, she was going to freak at how far away he'd be and for how long, but he wasn't going to let that stop him. He'd make it up to her when it was the right time to come home.

Chapter Six

Soon after opening her business, Sheridan learned Sundays didn't get busy until later in the morning because people slept in, so she changed her hours to open at eight instead of seven. It gave her a slower morning, which she enjoyed, as well as the time to make more cinnamon rolls and baked goods than usual to prepare for the run that would start shortly before nine o'clock and not let up until nearly one. After a few weeks of lines going out the door — even in the cold weather — she hired a crew of high school students who worked on the weekends to keep the counter line moving and the tables cleared. One or two stayed for the lunch crowd when the café added table service.

Waiting tables was Sheridan's first restaurant job. There weren't a lot of opportunities to make money in the small town where she grew up, and after one horrible encounter with a father when she was babysitting, she was willing to do almost anything else. She'd been surprised and pleased to discover she loved the work. By that time, her mother was divorced and on the hunt for her next husband, so being at home was cheerless.

Working got her out of the house, and the money meant she didn't need to ask her mom for much.

She'd enjoyed the short interactions with people, helping them choose the right meal and seeing them happy with their selection. After a couple of weeks, the head chef had pulled her aside. "How is it your customers always want something different than what's listed on the menu?" She was going to apologize but noticed he didn't sound annoyed. More curious. She explained how she talked with the guests to learn what they wanted, then suggested possible changes. Nodding and smiling, he said, "You have a flair for food and understanding what people want. Do you have any interest in working in the kitchen and learning more?" She was surprised that, at fifteen, it was allowed, and she'd jumped at the chance.

She took to cooking like a duck to water. Several weeks later, she transferred to the local vocational tech high school and enrolled in the culinary program. Kitchens were her happy place, her safe space, and she loved the one she'd created at the Just Right.

Shortly after the Open sign was turned, her first customer arrived. "Good morning, Mayor Keller," Sheridan said to one of her weekend regulars. "The usual for you?"

"Absolutely. Why fix things that aren't broken? I have enough to do," she said with a smile. Brenda Keller often stopped by on Sundays, and sat at a table with her coffee and cinnamon roll as she either read the newspaper or from her tablet. When the mayor made a habit of this, Sheridan understood it wasn't simply a nice way for her to start her day. People knew she'd be there and while some only stopped to say hi, others used the opportunity to have a more serious yet still informal chat. It was smart politics. Sometime after ten, Brenda would finish, come to the counter, and pick up something to take home to her husband, who liked to sleep later on the weekends. Sheridan always knew when the mayor was having a stressful week when she got an additional cinnamon roll.

With Wesley having the day off — he'd be working the next weekend after the wedding — it was a little more hectic than a typical Sunday, but it made the time fly. It did mean that she missed a text from Ryan, *Does it work if I pick you up at five?*

Sunday dinner with the Sinclairs. She'd almost forgotten. She'd been there a few times, usually because Laurel was going with members of her family, but tonight would be different. This time, she was someone's girlfriend.

Sort of.

Sounds good, she texted back when there was a lull. *Are you sure I don't need to bring anything?*

Nope. Mom wants you to have the night off. There was a pause and then he added, *But if you have any of those biscuits I've heard about, I'm sure no one would be upset.*

Sheridan smiled. She loved being known for her food. Put the right ingredients together and you got the results you wanted. If only life could be that simple.

Not a problem. I always keep some frozen.

He sent a tongue hanging out emoji, and she smiled again. She texted him her address and before she left the café for the day, she grabbed a bag of twelve biscuits from the freezer. After a quick trip home to drop them off so they could defrost, she went to Tailor Thrift.

She'd originally chosen a light blue wrap dress to wear for the wedding, but she did need something different now that she was participating in the group dance. Hopefully, her friend had something that would work.

"I have three dresses set aside for you," Janelle said as soon as Sheridan walked in, her hair pulled back in a ponytail, with two pencils visible. "I have a feeling I know which one you'll like best, but I'm going to hold my thoughts until you choose."

"You? Hold your thoughts? Shall I alert the media?"

"Very funny," Janelle said, her smile telling Sheridan she was kidding. "But shocking, I know. I'm curious to see if I'm right." Janelle was one of the most warmly honest people Sheridan knew. She could tell someone a harsh truth, and they'd thank her and ask her for more.

Janelle went to her back room and came out carrying the dresses. She showed Sheridan each one, not hinting at her preference. The first was a floor length seafoam halter dress with lace trim. The second was Wedgewood blue with a high-low hemline and lace inserts. But it was the third that caught Sheridan's attention. It was a pink A-line dress, with a sweetheart neckline and a gentle flare from the waist. If it fit, it would hit her slightly above the ankle. "It's lovely," she said, taking it from Janelle and holding it in front of her as she looked in the mirror. Over her shoulder, she saw Janelle's smile in the reflection. "This is the one you liked, isn't it?"

"It is. You are one of the few women I know who can wear a pink this pale. As an added bonus, the bridesmaids are in a dustier pink, so this will blend in nicely when we're all on the dance floor."

"We're going to be pink and pink? Like in *Steel Magnolias?*" Sheridan had to laugh. She loved the Southern-based film and all of its characters, but the description of Shelby's Pepto-Bismal colored wedding always made her smile and cringe.

Janelle gave a small head tilt. "If it looks good, that's all that matters. Go try it on so I can see where it needs alterations."

Sheridan did as she was told — she imagined everyone did as Janelle told them — and moments later, she was stepping out of the dressing room and standing in front of a three-way mirror. She hoped the dress would look good, but it was lovelier than she expected. "It's perfect," she said.

"Not yet, but it will be," Janelle said as she walked around Sheridan with a piece of chalk, making small marks. "The length is good, but I'm going to nip the waist in a touch. Give you more definition. And add a slit to the side to make it easier to dance. Wouldn't want you tripping. Besides, you've got great legs, may as well show them off."

As Janelle marked the dress with chalk, Sheridan blushed. She couldn't help but wonder what Ryan was going to think. Would he find her beautiful? Not that it mattered. They were friends helping each other out. Still, she didn't want him to be embarrassed to be with her, since everyone in attendance was supposed to believe they were dating. Normally, she didn't care how she looked or other people's opinions on the subject, but this situation was different.

"Are you okay?" Janelle asked, bringing her out of her thoughts. "You look lovely, honestly."

"I'm fine, sorry. Started thinking about all I have to do before the wedding, especially for the rehearsal dinner." Sheridan felt bad for keeping the truth from Janelle, but she'd already shared her situation with Laurel and Dani and wasn't sure how many more people could safely know before the truth ended up getting back to Millie. "The dress is great. I don't need to try on the other two unless you think I should."

"Do you have any doubts?"

She had a whole bushel of them, but that wasn't what Janelle was referring to. "None. And I have a pair of pink ballet flats that I can wear."

"All you'll need is blush and light pink gloss." She tilted her head to the side and added, "Maybe a lilac smokey eye. You'll look gorgeous."

Sheridan stared in the mirror and tried to see what Janelle did, but all she saw was her usual frizzy-haired self. After she changed back into her comfortable clothes, she met Janelle at the front to pay for the dress. "Thank you for doing this. Especially on such short notice."

"That's becoming my specialty. Did you hear about the Prince Charming costume I had to fix for Derek Ahern when he went to show Casey they belonged together?"

"I haven't." Derek and Casey had split for a while because Casey was worried a relationship was a bad idea so soon after Derek lost his wife. Apparently there was a story behind how they got back together. As Janelle rang her up, she told Sheridan how Derek had ordered a Halloween costume online, which had looked horrible when it arrived. Janelle's quick alterations had saved the day, or at least part of it. And things had worked out because the two were still together, and Casey spoke about Derek when everyone got together at the Seven Brothers.

Janelle handed Sheridan her receipt and said, "I'll have this for you no later than Wednesday."

"Thank you. And thanks for helping me."

"Always a pleasure," Janelle said, and Sheridan knew she meant it.

By the time she got back to her house, Sheridan needed to hurry. After a quick shower, she put on one of her nicer knit shirts and chose leggings over pants knowing Millie was going to serve almost as much food for this meal as Sheridan did all day. Okay, that was an exaggeration, but she'd been to meals at the Sinclairs', and there was always an abundance of food.

As she added eyeliner, she gave herself an appraising glance and considered what Janelle said earlier about wearing smoky eye makeup to the wedding. Maybe it was a good idea. She did a quick search and found a video called "Easy Purple Smokey Eye for Beginners." Sounded perfect. She was watching it for the third time, wondering what was supposed to be easy and if she'd be willing to try it, when Ryan arrived.

As she opened the door, he handed her a bouquet of daisies, which she accepted with a smile. "They're lovely." It was a thoughtful but unexpected gesture. "You didn't have to do this."

"I felt weird coming over empty-handed, especially since this is kind of like a first date. And I wanted to say thank you again."

She welcomed him in, and realized that other than Wesley, he was the first man to ever come to her house. Not even Nick or Hunter had been by with her friends.

Remembering her manners, she said, "Can I get you something to drink? I have water, ginger ale, one of Laurel's beers?"

"No need to serve me. I'm fine, honestly. Can I get a quick tour, though?"

"I can do that without moving." She pointed as she explained, "There are two bedrooms upstairs and a bathroom. We have the living room on one side, kitchen with dining area on the other. And there's another bathroom." It was small, but perfect for her. It had felt like home from the moment she'd moved in.

He peeked around her. "Tiny kitchen for a chef."

"I don't cook much here. Occasionally, some recipe development, but mostly I end up at the café. I'm going to put the biscuits in the microwave to make sure they're fully defrosted."

"No problem. Mom isn't expecting us until 5:30, and needless to say, it's not a long drive." She went into her kitchen, put the daisies in a vase with water and stuck the rolls in a low temperature oven to warm them. When she came out, she found Ryan in the living room.

"This is an amazing collection of records," he said as he thumbed through them.

"Thanks," she said, standing next to him. "They were my dad's. He loved music. My mother was going to get rid of them after he died, but I couldn't bear to lose another part of him. He put one on every night when I was growing up and told me about the performers. I didn't keep all of them, but I took my favorites. It feels like having him close."

"He was a classic rock and a jazz man," Ryan said as he continued to look through the albums, pulling out a few. Several of his favorites were also hers, and it was fun to exchange knowledge and memories they each associated with the music. "Some of these are very valuable."

"Doesn't matter if they are or aren't. They are valuable to me." And kept her company on the occasions when she was lonely and missing her dad. "All it takes is a few bars of Simon and Garfunkel and I'm back in the house I grew up in, sitting next to him as he sings along or tells me about a concert he went to."

"It's nice that you have something of his."

"My dad's records. My Meemaw's recipes, including those biscuits you asked for." It was her way of bringing the things she loved into her new life. "Do you have things from home where you're living?"

"Only pictures," he said, taking out his phone where she assumed most of the images resided. "They're easy to pack. For a while I had a toy truck my brothers gave me for Christmas, but it got lost in one of my many moves." She heard a touch of sadness in his voice, but because they were new friends, she said nothing. "Now everything I own fits in my car." They talked more about music, her café, and the job he'd finished the day before he arrived. When his phone buzzed, he took it out and looked at the time before saying, "Ready to go? Mom's making lasagna, which is my favorite."

"Which is why she's making it," she said as they went to the kitchen so she could plate the rolls and put them in a basket with a cloth over it to hold in the heat, but not add moisture. "She's beyond happy you're home. I think every time she's come into the café for the last few months, she's mentioned you."

"All the more reason to be a visitor. Trust me, if I were around more, she wouldn't enjoy it as much as she thinks she would. If I remember correctly, on more than one occasion, she's called me 'a handful'." He laughed and added, "Although a handful of what, I couldn't tell you."

As they headed out, Sheridan was suddenly nervous. What if she made a mistake? Embarrassed herself? Made Ryan regret this decision? She stopped walking and said, "I haven't been someone's girlfriend in a long time. Is there anything I should know to make it seem like we're dating? Your favorite color or food? Childhood pet?"

"Hey, don't worry." Ryan walked back and took her hand in his, giving it a reassuring squeeze. "We may be pretending about the dating thing, but we know each other. We've had months of those calls together, and in the last few days I've learned you're a quick study on the dance floor and have great taste in music. And you're willing to do a favor for a guy when he's desperate. All you have to be is yourself and relax." Still holding her hand, they walked to his car. "And if you think it'll help, the answers are forest green, peanut butter and fluff, and no pets unless you count a goldfish that didn't last a week." He put on a dramatic, sad face.

She laughed and immediately felt better. As she fastened her seatbelt, she said, "I never heard of fluff before moving up here." Ryan put his hand to his heart as though he'd been shot. "I learned it's a northern thing. If it makes you feel better, it's on my 'young at heart' menu and can be ordered with or without the crusts. It's one of my personal favorites."

He started the car and said, "Okay, tell me what a 'young at heart' menu is."

"It was something I promised myself I would do if I ever had a restaurant of my own. I never understood why things on the 'kids' menu' weren't available to adults, especially when some of them are so good. There are days what you most want is a peanut butter and jelly sandwich or chicken nuggets. Why should only children be allowed to order those?"

"Good question. Good point."

"When I opened the café, I added a menu with kid-friendly meals and sizes but made sure anyone could order from that part of the menu."

He raised an eyebrow. "Do many adults order chicken nuggets?"

"Surprisingly, no," she said, smiling. "It does happen on occasion, usually with a side of mac and cheese, but it's the fluff sandwich that gets ordered the most. Usually with a blush and an explanation."

"Is that what the bear on your logo is eating?"

"Perhaps, although I would think peanut butter and honey is more likely," she said. She loved her little bear holding a sandwich. Someday she hoped they'd be able to sell stuffed animals in addition to the T-shirts and sweatshirts they had now.

As Ryan had said, it took less than ten minutes before they were pulling up to the Sinclairs' red colonial. With a sigh of relief, she saw Nick's car and was glad to know she and Ryan wouldn't be Millie's sole focus, although Sheridan didn't kid herself. Millie did a big meal for

Sunday dinner every week, but this one was definitely for Ryan. Sheridan hoped she could pull this off and not disappoint him.

She also hoped that when things 'ended,' Millie would be okay that her son wasn't staying.

Chapter Seven

Ryan was glad he could reassure Sheridan as they went into his parents' house, but he wasn't being fully honest with her. Part of him was apprehensive. Bringing someone for Sunday dinner wasn't a small thing. It said, "This person matters to me."

He remembered the last time he'd done it. Caroline Osgood, his date for the senior prom. He and Caroline had been seeing each other and it seemed natural for them to go together. Unfortunately, as soon as he asked her, she'd become clingier, talking about the future and how easy it would be to stay together after graduation since she was going to college in state. All he'd been interested in was hanging out with his friends and losing his virginity. He'd decided against the latter because he figured Caroline would start choosing China patterns if they had sex.

Maybe it was because Sheridan wasn't a stranger to his parents or maybe because Dani and Nick were there, but as soon as they walked in, all of his concern melted away like butter on the biscuits. Sheridan comfortably received hugs from everyone, then went with Dani to the kitchen to help Millie while Ryan had his first chance to meet Otis and Lola, Nick's dogs. Pictures didn't do Otis' size justice and when he got on the floor to play, he was eye-to-eye with the Great Pyrenees mix.

They got up when Millie called them to dinner. As he brushed fur off his shirt, Ryan said to Nick, "Sometimes I still can't believe you've settled here with Dani and two dogs."

"Sometimes I can't believe it either," Nick said, holding Lola in his arms and giving her a kiss on the nose before letting the smaller dog scamper off. "But I can tell you this — I didn't settle. This was an eyes wide open decision."

Ryan almost stumbled as Nick's words hit him. He knew his brothers were happy with their lives. He saw it with Cole earlier, but hearing Nick's clarity — that there was no sacrifice in the choice he made — was powerful.

Before he could think more about it, he joined everyone at the table. His mother had him seated next to Sheridan and across from Nick and Dani. Food enough for twice as many people filled the table, which was fine with him. He'd look forward to the leftovers.

Memories of past dinners came flooding back. Times when it was just him and his parents; the first times the Hansons joined them. Nights when almost the entire Stewart clan was over, and they were seated shoulder to shoulder, hardly able to pass anything without jostling someone. But at the center — and at the head and foot of the table — were his parents. Happy to welcome and take care of whoever was there. He'd never tell them, but he often thought of them on Sunday, wondering who was there, what was being served. And, on occasion, he wished he were there.

As the meal went on, conversation flowed easily, not only regarding the weddings but plans for the Dog Days of Summer festival, which was coming up again in August. Apparently, three months wasn't a lot of time to prepare for an event which took over the town, and definitely not a lot of time when you were entering a new recipe in the blueberry competition as Sheridan was.

"I've never heard of blueberry rolls," Millie said after Sheridan swore her and Dani to secrecy about what she was planning. Rosie and Laurel were her competitors — and things got intense. Friendly, but fierce.

"It's not unlike what I do already, but I'm having trouble deciding between two different recipes." Her tone told Ryan that while she may be struggling, she was also excited. He watched her become animated as she spoke about her idea, her face almost glowing with excitement. "I'm trying to choose between a combination cinnamon-blueberry roll with blueberry cream cheese frosting and blueberry sweet rolls with a lemon glaze. I thought of having customers decide and vote, but I want to unveil it at the Festival. Maybe I should have everyone over to my place for a tasting? Not Laurel, of course."

Dani groaned. "I am never getting into my wedding dress with temptations like this. What if Aunt Rosie wants me to taste things, too?"

Nick leaned over and kissed her. "You're going to look gorgeous whatever you wear and whatever you weigh." Ryan was close enough to hear him add, "And the only thing that matters is that I can get you out of your dress later." Dani blushed.

Ryan had seen Nick over the years when a job brought him to New York. Back then, his brother was in his element, loving his work and his life. It was nothing compared to the joy Ryan saw tonight. Again, he found himself thrilled for his brothers. Love suited them.

It wasn't long before everyone was full, including the dogs, if the snores he heard from the other room were any indication. He and Nick stood to clear and clean, falling easily back into their old roles. Ryan took their time alone to tell Nick about the situation with Sheridan. Nick looked as though he was going to tell Ryan it was a lousy idea the way Cole had, but before he could, Millie joined them to parcel out the leftovers, making sure everyone, including Sheridan, had food to take.

There weren't any biscuits left, he noticed with a smile.

When it was time to leave, there were more hugs all around, and Millie said to Sheridan, "We're throwing a brunch for Theo and Eden before they head out on their honeymoon next Sunday. You'll come."

It was a statement, not a question. In case Sheridan was thinking of turning down the invitation, he said, "Of course she will."

"Thank you for including me. And for tonight," Sheridan added, and he gave her hand a squeeze. He owed her big time for this. "See you at the rehearsal dinner, if not before."

Once they were on their way, he said, "Now it's my turn to say thank you. I appreciate you joining me tonight."

"In case you couldn't tell, it wasn't a hardship. However, if you're trying to get me to give you my share of the leftovers, forget it. Your mom's lasagna is too good." He snapped his fingers as if to say "darn," which made her laugh. Minutes later, they were pulling up to her house. Before getting out, she said, "In case no one's mentioned it recently, your folks are wonderful."

"Yeah, I do hear that a lot, and I don't disagree. I know how lucky I am." Every time he was here or saw other people's families, he was aware of his good fortune.

It was a second before she went on. "But even with such a great example, you have no interest in either a serious relationship or settling down." She paused, as if considering her words, then continued. "You're welcome to tell me it's none of my business, but since we're pretending to be a couple, I'm curious. Why isn't there anyone in your life?"

He almost gave her a flip answer like "haven't met the right woman," but she'd agreed to this plan. She deserved better. "Because I've yet to be in a situation where the woman doesn't want a whole list of compromises. And by compromise, I mean me being the one who has to make all the changes, especially when it comes to the travel I do or the jobs I take." He tried to keep the annoyance from his voice, but he could tell from the double lines between Sheridan's eyebrows that she heard it.

"Sounds like you had some bad experiences," she said. He waited for her to say 'I'm sure she had to make compromises, too' or something else in support of the woman's side, but she didn't, and when he didn't sense any judgment from her, he went on.

"I had two, and that was enough. The first was the summer after I graduated from community college, when I got a gig with a marketing agency in Boston. In the fall, they offered me a job. It was what I wanted to be doing — and the salary was solid — so I accepted. I could come up and see Mom and Dad pretty regularly, but I was on my own for the first time, and it was great." Thinking back, he could remember how much he loved being away from Fable Notch. Not just the opportunity to do something new and different every day — which he did as often as his time and budget would allow — but not seeing familiar faces all the time or having to worry that what he did would get back to his folks. "I'd been there nine months when I met Lydia and fell in love for the first time. Man, that is a special kind of gut punch."

"I'd have to agree with that," Sheridan said. From her tone, it sounded like she had a story, too, but she didn't say anything more, so he thought she might not be ready to share that with him.

"After a year of dating, she moved in with me. At first it was fine — kind of like playing house. It's awesome when you want to have sex with someone and they're right there. But sex, I quickly learned, is only one part of a relationship. A few months after we started living together, I left the agency to do more freelance work. I already did some, but the jobs were getting bigger and the agency had me locked into a certain number of hours. Lydia wasn't happy with my decision and kept telling me it was too unreliable. She kept pushing me to find another agency gig, but all it took was an expensive dinner out after my latest paycheck came in and things were smooth again."

"But it didn't stay that way."

With a sigh, he said, "Not for long. The more I wanted to do, the more she got upset. I had taken two jobs back-to-back that required me to travel out of the area. Each time I was gone less than a week, but when I came back, she was annoyed. It took days before things were back to normal. When I got a third out-of-town gig, I turned it down so I wouldn't have to deal with her response when I got back."

Sheridan scrunched her face. "If we start changing what we want or who we are for someone, it's a bad sign."

He appreciated her understanding. "Yeah, but I was young and in love and figured that was what you did. I had seen my parents make compromises, so I figured I had to, too."

"What was the straw that ended things?"

"The next big job I was offered. I'd been approached by a travel company who'd seen my work. They offered me a chance to live aboard a ship and take photos during the pre-launch cruise that would be used for all of their non-video advertising. It was a hell of an opportunity and would have been the biggest payday of my career so far, but would have taken me away for much longer."

"She objected."

"Vehemently. I told her that part of the compensation was a two-week cruise we could take together at another time, but she wouldn't let it go. She said I couldn't keep putting my work before her or our relationship. This time I got the silent treatment before I made my decision. It was her or the job."

"You took the job," she said.

"No, I stupidly turned it down," he said and realized he still regretted it. He'd had some terrific opportunities after, but the decision set him back. “And I suggested they consider a buddy of mine. He jumped at the chance and got the job. By the time he returned, he had three more gigs lined up. If Lydia hadn’t been in my life, if she hadn’t insisted that I choose her over my work, that would have been me. I couldn’t stay with someone who was going to dictate what I could and couldn’t do. I broke up with her less than a month later.” And the lesson had been learned. Love was great, but so was his freedom. And they didn’t go together.

“I understand your priorities. I have nothing against love — in case you haven’t noticed, my two closest friends are head over heels for the men they’re with — but having your happiness depend on someone else? No thanks. I’ll stick to good friends and work I adore.”

“Sounds like you have a story, too.”

“I have a mother on her fourth husband.” He couldn’t stop his eyebrows from shooting up. “Yeah, not the best example. She’d meet someone and be happy. She’d marry, and we’d move. Then she’d get divorced and the whole process would start again. But you haven’t ruled out the whole marriage-family-commitment thing, have you?”

“No, I think what my parents have — and what my brothers have found — is amazing, and I hope to find it someday. But I’m barely thirty. That’s something for the distant future. Especially since I’m being considered for an amazing job that, if I get it, is going to take me overseas for at least two years.”

“I’d love to hear about it,” she said, but her enthusiasm was cut short with a yawn. “Oops. I am not a good date.”

"You're a terrific date," he said honestly, "with a job that requires you to get up early."

"I'm actually off tomorrow, but yeah, it was an early morning."

As she fought off another yawn, he said, "Go to bed. I'll see you soon."

"See you soon," she repeated, then reached down and grabbed the leftovers, hugging them to her chest. Lucky leftovers. "But I'm not leaving without these."

Minx, he thought with a smile as she let herself into her house and waved.

After wasting too much time on Monday on the phone talking to too many unhelpful and uninformed airline personnel and being no closer to finding his luggage, Ryan woke on Tuesday ready to drive to Concord to buy a new suit. The night before, he texted his brothers to see who might be around. Because they were all their own bosses, everyone was available for breakfast and Nick agreed to go shopping with him. They made plans to meet at the Kinsman before heading out.

"It's too bad you don't have the time to order something from Britches. That's where I'm getting my wedding tuxedo," Nick said, after Rosie fawned over Ryan and took their orders. At Ryan's confused face, Nick explained and added, "Who would have guessed there was a custom suit place less than an hour from where we grew up?"

"Who cared," Theo said.

"And who would have needed a suit all those years ago?" Cole said, then sipped his coffee before adding, "Or thought the day would come when we could all afford to shop there?"

"Speak for yourself," Nick said. They laughed and nodded. Nick had always been focused on and driven by money and success.

But when they were kids, none of them could have predicted how their success would look. Theo's work in arson investigation grew out of a tour in the army as a fireman. And while Nick and Cole had been more certain about what they wanted to do, both of their careers had taken unexpected turns. Nick planned to live in New York forever and stick to finance, and Cole expected his future to be with the band. Both made big changes in the last year.

Fortunately, Ryan didn't have to worry about that. He did, however, need to worry about the suit. "I looked online, and there's an on-the-rack store that should have what I need." He thought for a second and turned to Nick. "Remind me, do I need a tux for your wedding?"

"Nope. Black suit, vest and a tie," Nick said. Ryan groaned.

"Still hate to wear ties?"

"It's a noose," Ryan said. Theo agreed. "Hey, I'm wearing one for you, too."

"For Eden," he corrected. "A few times a year won't kill us, or so I've been told."

Their food arrived and conversation stopped as overflowing plates were attacked. Ryan had enjoyed a lot of good breakfasts over the years, but the Kinsman Diner was special. It had more to do with the people and the memories than the food, but that didn't stop him from sighing with appreciation at the first bite. "That is so good. I have definitely missed this."

"That's what you get for staying away so long," Rosie said from across the diner.

Ryan lowered his voice and asked, "How does she hear everything?"

Nick shook his head. "I have no idea. Dani says she's always been like that. Bat ears that could hear her, Xander, and anyone else getting into trouble from across the house."

"It's a gift and a curse," Rosie said as she came over with the coffee carafe and filled their mugs.

They continued to eat and chat about nothing important, until Theo changed the tone of the conversation when he said, "It still surprises me that of the four of us, you're the one who doesn't live here. You're the one who had the steady upbringing with the loving parents."

"I think that's the reason I could leave." Three pairs of eyes looked at him as if he'd spoken another language. Could he explain it? "Mom and Dad are great. You know that. If you look up ideal parents in the dictionary, their picture is probably there."

"Next to the Stewarts," Nick added.

Ryan nodded. The Stewarts had raised eight children — five of their own, and three nephews — while running their hotel business. Theirs had also been a loving and supportive home. "But as great as life here was, I wanted to see more of the world. Not to mention, as long as I was here, I was always Millie and Martin's son."

"It beats being Russel Hanson's sons," Cole said, not hiding the bitterness he held towards his father as he stabbed his omelet. Ryan wondered if Cole was aware he'd done that.

"No argument," Ryan said, "but while you were trying to live down your parents' reputations, I was supposed to live up to mine. I had the right home life, so, naturally, I would do the right thing. Trust me, that's more pressure than you might think, or at least a different pressure. When any of you made a mistake — or thought you did — I know you assumed people said 'Well, what would you expect from a Hanson?' I had the opposite issue. Any bad grade or behavior and it was 'What will your parents say' or 'I know Millie and Martin raised you better than that.' I know it sounds a little 'poor me,' but it was tough in its own way."

"You made mistakes?" Theo said. For a second, Ryan assumed he was being sarcastic, but Theo's expression was serious.

"I may not have set a shack on fire," Ryan said. "Or rearrange the teachers' desks..." It was one of Theo's most notorious pranks.

"Or pay the bills hustling pool," Cole said.

"Or get thrown out of town by your girlfriend's father," added Theo.

"Doesn't mean I didn't fuck up. Hell, I flunked math my junior year and had to take it over in the summer."

"How did I not know that?" Nick asked, looking confused. "I was around then."

"You were focused on leaving for college. And Dani." Nick shrugged and nodded. With a sigh Ryan said, "I forged Mom's signature on my report cards, so they didn't know until the school year was almost up and got a call from the school asking why I hadn't enrolled in summer school. Letting them down sucked in every way, and I swore I would never do that again. The three of you wanted to get away from the expectations people had of you. Mine may have been more positive, but I needed to create a life and a reputation that were mine and mine alone." He hadn't realized his voice had gotten louder until he stopped talking and there was silence throughout the diner.

"Guess this is something you're passionate about," Cole said.

It was. He'd never tried to put it into words, but he wanted his brothers to understand. "Besides, what was I supposed to do here? Photography is 'it' for me the way finance is for Nick or music for Cole." He held up a hand before they could interrupt him. "Yes, I know. Nick's gone part time and Cole teaches, but you still do what you love. There's only so many pictures of foliage the world needs. How many school dances and weddings could I do here?"

They were silent for a moment before Nick said, "I guess we assumed you had it easy."

"Compared to the three of you? Damn right. But I had my own goals and things to prove." He took a deep breath and continued. "Fable Notch is home. It's always been and always will be. Knowing Mom and Dad are here makes it easier for me to be out in the world. Mom asks me how I can keep moving, but the truth is, I don't need a home base because I have one. Just because I don't live here, that doesn't change." His life might seem rootless, but it was emotionally tethered to their town, even if he wasn't. "I have my freedom and can go wherever I want, whenever I want, and know there is somewhere to come home to. And now when I visit, I'll have the three of you to see and any of your future rug rats to spoil. I've said it before. Give me another decade. Then maybe the time will be right."

Chapter Eight

On her day off, Sheridan spent most of her time planning out the details of what she had to do for Eden's rehearsal dinner on Friday. Everything was ordered, but she needed to figure out her timeline. The cookies would be made on Wednesday, the main courses would be done day of, but cutting and other prep work could be taken care of early. The supplies arrived as scheduled by Tuesday afternoon, and she was almost sorry Wesley had the day off because getting everything into the freezer and refrigerator had been like playing Tetris. He was better at organizing than she was.

And in between, she unexpectedly thought of Ryan. She'd enjoyed spending time with him on Sunday and appreciated him opening up about his dating past. There had been no need for her to tell him her mistakes, but she felt like if she did, he would listen and understand. There had been two relationships in her life. One where she forced herself to want what "everyone else" did, which had been a disaster, and one where she'd been too naïve to see she and the guy wanted completely different things.

Live and learn. And from that she built a life that worked.

"What have you done to Dorothy?" Wesley said when he arrived on Wednesday, using the name they'd given their refrigerator as he peered into it to get breakfast supplies. She reminded him about the large order, and he grumbled while he rearranged everything.

Thinking about the week to come and what had transpired in the last few days, she said, "I need to give you a heads up on some rumors you might hear about me."

He took his head out of the refrigerator and gave her a look she couldn't read. Confused? Concerned? "Are they true?"

It was a reasonable question. She'd gone back and forth on what to tell Wesley about the arrangement and decided to tell him part of the situation. "If you hear that Ryan Sinclair and I are dating, it's true." Technically, it was.

He stared at her for a second longer, then grabbed his apron from the back of the office door. She waited for him to ask another question, but instead he said, "And the rumors about you deciding to raise alpacas?"

"False, and I don't want to know what made you think of that," she said with a laugh. He was a peach. "But now that you mention it, I find myself curious what that might entail and if Dani would know how to take care of them if they got sick."

"I think we've got enough to keep us busy without adding furry animals, don't you?"

With a shrug, she said, "Yeah, one business will have to do." Someday she might want a second location, but that was years away.

Later that afternoon a familiar voice at the kitchen door said, "Knock, knock."

Sheridan looked up from kneading dough that would become tomorrow's biscuits to see Ryan standing there with a grin on his face she couldn't help returning. He was so immediately likeable. "What brings you by?"

"Can't a guy stop by to see the woman he's dating?" She gave him a look that she hoped said 'very funny'. His chuckle told her he got the message. "I was in the neighborhood. The guy out front told me I could find you here."

"The whole town is 'in the neighborhood', so that isn't saying much. And that guy is Wesley, my co-owner." She told him a short version of how she came to hire him.

"He's built more like a linebacker than a baker." He wasn't wrong in his visual assessment of Wesley, but she knew the comment came from him not understanding what it took to keep a restaurant going.

"Trust me, you need more strength for this work than you might think. Between the upper body workout of stirring, rolling and kneading, and standing for hours, it takes endurance." He tipped his head at her. Yeah, she could hear the edge of defensiveness in her voice. "Sorry, I don't like it when people think what we do back here resembles what they do at home. A lot goes into running a food service business. But you didn't answer my question. What brought you by?"

"I had to come get one of these cinnamon rolls everyone's been talking about and forgot you'd be sold out." She couldn't say what it was, but something in his tone told her that wasn't the full truth, so she said nothing. Finally, he gave an embarrassed shrug and said, "I'm bored." And he looked kind of adorable admitting it. "I prefer being busy. It didn't occur to me when I planned to be off for this wedding that I'd have so much downtime. I'm not used to it. Everyone else has things they need to be doing, and I don't want to hang out at my parents' house. I remembered the café closes at three, so I came to see if you're free."

She heard the frustration in his voice and understood. She wasn't good at doing nothing, either. As she put the finished dough in the refrigerator, she said, "Not for a few more hours, but if you're up for it, you can hang around and give me a hand."

"Are you sure? I'm not much of a cook. I'm more of a takeout and leftovers kind of guy."

"If Eden can teach us to dance, I can teach you to cook. Or at least to help." She pointed at the sink. "Go wash your hands."

"Yes, ma'am," he said and gave her a salute. Sass, her mother would call it.

"Do I look like ma'am to you?" she said, putting her hands on her hips and trying to sound annoyed rather than amused.

"No, ma'am," he said with a dimpled smile and a wink. He put his ever-present camera bag in her office, went to the sink to do as he was told, then came to stand beside her, close enough that she could see the spot he'd missed shaving that morning. "What are we making?"

"Scones for tomorrow's customers. Cookies for the rehearsal dinner on Friday," she said. "I'm making the dough in advance. I'll bake them that afternoon before everyone arrives, so they'll still be warm."

"Oh, I can manage cookies. You take the tube it from the refrigerator, cut slices from the tube, and whatever you don't eat raw goes into the oven."

"Not exactly, Pillsbury Dough Boy." She poked him in the stomach as if he were the brand icon, and he gave the appropriate giggle. "Making them from scratch is different."

"Yeah, I kind of figured. What do you need me to do?"

"Take whatever I hand you and put it on the island." She went into the refrigerator, followed by the storeroom and handed him item after item and watched the surprise register on his face as the island became crowded. "Didn't know we'd need so much, did you?"

"I've seen my mom prepare big dinners, but I don't think she's ever started with so many ingredients."

"Like I said, different from home. And that's why we have Rose over here." She put a hand on top of the floor mixer she used on a regular basis.

"You named your mixer? For Dani's aunt?"

Sheridan gave a laugh. "No, not Rosie, Rose. Over there is Blanche," she said, tipping her head toward the oven. Then she pointed to the refrigerator and said, "And that's Dorothy."

His smile told her he got the reference. "The Golden Girls. No Sophia?"

She thought for a moment. "I haven't named the dishwasher, which is as vital as any of our other machines, so she can be Sophia."

As Sheridan handed him bowls, spoons, and measuring cups, Ryan said, "Is it typical for a restaurateur to name their equipment?"

"I don't know if it's typical, but it's probably not unusual. Laurel named her fermentation tanks for the Sanderson Sisters and the Powder Puff girls, so when I got my pieces, I decided to do it, too. I know chefs who name their knives. I guess when something is important, naming it boosts that importance. Have you ever considered naming your cameras?"

"No," he said, and she could see him thinking. "Not sure what I'd chose if I did. And if any of my colleagues have, they don't share those names with anyone else."

The scones were in the oven when Wesley brought in the few remaining baked goods from the day's inventory and announced the last customers were gone. "You're still here," he said, stating the obvious when he saw Ryan. "And I see you've been put to work."

"I'm trying not to mess anything up too badly. Or slow her down."

Wesley gave a short laugh. "Don't worry. She won't let you do either."

As Wesley put pastries in a bag, Ryan asked, "What are those?"

"Day-olds. We'll sell them tomorrow."

"Not many," Ryan said.

Wesley twisted the bag closed. "Rarely are." Sheridan shook her head. What they said in ten words would have taken her and her friends three times as many. "Need my help for anything?"

"Nah, I'm good," she said. He always asked. She usually said no. "Besides, you're working extra shifts during the wedding. I've got this covered."

Wesley said goodnight, and Ryan and Sheridan kept working. "I'm sorry I don't have any cinnamon rolls for you. I'll put one aside for you tomorrow if you want."

"Yes, please. Everyone says your cinnamon rolls are the best," Ryan said. "Do you always run out of them?"

"Every day. It's what we're known for. That and my grilled cheese sandwiches. But cinnamon rolls are my favorite thing to make. They are the only food that gets better the more you eat it." He raised an eyebrow. She'd seen him do that during the Attendants calls, but in person it was cuter. "Have you ever noticed that the first bite of any food is the best? And after, it's not quite as good anymore."

"No, that's not…." His voice trailed off as he thought about it. "Wait, is it?"

"I think so. That first bite is everything. It's either what you've been looking forward to or it's something new you're discovering, but either way it starts off wonderful and then? It's either more of the same or not quite as good. Maybe it's because the meal is getting colder or the ratio changes — like when you get to the end of a sandwich and it's more crust than filling. And as you go on, you're getting full so you don't quite enjoy it as much."

As they finished the cookie doughs, she watched him remember his experience with foods. "You're right. Ice cream melts. Pizza toppings are gone before you finish the slice, and I can never make the cheese last as long as the soup on French onion soup."

"Exactly. It's frustrating. But with cinnamon rolls, the more you eat, the closer you get to the best part. The gooey center. There's more of everything in the last bite than there was in the first. Nothing else is like that."

"Maybe sex," he said.

"What?" That wasn't something anyone ever suggested before, and it certainly wasn't something she expected him to say.

"Okay, sure, sex is different from food, but when it's good, it gets better with each part. You start out with kissing, and that's great, but then you get to touching." Had his voice deepened? He was certainly talking slower, drawing out every word as if he were picturing what he was doing. "From touching, you can move to undressing — and more touching — and to licking and tasting. Until you get to the center. The climax."

Sheridan's mouth had gone dry. As Ryan talked, something unexpected happened. Sheridan could feel what he was saying. And wanted more. With no warning or hint that it might happen, she found herself drawn to him, wanting to know what his kisses felt like, his touch. What it might be like to....

BUZZ

Like an electronic chaperone, the timer on Blanche rang, breaking the spell and saving Sheridan from doing something foolish. Like kissing him.

She took out the tray of scones, slid off the silicone sheet, and placed them directly on a cooling rack where they'd be waiting for her in the morning. She took off her apron, not daring to look at Ryan for fear he'd see what she was imagining. "I guess we're done for the day. Thanks for your help."

"Thanks for keeping me busy," he said. "And sharing about cooking. I actually learned a lot and will *not* take cookies for granted again. Are you free for dinner?"

She liked the invitation more than she expected, but she needed to remember he wasn't interested in more than what they'd established. "You really want to make sure word gets around that you're with someone."

His slightly sheepish expression said she was partially right. "Maybe there's a little of that, but I'm enjoying spending time with you. And since you've been doing all this cooking and prep work, I'm guessing you're not eager to make yourself dinner."

It was true that most nights she kept her meals simple or brought home leftovers from the café. She didn't think of it as takeout because she was the one who made it. Still, she was enjoying the company too, so she said, "Sounds good. But you have to have me in bed by ten or I'm a grump in the morning."

She didn't realize what she'd said until he gave her a devilish grin. "That works for me."

Crap! "Home. You need to have me home early. Sorry, slip of the tongue."

"That sounds good, too."

She dropped her head into her hand. She wasn't usually like this, making casual comments that could be construed as flirting. He was bringing out something unexpected in her, and she was more comfortable with it than she expected. Was that because nothing between them had a chance of lasting? Maybe. "Okay, one more crack like that and you're eating alone."

He put his hands up in surrender. "You win."

"Let's talk dinner. What are you in the mood for?" He gave her a look that she thought might say "you," but she wasn't used to wanting to respond to those kinds of signals. Deciding the best course of action was to ignore it completely, she said, "Have you been to the Seven Brothers yet?"

"No, although I had one of their beers. Nick put some in the fridge at the house."

"It's the best around," Sheridan said. People might call her biased, but to her it was truthful. "Let's go."

Her car was at her place, and his was out front, so he offered to drive. "I can't get over how many places I haven't been to," he said as they drove. "That bookstore and the pet supply store weren't here. I think Pie in the Sky is new, too. And your place, of course."

"When were you here last?"

"After my dad's heart attack."

"I remember hearing about that. It was around six months before my place opened. I was here, but I was working with Laurel." She explained how she'd come to help her friend open the business.

"And after Laurel was set, you stayed?"

She nodded. "You love the unpredictability of your career, but I love knowing what my day is going to hold. Most of it, anyway." She didn't mind that they saw things so differently, wanted different things. It meant any attraction she felt for him wouldn't change her life in the long run, and that was perfect. "Before I moved here, I was always trying to fit in. Here, I belong. I can be myself in a way I've never been able to."

"I can see the appeal, even if I'm not ready for small town life. Although there have been more changes since

I was here last. I should take time to play tourist. I also need to take another drive through the mountains to get more local shots to post to my commercial usage portfolio."

"What's that?"

"Have you ever seen sites where people can buy stock photos?"

She nodded. "Sure. I use a couple on our site. It was easier and cheaper than taking ones ourselves, although Chris Farrell — he manages my site — did come in and take a few of the place for us to use."

"Which is smart. Your place has a specific look and charm, but when you need something more, stock photos come in handy. Those images come from photographers like me. We upload our work and get part of the fee when people license our images. Whenever I'm traveling, I build in time to take extra pictures separate from the shoot that I can use to expand what I offer. Gives me an excuse to have fun and explore more of a place I'm visiting."

"Having fun while making money. What could be better?"

The devilish grin he gave her had her blushing. If she hoped he wouldn't notice, his smile told her otherwise. "I... am going to let that go."

She was grateful. Fortunately, she was saved from more banter as they pulled up to the Seven Brothers Brewery, easily finding a parking spot because it was early in the week.

"Hey, Sheridan. Not your usual day for coming here," Cameron, the front desk host, said as they walked in. "Unless it's Friday already, and I've totally lost track of time, which, considering my course load, is entirely possible."

"No, you're good. It's Wednesday, and I know Laurel isn't here tonight." Since falling in love with Hunter, Laurel was better about taking a night or two off during the week so they could have time together. "Cameron, this is Ryan Sinclair. He's in town for a wedding. He's never been here, so I decided to fix that."

"Absolutely. We are one of the places you shouldn't miss in Fable Notch. Follow me," she said. Sheridan was sure when Cameron said that most men — and likely women, too — took it as an invitation to check out the curvy blonde. Glancing at Ryan, Sheridan was happy to see he was looking at the decor.

"I'd heard they'd done things with several of the abandoned paper mills, but this is my first time inside one." He almost walked into a chair as they made their way to a booth on the side.

"You should check out Ash Royce's clothing store, Fluid," she said. "That's also in a repurposed mill."

"Nice to know not all of the businesses are in old Colonials."

Sheridan had to laugh. That was one of the first things she'd noticed when she came to town. While it wasn't as true on the main street, it seemed as though every third or fourth business was in a building that used to be a house. This was the case for Dani's veterinarian practice, the hair salon, and others. Even the Triangle General Store had started as a residence, and the Fishers still lived on the top floors. "You've got to admit, living and working in the same building makes for a short commute."

"Cole is about to have that." He told her his brother's plan for the school.

Cameron put their menus on the table. "Specials are on the board over the bar, and your server will be over shortly." She took a step toward her post, then turned back. "Ryan Sinclair? Your mother wouldn't be Millie, would she?"

"The very same. Let me guess. You took piano lessons from her." Sheridan didn't know why, but she thought his smile looked forced.

"I did when I was in middle school. And now my little brother does. He's going to the new music school so he can also take guitar from Cole Hanson." Something else clicked, and she snapped her fingers. "You're here for Eden and Theo's wedding."

"I am," he said. He chatted with Cameron for a few more minutes, keeping his answers short before she left them alone, and Ryan turned his focus to the menu.

They sat in silence, looking at the choices before Sheridan's curiosity got the better of her. "Are you okay?"

He looked at her over the top of his menu. "Why wouldn't I be?"

She'd opened this can of worms. No avoiding it now. "I realize we haven't known each other for very long, but while you were talking to Cameron, it seemed as though something was bothering you."

For a second, she didn't know if he was going to answer her. Finally, he said, "In California — or wherever I'm living — I'm my own person. I'm known for my achievements and my abilities, my creativity, and my talent. With new clients, I get to prove myself and impress them with what I'm capable of and how that can help them. Past clients hire me again because they know what I can do for them." There was pride in his voice, but also frustration.

"But not here," she guessed.

"When I'm here, everywhere I go, I'm reminded I'm my parents' son. It's like when you win a major award, and you give up your first name." She must have given him an odd look because he explained, "You become Academy Award Winner Jane Jones or Pulitzer Prize Winner Joe Smith. In Fable Notch, it doesn't matter what I've done or where I've been, I'm Martin-and-Millie's-son Ryan. I can't just be me. I come with this whole history that's both mine and theirs." He sighed and ran a hand through his hair. Sheridan wished she knew what to say to make him feel better. She'd never imagined there might be circumstances where there were downsides to a loving upbringing. Turning the conversation he asked, "Do you ever go home?"

She shook her head. "Rarely. The occasional holiday, but work keeps me pretty busy, and I don't like taking time away. And remember, my mother is on her fourth marriage. I can't say any place I lived in as a child felt like home, not after my father died."

He winced. "Sorry. That was insensitive of me. I should have thought twice. I know what a tough household did to my brothers."

"It's okay. I had my sister, Paisley, and once I learned to bake, I never had to worry about not having friends." Baking always brought people together. "If it's any consolation, I don't see you that way. I mean, I know your folks, but I'm enjoying getting to know you, No-First-Name-Other-Than Ryan."

The smile he gave her showed his dimple. This one was real. "I'm enjoying getting to know you, too, Fable Notch's Southern Belle."

"Is that my name's precursor?"

"Pretty much. It was how I first heard you described. Does it bother you?"

"Not in the least. When you sound like I do and live in New England, it's going to be remarked on."

"And I suppose with everyone living here now, I'll have to get used to being asked about my family, since I'll be back more often. Holidays and things." He gave a shrug and went back to looking at the menu. "So, what's good here?"

"Everything, of course," she said, glad to focus on something other than the fact he was going to be around after the weddings. Being his date was supposed to come without string. Would this unexpected attraction cause a problem in the future when he visited? She didn't have much experience with this, so she didn't have an answer. It was a touch worrying, but there wasn't anything to do about it now.

When their server came by, they chose beers and an appetizer to split, then put in the order for their entrees after their drinks came. During the meal, she noticed familiar faces and smiled when she met people's eyes. Yup, the news of them being seen together would soon be all over town.

At the end of the meal, Ryan said, "You were right."

"About?" They'd discussed so much she wasn't sure what he was referring to.

He tilted up his empty plate. "The food. It was terrific."

"I'll pass your compliments on to Laurel when I see her." She let him pay when he insisted and didn't mind when he put his hand on her back as they walked out. Soon after, they were pulling up in front of her house. "Thanks for dinner. And the help in the kitchen earlier."

"Thanks for keeping me out of trouble. I had fun," he said as he parked the car. "I feel as though I should walk you to your door."

"It's nice that your momma taught you manners, but this wasn't a real date, so there's no need."

As she reached for the door handle, he said, "If this *were* a real date, I'd ask if I could kiss you good night."

She smiled at him and answered without thinking, letting her increasing awareness of him speak first. "If this were a real date, I'd let you."

Not waiting for his response, she got out of the car and went into her house. Closing the door behind her, she dropped her bag onto the floor and leaned against the wall.

I'd let you. I'd let you. I'd let you.

Oh shit, said a voice in her head. This was not part of the plan. It was all supposed to be an act.

But she'd gotten to know him. His passion for his work, and his love for his family. The sound of his laughter, the way he asked thoughtful questions, and his willingness to listen. And something had definitely shifted.

Because as she stood there, what she really wanted was for Ryan to kiss her.

Chapter Nine

Ryan was the first thing Sheridan thought of when she woke the next day. He'd also been on her mind when she went to sleep, so it shouldn't have been a surprise.

The zing was the surprise.

It had been so long since she'd felt attracted to someone, and she had put Ryan firmly in the casual friend category. She'd never expected to be drawn to him as she got to know him better. And now that she was, she didn't know what to do. She'd been so quick to brush off Laurel's and Dani's concerns about this arrangement.

Could they have been right?

Neither she nor Ryan had any interest in a relationship — that was the whole reason for pretending to be dating. Reminding herself that friendship and a new attraction didn't mean her heart was in danger, she made a new plan to enjoy what they had for as long as it lasted and be fine after he left.

She focused on her work, but the tingles returned when Ryan walked in at eight thirty. His eyes locked on hers and his smile, complete with dimples, warmed his face when he saw her. He waited patiently in line with the other customers and when he came to the front, he said, "Please tell me I'm not too late for a cinnamon roll."

"You are not too late." She'd done what she said and put one aside for him the way she did for Ash. "For here or to go?"

"Here, please." And she was inappropriately glad he'd be staying.

She headed for the kitchen, stopped and turned back. "Do you want it warmed?" He gave her a half smile as an answer, and she blushed. Oh, this was not good. When she brought him the plate with a fork on the side, she asked, "How do you feel about icing?"

"I'm for it," he said, but looked confused.

She laughed. "Some people like a little, some a lot. We offer an extra container for those who like more."

"More always sounds good," he said. Yeah, tingles. Which she did her best to ignore as she put a side of icing on his plate and handed it to him. He bought a coffee to go with it and settled himself at a table by the window.

Curious what he'd think, she watched him take his first bite. His eyes closed and his shoulders dropped. Exactly the reaction she wanted. When he opened his eyes, he caught her staring. Before she had a chance to look away, he gave her a wink and a thumbs up. She went back to her customers, trying to keep her focus on them, although she did notice him take out his camera and photograph the food. Pride mixed with the tingles. She appreciated it when customers shared their love of her food.

She was with a customer when Ryan got up and cleared his table. He waited to the side until she was free. "Well?" she asked, knowing the answer.

"Rarely does something live up to the hype, let alone surpass it. This did. Sheridan, those are amazing. Every bite better than the last, and the center?" He made a chef's kiss with his hand. "Everything you said it would be."

She flushed, both from the compliment and from remembering what he said about sex being something that got better as it went along. "I'm glad you enjoyed it."

"Very much. I want more already." Yeah, still thinking about sex — and it was unnerving. Fortunately, an order came up, and she needed to go back to work. "I'll see you tomorrow at the rehearsal dinner, right?"

"Considering it's here? Absolutely."

"I'm off to spend the day taking pictures of the area. Have fun at the bachelorette party tonight. We'll be eating nachos and playing pool at the Varnum."

"We're going dancing at Flurry. Eden can't get enough." For a second, Sheridan wondered if he might kiss her the way couples did when they say goodbye, but the moment passed. She had mixed feelings about that.

On Thursdays, business picked up as the weekend started early for some folks, so she didn't have much of a chance to think about Ryan as the day went on. After the café closed, she spent the next two hours doing prep work for the meals on Friday before going home and making herself a sandwich for dinner, then jumping into the shower.

As she stood looking through her closet, she decided on a long, bright pink shirt to go with leggings and flats and a touch of eyeliner — the bigger production for that could wait for the wedding. She thought she looked good, until Dani showed up at her door wearing a mini skirt, a green short-sleeve knit top with sparkles that looked perfect with her auburn hair, and low-heeled shoes. It was such a change from the casual clothes Sheridan was used to seeing her in, she couldn't stop the "Wow."

"Thanks," Dani said as she rubbed her hands down the side of the skirt as if she wasn't sure. "I have no idea what people wear to clubs these days. I hope this is okay."

"It's more than okay. You look great. But I look underdressed." Sheridan had a terrible realization. "What's Laurel wearing?"

"A dress, I think."

Sheridan groaned, her head falling back. She was certain Eden would be wearing something that floated around her as she danced, and Janelle? Who knew what she'd choose, but whatever it was, it would be fabulous. Everyone would look like they belonged. Except her. "I need help. This isn't going to work," she said, indicating her outfit.

"I think you look fine, but if you want to change, we've got time. Do you have any dresses?"

"Maybe?" She never wore them, which was why she'd bought a new one for the wedding and was planning to get another for Mia's. "There could be something buried in my closet. What am I going to do?"

"We'll search through your closet and call for help," Dani said, taking her phone out of the tiny bag she was carrying. Seconds later, she'd filled Laurel in on the situation, and Laurel offered to swing by instead of meeting them at the club. "She said she'll bring options. Just in case."

"You look terrific," Sheridan said when Laurel arrived. Her friend was wearing a multicolored dress that reminded Sheridan of the one Jennifer Garner wore in *Thirteen Going on Thirty*. "I can't believe Hunter let you leave the house looking like that."

Laurel blushed. "He almost didn't." Sheridan snorted and put her hand to her mouth to cover the sound. "Exactly. And don't worry, you're going to look amazing, too." She held up a navy-blue dress that had simple lines but the added touch of being in an iridescent fabric. "Maybe not your favorite color, but it will be fine if we can't find anything else."

Without another word, Dani and Laurel dashed upstairs to Sheridan's bedroom and made a beeline for her small closet. She could have told them exactly what they'd find. The front part was nothing but long knit shirts, most of which she wore to work followed by two blouses and one black skirt. At the end was a long fuzzy robe she loved to curl up in during the colder months.

"Nope, nope, nope," Laurel said, as she went through each piece, getting through what little Sheridan had fairly quickly. Then she perked up. "Hey, do I see a Little Black Dress all the way at the end?" As Laurel moved the clothes forward, Sheridan suddenly remembered what was also at the end of the rack. She tried to stop Laurel, but it was too late. Laurel went past the black dress – which wasn't suitable for dancing – to one she hadn't seen in so long she'd forgotten it was there.

"Um, what is this?" Laurel said, pulling out a dress Sheridan hadn't thought of in years. She winced. She'd kept it as a reminder that even when her body and heart agreed on something — they couldn't be trusted.

Dani took it from Laurel, who was waiting for an answer. "Okay, I know white can be worn other times, but as someone who's gone shopping for one recently, this looks a lot like a wedding dress."

Sheridan wanted to deny it or make a joke, but these were her friends, her family. She wasn't going to lie to them. "That's because it is. And before you ask, yes, it was supposed to be mine." Dani nearly dropped the dress, so Sheridan took it from her and hung it on the hook on the back of the closet door. When she turned to her friends, they were still staring, their gazes glued to the dress.

Dani found her voice first, "You were engaged?"

"No, but I thought I was going to be." She had been so certain where their relationship was going that when she'd seen the dress, she couldn't stop herself from trying it on. And when it had fit perfectly, she'd bought it on the spot. Foolishly.

"Who was he?" Laurel asked. "When did this happen? Why have you never told me?" In this moment, Sheridan was more upset not to have shared something with her friends than she was embarrassed about what had happened. Back then, she'd been so devastated to be wrong, she'd never wanted to talk about him again. Before she could answer, Laurel said, "Wait, was this Paul something-or-other?"

So, Laurel did remember. Sheridan mentioned him much because the relationship had happened at the same time Laurel had moved back to Fable Notch when her mom Valerie had breast cancer. It hadn't felt right sharing her newfound happiness while her friend was going through so much. She'd expected there would be plenty of time to tell Laurel later. After all, the relationship was going to last forever.

She'd been so very wrong.

Sheridan took a deep breath and sank onto the bed. "It was."

"Who is Paul? What did I miss?" Dani asked, her head going back and forth between Laurel and Sheridan. Sheridan could see the uncertainty in her friend's eyes. Because of old wounds, Dani was sometimes worried about their friendship.

This was not something she wanted Dani to worry about. "Paul was a coworker of mine at a restaurant in Memphis. We worked well together, became friends, and after he moved to another restaurant, things changed, and our relationship became something more."

"It must have been serious for you to buy this dress," Laurel said, her voice soft and concerned as she sat next to Sheridan on the bed.

Dani sat on the other side. "I feel the need to state the obvious. It didn't work out. Will you tell us what happened?"

It was odd to talk about him. It felt like it happened a lifetime ago, but her friends deserved to know. "Paul was ambitious. He wanted to work in better restaurants in bigger cities. He cooked on his days off, making videos of his work and sending them to other establishments. Eventually, one of them flew him out to San Francisco for an interview and hired him." And everything changed. She hadn't thought of their last night in a long time, but the memories came back as vividly as if she'd pressed 'play' on a recording.

The joy on Paul's face made him more handsome than usual. "I did it, Sheridan," he said, his excitement palpable. He couldn't sit still, and he paced around his apartment. It looked like he might start packing right then and there. "I am getting out of this would-be-city and moving to the big time. My career can truly begin."

Sheridan was thrilled for him. She didn't know how long it might take her to find a job in California, but there had to be more opportunities there than here. She liked the restaurant she worked in, and she was getting great experience, but it wasn't the job of her dreams. There was no baking and no opportunity for her to be creative. Maybe in a new place, she'd get closer to doing what she wanted. Already she was wondering how she could get out of her lease, and if her employer would care if she quit. "When do you need to be out there?"

"I told my boss about the offer. He asked if I'd stay a week, and I agreed. I called the new restaurant, and we decided I'd start in two weeks. Gives time to drive out there. They have an Air BnB they use for visiting chefs I can stay in for the first month until I find a place of my own, so I don't have to worry about that." He stopped moving as if the enormity of everything hit him. "Holy shit! In eight days, I am California bound." He gave another whoop, picked her up, and spun her around. "I. Am. Outta. Here!"

Laughing as he put her down, her arms still around him, she said, "This is so exciting. I don't know how much notice I need to give, but it shouldn't be long."

He stopped smiling. "What do you need to give notice for?"

"So, I can join you," she said. Paul let her go and took a step back, then ran a hand through his hair and put more distance between them. Sheridan's heart jumped for a different reason. Why was he acting like this? Maybe he was surprised. That was it. He didn't expect her to be willing to join him so quickly. Right? As alarms went off in her head, she said, "You do want me to come with you. Don't you?"

The fact that she had to ask should have told her the answer, but she waited. She needed to hear it. He probably responded after a few seconds, but in her memory there was a long, uncomfortable pause. "Sweetheart," he started, and she bit the inside of her cheek. His tone told her everything. As did the endearment he'd never used before. "You knew this was temporary." Sure, she knew that about his work, but it never occurred to her it was true about their relationship. "I'm sorry if you thought things were serious between us. I mean, it's been great and all, but I can't be worrying about a girlfriend while I'm working my ass off. This is the best thing that's ever happened to me. I can't be tied down."

But they were a couple. What they had was special to them both, wasn't it? She'd turned down a job when he was frustrated it would mean she needed to work mornings and they'd never see each other. She'd imagined a future with him, both of them cooking and creating what they loved, maybe opening a place together. "But... I love you. You said you love me." She sounded foolish, like those horrible clingy women she'd never imagined herself to be.

"I did. I do. We've had a lot of fun together, but that doesn't mean this is long term. Look, I know you haven't had a lot of relationships because of that demi-thing. Maybe that's why you thought this was more than it is."

He might be right, but she didn't like him throwing it in her face, and she wished she'd never shared that with him. She was wishing she hadn't shared a lot. "Damn it, Sheridan. Why are you ruining this for me?"

Ruining it for *him*? That was a laugh. She pictured the beautiful dress in her closet, bought for a wedding that was never happening. "I'm sorry. I guess I didn't realize what we had was only for now. My mistake." A big mistake. And one she promised herself she would never make again. She would never allow herself to be more committed to a relationship than she was to her own dreams. Had she learned nothing from her mother, whose only goal was to be married?

When she was done sharing the worst day of her life with her friends, Laurel said, "Everything about that sounds horrible."

"He was a jerk," Dani added in solidarity. "He didn't deserve you, and you deserve better."

"Thank you and, Laurel, before you ask, the reason I didn't tell you when things were going well was because it was when your mom was sick. With all you and your family were going through, it never seemed like the right time to mention him. And I didn't tell you after because I felt like a fool."

"*He* was the fool," Laurel said. "Dani is right. You deserve better. Is he part of the reason you offered to move here to help me when the brewery opened?"

Sheridan wasn't surprised Laurel made the connection. "Yes. You opened the Seven Brothers shortly after everything fell apart. I was looking for a new job, and it was the perfect opportunity to get away. I didn't expect Fable Notch would end up being the perfect place to stay."

"Well, I could have told you that," Dani said, bumping Sheridan with her shoulder. Sheridan had heard the stories of how Dani was happiest when she was in Fable Notch for the summers and couldn't wait to move back when the opportunity arose.

Laurel put her head on Sheridan's shoulder and said, "And as sorry as I am that you had to deal with that asshole, I can't help but be happy for the way it turned out." She stretched her arm across and grabbed Dani's hand. "Because I have my two best friends living here."

Laurel was right. The experience may have sucked, but the results were kind of perfect. "It was a good lesson, if a hard learned one." She supposed all the big ones were. She put her arms around them and gave them a squeeze. She was so lucky to have them.

"I'm curious," Dani said. "Why did you keep the dress?"

"As a reminder and a warning." When she moved to Fable Notch, she almost left the dress behind, but decided to take it with her in case she ever got carried away again. Was it a sign that it reappeared as she found herself attracted to Ryan? "Marriage isn't for me."

"Plenty of people who identify as demi marry," Laurel said.

"Yes, they do. And I hope they're happy. But I'm good with my decision. Honestly, given my mom? I think I'd feel this way even if I wasn't on the ace spectrum," she said as she took the dress and hung it on a hook on the back of the closet door. Relationships created an unpredictability and chaos she had no interest in having in her life. And she knew better than to ever be dependent on love to make her happy.

Dani came over and gave her a quick hug. "I'm sorry. I shouldn't have asked. I mean, you keep the dress hidden and with all the wedding talk the last few months, you've never mentioned this jerk. That should have told me enough."

"It's okay. Truthfully, my life is so wonderful now, and Paul is so far in the past that until you were headed to the back of my closet, I completely forgot about him and the dress." She hadn't forgotten the lesson, but she didn't mention that. Instead, she said, "And I have every intention of forgetting again. Now, text Eden to let her know we'll be there soon, and let me get dressed so we can go dancing."

Chapter Ten

Ryan was surprised Theo chose the Varnum Bar and Grill for his bachelor party. Ryan had been eleven when Susan Hanson died, but the first year the Hansons were at his house, he'd overheard several stories of how Cole and Theo had to pick her up from the bar when she was drunk. They never had anything good to say about the place, although Nick knew the food was respectable. The bar may not have changed much, but his brothers certainly had.

Theo planned a low-key night with his brothers, three of the Stewarts, and Derek Ahern, a friend of Nick's who ran the auto shop and who, he learned as they were introduced, moved to town at the end of last summer. They ordered beers and all the typical appetizers, then headed to the pool tables. They took two tables and divided into teams of two, managing a round robin, so each pair played the others. Winners got bragging rights, which could last for years in a small town.

"What is your bride doing tonight?" Adam asked as he chalked his stick while Theo racked the balls.

"Dancing, of course," Theo said with a smile so full of love it would have been sappy if Ryan hadn't known what it had taken for Theo and Eden to be together. "She's at your brother's place with her friends." Theo's words reminded Ryan that Jeremy Stewart owned Flurry. It also made him think of Sheridan and wonder what she was doing, wearing, and if she'd catch the attention of anyone while she was there. Probably. The woman had a sparkle that men found irresistible.

"Isn't Flurry where you met Casey?" Nick asked Derek, nudging him on the shoulder.

Derek pulled in his lips before saying, "It is. Then I ran into her two more times before the weekend was over." Derek's tone said there was more to the story, but his expression suggested it wouldn't be a good idea to ask.

As they tried to decide who should start, Nick said, "Age before beauty," and swept his hand toward the table. Cole gave him a "fuck you" look, but it didn't stop him from breaking.

"What are we doing for your bachelor party?" Lucas asked Cole as he walked around the table, deciding on his first shot. Cole and Lucas, the second oldest of the Stewart clan, had reconnected when Cole moved back, not only because they had been friends in high school, but because Lucas was Mia's lawyer when her custody of Dean was threatened.

"Mia and I have decided on the same thing — movie night."

"So we're all going to be together?" Ryan asked. It could be nice sitting in the dark with Sheridan watching a movie, learning which ones she liked, listening to her laugh. Finding a way to put an arm around her, being close enough to smell her shampoo.

Damn, his thoughts were moving into dangerous territory.

Cole shook his head as he bent over the table. "Not unless you want to watch *While You Were Sleeping*, *Crazy Rich Asians*, and *The Notebook.*" There were groans all around.

"If that's guaranteed to get me laid, sure," Lucas said. "Only reason to watch those is to get her in the mood."

"Which is why Mia and her friends will be at our house, and we will be at Nick's place," Cole said, knocking in another ball. This time, the groans were about Cole's skill. The man had played pool to earn extra money when he was younger. He hadn't lost his touch, and Ryan wondered if any of them were going to get a turn this round. "I thought it was time to introduce Dean to some classics. *The Big Lebowski*, *Animal House*, and *Harold and Kumar Go to White Castle.* Maybe a little *Evil Dead*."

"Now that sounds like fun. I haven't seen *Lebowski* in years," Nick said.

"Isn't anyone going to hire a stripper?" Ryan asked. It earned him several raised eyebrows. "Fine, isn't anyone going to a strip club? We've got three weddings. What happened to tradition?"

"It grew up," Cole said.

"Like the rest of us," Theo finished.

Ryan had been kidding when he suggested it, but Cole's and Theo's comments brought him up short. Yes, unlike them and Nick, he wasn't tied down, but that didn't mean he hadn't grown up. Okay, he owned nothing but his car and his camera equipment, but he paid bills, met deadlines, and had built a business. He was plenty grown up.

He was going to make a comment to that point, then realized the conversation had moved on. Maybe Theo was referring to himself. None of the others were looking at Ryan as if he needed to defend himself, so he let it go. Talk turned to work, movies, sports, and questions for him about life in California, which, he had to admit, felt like a world away.

Theo chalked his cue as he walked around the table and said, "I've been meaning to ask you, Ryan, did your luggage ever arrive?"

Ryan rolled his eyes. "This morning. Practically tripped over it leaving the house. Hardly need it except to pack all the new clothes I ordered since I got here."

"No one's in the house again before you come back for the next wedding," Nick said, "so feel free to leave things there."

"Thanks, I might do that." He hadn't intentionally left anything in Fable Notch in over a decade. But then again, he hadn't visited so often in such a short span of time either.

As they continued to drink and play, Ryan couldn't help but notice how comfortable he was with everyone. He couldn't remember the last time he'd gone out with such a large group of people and felt so relaxed. Because he traveled so much and lived in so many different places, he knew people all over the country — and several overseas as well — but almost all of them were casual relationships. People he could grab a meal with or bunk with for a night or two, but no one he wanted to call if things were tough. The more he considered it, the more he realized there were very few people he called friends.

If he were getting married, besides the people here or those coming to one of the next weddings, who would he invite?

And what was he doing thinking about marriage?

He shook his head to dislodge the idea.

It was a good thing he was leaving Monday. Whatever held his brothers and their friends in this town was influencing him, too. He needed to get back to the work he loved and not get sucked into life in Fable Notch.

Play went on until ten, when guys started to head home. Whether that was because of the time or because no one could beat Cole, Ryan wasn't sure, but either way, it ended up being an earlier night than he expected. He almost made a crack about folks getting old and needing sleep but remembered that not only had most of these guys put in a full day of work before coming here, but some, like Adam, were going to work tomorrow before the wedding.

As Ryan was driving back to the house, fully intending to go to sleep early, he had another idea, and he headed to Flurry instead. He'd been there once, when he'd come to town to help his parents, Millie told him to get out of the house and have fun with people his own age. He'd danced with a handful of women and was given three phone numbers, including one from someone he'd known back in high school, which he tossed on the way to his car.

Tonight, he was hoping to dance with one woman in particular.

He paid the cover at the door and wondered how long it would take before he'd know if Sheridan was still here. The place was busy. Apparently, Jeremy Stewart was another local with a strong business. Both the dance floor and the bar were crowded.

Seconds after stepping inside, he spotted Sheridan at the bar wearing a blue dress that hugged her curves and makeup that made her eyes look bigger.

As he walked over to tell her how great she looked, he could see something was bothering her.

There was some jerk standing next to her, and whatever he was saying was making her uncomfortable. While he was leaning forward, she was leaning back, practically screaming 'go away,' but the guy didn't notice. As Ryan watched, whatever she was waiting for from the bartender arrived. She took the glasses off the bar and turned to go, but the man grabbed her upper arm, and she stopped. He was gripping her hard enough that Ryan could see his fingers press into her skin. She couldn't move without spilling the drinks.

Without thinking, Ryan rushed over. "I think the lady would like you to let go of her."

Sheridan took her eyes off the man and met Ryan's. From her expression, he could see he'd read the situation right. He got additional confirmation when, without turning around, the man said, "Scram, asshole. The lady and I are getting to know each other."

Ryan wouldn't say he was the touch-her-and-die type of guy, but he was not going to let this man intimidate Sheridan. For a split second, he considered what the consequences would be if he assaulted the dude. Scenarios and questions ran through his head. Would someone call the cops? Would he be held at the police station? Would he be out in time for the wedding if he was?

Fuck it. It was worth the chance.

He put his hand over the man's and pulled back one finger, instantly forcing him to release Sheridan. "I said, let her go."

The man spun around, and Ryan hoped he didn't have to fight. The guy wasn't small. And his brothers would be pissed if he showed up bruised for the ceremony, but he would do whatever was necessary. "Who the fuck do you think you — Sinclair? Ryan Sinclair?"

Shit. Ryan should have realized there was a chance the person was someone he knew. At least a fight was off the table. "Harry Newman." Harry had been the year ahead of Ryan in school, but they'd had elective classes together. He'd also been a jock who had his pick of the girls and liked everyone to know it. "Didn't I hear you got married a few years back?"

"Got married a lot of years back. The divorce was a few months ago."

Ryan gave him points for not cheating on his wife, but he wasn't letting him off the hook for upsetting Sheridan. With Harry's attention on him, Ryan tipped his head to the side and hoped Sheridan would get the message. She did and left the bar to join her friends. One problem solved.

"You in town for the wedding? We've all heard about your brothers moving back. Guess that means you will be, too."

As if his mother's assumptions weren't enough. "I'm just here to make sure my brothers don't get cold feet."

Not that any of them would. "And to have a good time. So, if you'll excuse me. Nice seeing you." Even though it wasn't.

"Yeah, sure." Harry turned back to the bar, then looked around for Sheridan, as if she'd still be there. Idiot.

Ryan went over to the bridal party, gave hugs to Eden, Dani and Mia, and said hello to everyone else. Eden asked the question everyone was probably thinking. "What are you doing here?"

"Your groom-to-be and his friends stopped partying early. I wasn't in the mood to call it a night yet."

"So you've crashed our party?" Mia asked. Her smile told him she was teasing.

"You seem to be the more fun group." They laughed. Still worried about Sheridan, he walked over to her and rubbed her back. It was intended to be reassuring, but he also wanted to touch her. "You okay?"

"Yes, thank you for the save," she said. "I go out so rarely, I'm never quite sure how to handle it when those things happen. And I have to be careful how I respond because the person could be a customer. Don't want to create a situation that could be bad for business."

"I hadn't considered that," he said. That could keep a person home at night. "I don't think you have to worry about Harry. He thinks I'm the one who ruined it for him. Not you." Wanting to lighten the mood, he continued, "I owe you a beer from our 'jinx' during the dance practice."

"You do, but I had one earlier and since I have a full day tomorrow, that's my limit." She lifted her glass. "I'm on club soda."

"In that case, wanna practice?" he said, holding out a hand and motioning to the dance floor. For a second, he thought she might turn him down, but she put her drink on the table and took his hand. He pulled her close, liking the feel of her in his arms, and spun them out to join the other dancers.

They had fun for the first few songs and laughed when the Michael Bublé song started playing. As they practiced, Eden rushed over and danced next to them, mirroring Sheridan, and helping them along. When the song ended, she gave each of them a hug. "You're both awesome. Thank you," she said before rejoining her friends.

With the next song, the music slowed, and couples came to the floor. Ryan wanted to continue, but he didn't want to presume, especially after her earlier encounter with Harry. "Shall we?" he asked. When she stepped closer, he put his hands around her waist and drew her to him. She encircled his neck, and they swayed to the music, not worrying about the right steps.

"This is what I assumed we'd be doing at the wedding," she said. "I should have known better."

"Depending on the music, we still can." And he found himself hoping they would. Last night she'd said if it were a date, she would have let him kiss her. Now that she was in his arms, he couldn't stop thinking about it. Staring at her lips, he wondered what she would taste like. Cinnamon and icing? A hint of the beer she'd had earlier? What would it be like to turn her laughter and smiles into moans and sighs?

He was considering taking a first step when they were jostled by another couple, causing them both to stumble. There were apologies all around, but before they could start dancing again, the song ended, and Sheridan's watch lit up. "That's my cue," she said, turning off what must have been an alarm.

He checked the time. "It's only eleven."

"Which is already an hour past my usual bedtime on a work night. Weekends are busy and they start on Friday. I'm even working Saturday morning. If I don't go now, I'm going to be worn slap out."

He loved her southern phrases. "I'd say I'm surprised that you're working the day of the wedding, but considering I'm sort of working *at* the wedding, I suppose I can't comment."

"We do what we must for what we love," she said. He liked that sentiment. She might have chosen a settled and predictable life, but she was as committed to her profession as he was to his.

He walked her back to the group, and she said her goodbyes. "Is it already that time?" Dani asked.

"It is. My personal pumpkin hour," she said, giving Dani a hug, then going to each of the women. To Eden she said, "Sweetest dreams. See you at dinner tomorrow. Call me if anything changes."

Ryan waved to the women and fell into step next to her.

"What are you doing?" she asked.

"Walking you to your car." Before she could tell him it wasn't necessary, he put a hand up. "I came to see you and now you're leaving. And I wouldn't want Harry or anyone else following you out. Besides, an early evening and a good night's sleep aren't a bad idea for me either."

They got to her car, and he held the door for her. "I promise to report back to Millie that you're a perfect gentleman," she said as she got in.

"Oh, I am not as perfect as you think," he said. She arched an eyebrow, suggesting she might want to know more, but instead of saying anything, she closed the door, started her car, and gave him a wave as she drove off. Probably a good thing because one more minute together and he was going to kiss her.

This was fake, he reminded himself. It was supposed to make his life easier. He wasn't supposed to want to kiss her, but he did.

And he wanted more than that.

Chapter Eleven

The Saturday of Eden and Theo's wedding dawned sunny and beautiful, and Sheridan would know because, as usual, she was up before the sun and getting ready for the day's customers less than a half hour later.

As she walked into the kitchen, she realized she'd only left it a few hours before, after the rehearsal dinner. She'd been nervous to host the event for Eden and Theo, but everything had gone smoothly and even Eden's father, Patrick, enjoyed himself and the food — taking the time to come into the kitchen to compliment her. The biggest surprise was when Eden insisted Sheridan join them at dinner. Sheridan had been planning to spend the time in her office, doing paperwork, but as she and Wesley were about to bring out the food, Eden appeared. She gushed about how lovely everything looked, and said, "Ryan tells me you weren't planning to join us for dinner."

She was going to have to give that boy a kick. "Nope. I'm your friendly caterer for the night."

"Nonsense," Eden said, as though Sheridan had suggested going swimming in the Pemigewasset River, which at this time of year was not much above forty degrees. "You're coming to dinner. Unless you don't have enough food."

Wesley barked a laugh. "She has enough food for at least ten more people. Although I hear there's a teen, so maybe eight."

"Then it's settled. Get another chair." Eden would not accept anything other than a yes.

Sheridan said yes.

Dinner had been fun and relaxed, not unlike Sunday dinner at the Sinclairs, and it had given her more time with Ryan, to see him interact with his family and learn more reasons to like him – including his quick sense of humor and willingness to help her when it was time to clean up after.

But it had been a late night. And two late nights in a row couldn't be made up by the equivalent number of cups of coffee. Wesley noticed immediately she didn't have her usual levels of energy, and he shooed her out of the café before noon. When she protested, he said, "I've got everything handled, and we have a full staff of servers. Give yourself time to take a nap before you have to get ready."

"I don't need a—" A yawn made her a liar.

"I believe you're plumb tuckered out," he said, using one of her euphemisms. "You had a great time the last few nights — and I'm glad you did — but you're going to want to have fun again tonight. Get some sleep and extra time to get ready. You hate feeling rushed."

The last part was true, but she was also leaving him to run the kitchen alone on Sunday, so she was hesitant. As she took off her apron, she kept looking at the shelves.

"I can't shake the feeling there's something more I need to do." She peered into the refrigerator for the third time to check on the dough he'd be using the next day for all of the baked goods.

Wesley stepped next to her and closed the door. "You're going to give me a complex, Dollface," he said. "I can handle tomorrow. And Monday. I've done this before. You're worse than a hovering mother. Go."

After one last check of everything, she did.

Her house, in good weather like they were having today, was walking distance from the café. When she'd first decided to put down roots here, she'd looked at renting an apartment or getting a condo. But Laurel's parents, Valerie and Robert Stewart, who were co-signing her business loan, suggested she consider finding something to buy.

"You don't want to be at the mercy of sharing a wall with a noisy neighbor, especially given how early in the morning you wake up," Valerie said. As a woman who ran an inn while raising eight kids, Valerie understood noise — and the value of a good night's sleep. Sheridan had heeded the advice. It took longer to find a place in her price range, but she was thrilled when she discovered the small, two-bedroom colonial so close to the café. As if she'd needed another sign that she was in the right place.

When she got to her bedroom, one look at her bed and she knew Wesley was right. She needed a nap. Ninety minutes later, she woke refreshed and grateful for his recommendation. She sent him a quick text to thank him, and while she was in the shower he sent a smiley face and *Have fun.*

Her thoughts immediately went to Ryan and how it felt when they danced together the other night. Yes, fun was a definite possibility.

She was glad to have given herself plenty of time to get ready because the smokey-eye look took several tries before she was satisfied. She was glad Dani hired a professional to do their makeup for her wedding. Sheridan was sticking to liner and lip gloss after this.

Arriving for the event, Sheridan ran into Casey and Derek in the steadily filling parking lot of First Congregationalist Church, where two of the three ceremonies were being held.

"No Samantha today?" Sheridan asked. Derek had a young daughter who could often be found in the office of her dad's garage. Sheridan had brought her car to Derek's garage, and he occasionally brought Samantha in for lunch on the weekends. The girl had a penchant for fluff sandwiches.

"No, she spends Friday nights and most of Saturday with her grandparents," he explained as they walked up the church's front steps. "I asked them to watch her until this evening. She might enjoy seeing the bride, but I think she'd get bored with everything else pretty quickly. Nick and Dani asked her to be a flower girl for their wedding, so she's excited about that."

Stepping into the church, Sheridan couldn't stop the smile. Unlike the scene she'd been imagining from *Steel Magnolias*, the place wasn't covered in pink flowers. Instead, there were a pair of pink and purple flower arrangements on pedestals by the door, as well as a larger one at the front of the church. White ribbons decorated the aisle and matched the runner the wedding party would walk down.

People were standing in groups talking. Casey and Derek went to talk to Mia, Casey's closest friend, and Sheridan looked to see if Laurel had arrived but didn't see her or Hunter anywhere. It was harder for Laurel to leave work on a Saturday than it was for Sheridan. The café had closed two hours ago. The brewery's busiest time would be starting.

She was hoping to find someone to chat with so she wouldn't have to stand there feeling foolish when she heard the shutter of Ryan's camera. He was taking pictures of guests at the front of the church and she headed in that direction. As if he'd sensed her, he turned and smiled, then walked over. Involuntarily, she smoothed the front of her dress. When he was close, he put his camera to his face again and snapped one of her. "You look lovely," he said, his eyes skimming over her body in a way that sent shivers through her.

"You shine up nicely, too," she said. And he did. Gone were the jeans and T-shirts. Instead, he was wearing a dark blue suit and vest with a light blue shirt and matching tie. "Quite dashing, although if I miss my guess, you are not happy to be wearing that tie."

"Does it show?" he asked, fiddling with the knot. "I hate these. When I was a kid, the only thing I knew about the job I would eventually have was that it would never require a tie."

"You got your wish," she said.

"I've gotten several," he said. He put a finger under his collar and pulled. "And this is getting removed the minute we're at the reception." He changed the subject.

"I like what you did with your eyes. Makes them stand out more."

Sheridan couldn't help but blush. She should have known Janelle would be right, but she hadn't considered the possibility of it being commented on. She wasn't good at accepting compliments, although she found herself unexpectedly pleased that Ryan noticed. "It's not often you meet a man who notices makeup."

"Occupational hazard," he said with a smile, and snapped another picture of her. "Being observant pays the bills."

Before they could say anything else, Laurel came over, Hunter Davis behind her. The glow on her friend's face whenever she was with the man she loved made her more beautiful than usual. Sheridan imagined their relationship was heading towards marriage soon, too, or at least a proposal. Although Hunter had only moved back to Fable Notch late last August, Laurel had fallen hard for her brother's best friend, and he felt the same way. Sheridan hugged them both, and Laurel asked, "Have you found a seat yet?"

"No, I arrived a few minutes ago."

Laurel took her hand. "Then come with me. Ryan, we'll see you at the reception." She dropped her voice as they walked, "You can flirt with him later."

"I wasn't flirting," Sheridan said quietly as they made their way to an open pew several rows from the front. "You know this is fake."

"Then the two of you should consider acting as back up careers. Seriously, that man looked like he wanted to have you as a meal. And possibly dessert too."

Sheridan smiled and said nothing, especially not how much she liked the possibility that Ryan was attracted to her, too. Her reaction to him was still surprising and, having spoken about Paul recently, she was reminded her instincts weren't always reliable. Maybe Ryan was a good actor.

To change the subject, Sheridan asked Hunter, "Is Zoe coming?" Zoe was Hunter's younger sister, who had moved back around the same time he did. Last Christmas, she'd given birth to a baby girl, Stella. She'd been getting to know everyone in Laurel's friend group for the last few months, but the baby's arrival curbed her social life, so they didn't see her often.

"Only to the reception," Hunter said. "She didn't want the baby causing a fuss during the ceremony. I tried to get her to let Janice watch her, but she's not quite ready for that."

Before they could settle into their pew, Millie caught her eye and waved. As the mother-of-the-groom, Sheridan assumed she was too busy talking with people, but Millie came over and gave her a hug. "You look beautiful, my dear. Pink is a good color on you."

Sheridan managed to say thank you and return the compliment — Millie was lovely in a salmon-colored dress with lace inserts and as happy as if she were the bride — before Millie was called by Martin to talk to more people.

She sat with Laurel and watched as Ryan continued to take pictures of the church and people arriving while waiting for the ceremony to begin. When he turned his camera over to Devon, Sheridan knew they were about to start.

As the late afternoon sun set through the stained glass at the front of the church, a string trio played Pachelbel's Canon in D. Theo stepped out from a side room to stand at the front with Cole, Nick, Adam, and Ryan behind him.

She might not know Ryan well, but she could see that giving his camera to Devon for the duration of the ceremony made him nervous. She saw him whisper to get her attention then make a few hand motions. Devon changed locations, and Ryan gave her a thumbs up. Devon would also be taking pictures during their group dance, and Sheridan hoped he could concentrate long enough to keep them from tripping over one another.

Dani walked down the aisle first, followed by Mia and then Janelle, whose dress was the same color as the other two, but, as maid of honor, in a different style. Looking closer, Sheridan realized it was actually the same dress, but the neckline and sleeves were different. She imagined Janelle made the changes. After a pause, everyone stood, and Eden stepped in. Sheridan looked to the front in time to see Theo's hand go to his chest, and his eyes fill with tears.

So that's what lasting love looked like.

She couldn't say she'd ever seen that expression on any of her mother's grooms. Or on her mother, for that matter. She hoped Hazel felt that way for Sheridan's father, but she never wanted to talk about him, so Sheridan didn't know.

Turning from Theo, Sheridan got her first look at Eden coming down the aisle with her arm hooked through her father's. To say she looked magical would be an understatement. The gown, which had been redesigned for her by Janelle from a dress that originally gave new meaning to the word "poof," was a diaphanous, off-the-shoulder lace creation that would have looked at home as the final piece of a couture runway show. Eden wore her hair up, tendrils around her face, and a veil cascading down her back. Because of years of dance training, Eden always exhibited a natural grace, but the way the material draped and moved around her, she seemed to float down the aisle. And the joy and love on her face mirrored Theo's. Sheridan wouldn't have said she was the type to cry at weddings, but as her eyes filled, she reached into her bag for a tissue.

"Do you have an extra?" Laurel whispered. Sheridan took out two and gave her friend one.

When Eden and Patrick arrived at the front, Patrick shook hands with Theo, then gave him a brief hug before guiding Eden to her place across from him. He took his seat in the front pew, and everyone sat.

"Dearly beloved," said the pastor. "We are gathered here today to join this man and this woman in the bonds of matrimony. If anyone has any objections... there's the door. Nothing is stopping this ceremony." There were laughs all around and whoops from the groomsmen.

Before long, the pastor told Theo and Eden to kiss and seal their vows. Sheridan heard sighs in the audience, and she had to agree. Seeing two people who were so in love have this moment was special, and she was glad to be there. She looked at the attendants and noticed Dani smiling, not at the couple, but at Nick. Glancing over, she saw the same was true for Mia and Cole, whose eyes were locked on each other. So much happiness and commitment. It was breathtaking, and so different from her mother's weddings. It gave her hope.

When Eden turned to Janelle to take back her bouquet, Sheridan watched Ryan dash away from the other groomsmen, run to Devon to get his camera, then race to the back of the church so he could be in position to take the first post-ceremony photos. She appreciated his commitment to the role he most wanted to play at the event. She had a feeling after their first dance, she wasn't going to see him much at the reception.

Eden and Theo walked down the aisle hand in hand, smiling more at one another than the guests they passed. If Sheridan hadn't spent the last year and a half seeing Dani and Nick together, as well as watching Laurel's relationship with Hunter bloom, she might have believed this was something rare. Maybe it was something magical in the town. It seemed to Sheridan that there was a lot of true love in Fable Notch.

Of course, she'd found her own kind of love here. Friends, her work. She was alone when she wanted to be and rarely lonely. That was a fairy tale come true as far as she was concerned.

As the happy couple got into Theo's car to drive to the Community Center where the reception was being held, Dani and Nick came over. "Wasn't that beautiful?" Dani said.

"Absolutely perfect," Sheridan agreed.

Nick stood behind Dani and put his arms around her waist. "Gotta say, less than two years ago, if someone had told me all three of the Hansons would live here and with the women they loved, I would have said it was impossible. And now Theo is married."

"And I'm next," said Cole, coming over with Mia and their son, Dean. Cole gave Mia a quick kiss. "Which I couldn't be happier about."

"Still doesn't seem real sometimes," Mia said.

"Oh, trust me, it's real," Ryan said, joining them and tugging again at his tie. It was kind of cute. "Why else would I be here so many times in five months?"

Everyone laughed, and Sheridan thought it was a good reminder. Her attraction to him was something to be enjoyed for now, because when he left, it would go with him.

"Poor baby," Cole said, sounding like a big brother and not sympathetic at all. "Shall we?" He offered his arm to Mia and the three of them headed to their car.

"Guess I'll see everyone at the reception," Sheridan said, opening her bag to get her keys.

Nick nodded. "We're going to run home first to take the dogs outside, then we'll be there." Thinking of her own responsibilities, Sheridan considered texting Wesley to make sure everything went well, but knew it wasn't necessary. He was as good at running the place as she was.

"Not bringing Otis to the party?" Laurel asked.

"He'd take up the entire dance floor," Dani said with a laugh. Otis was her Great Pyrenees mix and the biggest dog Sheridan had ever seen. "And don't get me started on the shedding."

"We keep the lint roller people in business," Nick said. "I think I need to buy stock in that company."

"If you do, let us know so we can get in on that action," Hunter said. Nick might mostly work in home design, but he consulted with his old finance firm when they needed him. When it came to investments, he was still good at making people money.

The drive from the church to the center didn't take long, and soon Sheridan accepted a flute of champagne and found her seat. There weren't table assignments — that would wait for Dani's more formal wedding — but Laurel made it clear they would all be sitting together.

The moment she put her things down, Ryan was next to her. "Save this seat for me," he said, pointing to the one on her left. He handed her his camera bag, kissed her on the cheek, and disappeared to take more pictures. A man with priorities and goals. She understood that.

The warmth in her body that followed the easy way he kissed her, she understood less. Yes, many people showed affection easily, but she usually didn't enjoy it. From Ryan, she did.

Before she could overthink the gesture, she was joined by Laurel, Hunter, Dani, and Nick, as well as Zoe and Adam. "What did I miss?" Zoe asked as she sat down, taking Stella out of her carrier. Everyone was happy to talk about the ceremony as Hunter bounced his niece on his knee, making her giggle. As they finished giving Zoe the details, the DJ spoke into the microphone. "Ladies and gentlemen, please join me in welcoming to the dance floor, Theo and Eden Hanson."

The cheers that went up were almost deafening as the happy couple came into the room and went to the dance floor. Once there was quiet, strains of Christina Perri's "A Thousand Years" played. With every eye in the room on them, Theo and Eden began their dance.

At first, they did little more than sway to the music, but as the lyrics began, they switched into what Sheridan believed was a waltz. They moved together beautifully, and although Sheridan knew it was choreographed, it looked as though the dance came from their love. They swept across the floor, using all of the space as they spun, completely lost in one another. As they smiled and whispered to one another, for the first time in years, Sheridan wondered what it might be like to be loved like that, to want to be with someone and for them to want to be with her.

As Christina sang about believing her special love would come even after so long, Sheridan heard the appropriateness of the lyrics. There had been a long period where these two hadn't believed that, but even apart, they'd continued to long for and love each other. And now they were together. More unexpected tears filled her eyes.

When the song neared its climax, Theo gave Eden a small smile. She stepped away from him, still holding his hand, then as he pulled her back, she twirled into his embrace. At the last moment, he lifted her into his arms, and he spun them around as applause broke out around them. With their foreheads pressed together, Sheridan wondered if they heard any of it. They were completely wrapped up in each other.

As they should be.

Moments later, the applause burst again as the dance ended. Theo and Eden remained in each other's arms. She saw Theo say, "I love you," and kiss his bride. For a second, Sheridan wondered if the reception would end there so the newlyweds could leave and be alone, but the strains of "Everything" began and Theo and Eden started to dance again. Sheridan found herself nervous for what was going to happen next. Then Ryan was in front of her with his infectious smile.

"Ready?" he said as he held his hand out to her.

"As I'll ever be — which may not be a lot," she confessed. Still, she returned his smile and chuckled when he gave a small bow, took her hand, and lead her onto the dance floor. He put his arm around her waist, brought her appropriately close, and they were off.

She was grateful they'd danced the other night because she was able to easily fall in step with him. Although that might also be the zing she was experiencing. She liked being in his arms. His touch gave her pleasant tingles and his nearness was comfortable, which allowed her to relax and enjoy the moment.

"You're a natural," he said as the song continued. She wasn't convinced of that, but Eden had taught them well and the steps flowed. And having Eden and Theo at the center allowed them to mirror what to do — or catch up in Janelle and Adam's case when one of them missed a step. Laughter followed, and Sheridan realized this wasn't about doing it perfectly. It was about having fun. This wasn't a performance; it was a celebration. And she was more pleased than she expected to be a part of this.

Then she saw Millie, and it was her turn to nearly miss a step.

The woman was looking at them with bright, shining eyes. Her gaze took in everyone on the dance floor, but Sheridan couldn't help but wonder if she was picturing the day when it would be Ryan's turn to get married. Returning her attention to the dance and her partner, she said, "I don't want to alarm you, but I think you should know. Your mother looks hopeful."

Ryan glanced over her shoulder. She knew when he caught his mother's eye because his smile got bigger, but it looked forced, not like the ones he gave her. "Yeah, she does. Maybe I didn't think this plan through entirely. I am going to be on her shit list for a while when this is over."

"Good thing you live in California," Sheridan said. "You can stay away long enough for her to miss you. Maybe even forgive you."

He nodded but didn't say anything. She was sorry he was regretting his choice, but after dinner last Sunday, there was no backing out. They were "together" for the next few months.

When the song ended, there was more applause, and everyone was welcomed onto the dance floor. Before she could decide if she wanted to dance more, Ryan dragged Sheridan aside, put her hand to his throat and, in a pleading tone, said, "Take this off of me before I choke. I cannot stand it one more minute."

Cole's "Poor baby" comment came to mind, and she smiled. Ryan really was the little brother in all of this. She found it endearing. Removing the tie must be important if he chose to do it before taking back his camera.

He lifted his chin, and she loosened the knot. As she popped the top button of his shirt, she found herself thinking what it might be like to undress him entirely. He gasped for air as if it had been truly cut off. After she undid the tie and pulled it from his collar, he unbuttoned his shirt more, and she glanced at the exposed skin and the hair on his chest peeking out, wanting to touch. Is this what it was like for other women? This awareness? No wonder they chased the feeling.

Bringing her focus back to the present, she kept her hands to herself. "You're free, Sugar."

"Thank you. I am forever in your debt," he said, sounding gallant and playful. Devon came over with his camera. He took it from her and bowed with a flourish, then disappeared into the crowd. She didn't see him again until he joined them as the main course was being served. He put his camera in its bag before sitting down and saying hello to everyone. Priorities.

Over the meal, the eight people at the table chatted about nothing in particular. After Ryan left to take more pictures, Sheridan took a turn holding Zoe's daughter and enjoyed making the little one smile. Someday soon, she'd be doing this for Dani and Laurel's children. She was looking forward to being an auntie. She'd teach them to bake, babysit so their parents could have adult time, and spoil them every way she could.

As she chatted with Zoe about business and what baked goods of hers Zoe wanted to carry at the Davis Market, Ryan tapped her on the shoulder.

"May I have this dance?"

"Are you sure? Is it okay for you to take a break?" It wasn't that she didn't want to be in his arms again, it was that she did.

"I've got plenty of shots —more than I need — and I'll get more later. What I want now is to dance with you."

She wasn't going to wait for him to ask again. They walked onto the crowded dance floor and joined in the fun. The music was a mix of classic rock and current pop tunes, same as at Flurry, probably because it was the same DJ. With no one staring at them or needing to get the steps correct, she relaxed into the dance the way she had the night before.

Looking at the familiar faces around them, Sheridan felt a warmth in her chest and could sense the smile bloom on her face as a wave of joy overtook her. This was why she built a life in Fable Notch. Connection and community. It was what she saw Laurel had, and now it was hers as well.

And this attraction to Ryan?

Well, it was unexpected, but it had been so long since she'd felt this for someone that no matter if nothing came of it; she would enjoy it. Maybe she could try flirting and see if Laurel was right about him feeling something, too.

She was so caught up in her thoughts she didn't notice when the music slowed, and Ryan pulled her close. "Can we continue?"

She appreciated that he asked. "Yes," she said. She sounded breathless because they'd been dancing, right?

He put his hand on her back, and she let herself enjoy the warmth of his touch through the material of her dress. She wrapped her arms around his neck, and they swayed to the music. Instead of being in the midst of a large crowd, now they were dancing among couples — all the upcoming brides to be, as well as Laurel with Hunter, Janelle and Ash, Casey and Derek. Even Martin and Millie, and Rosie and Helen were on the dance floor. And she was perfectly at ease. A lovely surprise. For most of her life, she was used to being the fifth wheel when there were couples or sitting on the sidelines. It was nice to be a part of things.

And nicer to be attracted to the man who currently had his arms around her.

Without thinking, she moved a hand from Ryan's neck to run it through the back of his hair. His dimpled smile had her tingling with hope. "Are you doing that for my mother's benefit or for me?"

She honestly hadn't thought about Millie. "What if the answer is you?"

"Then I'd say don't stop." And to show his interest, he caressed her arm. Shivers. They were nice, too.

"You smell like cinnamon and magnolias," he said, snuggling into her neck.

"How does a northern boy recognize magnolias?"

"I lived in Charleston, South Carolina, for almost two years. They are a very distinctive flower. Once you smell them, they are hard to forget."

"How many places have you lived?"

"Let's see." He pulled back to look at her as he spoke. "I moved to Boston after I got my Associates Degree, followed by Colorado two years later. Got to live with Cole before getting my own place, which was fun. South Carolina was next, then Arizona for a year, and now I'm in California. Been there almost three years."

"You stay in locations less time than my mother stays in marriages. And I can tell you that's saying something."

"That was five states. How many times has your mom been married?"

"Four. But don't count her out. If you don't move soon, she could catch up."

Not knowing what else to say, Sheridan rested her head on Ryan's shoulder, and he tightened his arms around her. They stayed that way through the next slow song, and when the pace sped up again, he took her hand and led her back to their seats.

Now what, a voice in Sheridan's head said. There was chemistry and interest between them, but that didn't mean anything was going to happen. The whole reason Ryan wanted to do the fake dating thing was to avoid getting pushed into any possible relationship. She didn't want one either, but she wouldn't object if something physical happened between them while he was visiting. Nothing wrong with acting on attraction. People did it all the time.

"Can I get you another drink?" he asked before he sat down.

"I like the champagne," she said.

"Another bubbly coming up. Anyone else want something?" When there were several orders, Nick offered to go with him.

As they left, Dani slid across the empty seat between them. "Did I see a spark between the two of you?"

Why did her friends have to be so observant? "Yes, and I think he feels it, too, but I'm not sure what to do about it."

"Do you want to do something about it?" Sheridan nodded. "Then let him know. Subtly."

"Define subtly," Sheridan said, because this was not in her wheelhouse.

"Show your interest and watch for his response. Touch his hand if you can. That usually sends the right signal."

It seemed like good advice and doable. She'd show her attraction to him and see if he wanted to change their 'status'. Soon Ryan and Nick came back with drinks for the table. "Your champagne, my lady," he said.

Taking Dani's advice, she put her hand over Ryan's as she took the glass from him. She didn't miss how his smile got bigger. Good, that worked.

When the next song ended, the DJ asked for people to sit as the wedding cake was brought out. "Time to get back to work," Ryan said, grabbing his camera. For a split second, he hesitated. Sheridan wondered if he might kiss her, but the moment passed, and he made his way to the center of the room. She watched him take pictures of the cake and then the couple as they cut a piece and fed one another.

As traditions went, it was one of Sheridan's favorites. She liked the symbolism of sustaining each other physically, being a sign of the ways the couple would be there for each other.

When the cake was wheeled off, Ryan joined them at the table again. "Damn, I was hoping she'd smash the cake into his face," he said. "Guess that's the difference between a brother and a wife."

"Oh, there are a lot more differences than that," Nick said, which got everyone laughing.

"I don't know who came up with that part of the tradition," Dani said looking at Nick, "but we're not doing it."

The other women agreed. "It would make a particularly sticky mess for Mia and Cole if they tried," Sheridan said.

"That's right," Zoe said, excitedly. "I heard you were making them a cinnamon roll cake." Sheridan nodded. She had been as flattered when Mia asked her for the special dessert as she had been when Eden wanted to have her rehearsal dinner at the café. "Are there going to be several big ones, or a lot of little ones?"

"Something in between. For the top tier, it will be one big one. That way, they can take it home and have it later, and so any topper they put on it will stay put. But for the rest, I'm making my regular sized ones." She'd found a large tiered cake stand, like what people served cupcakes on, and was planning to place them on that. "I'm still trying to figure out how many I need to make total."

"One for all of us, of course," Laurel said. "At least."

"Note to self, save room for dessert at the next wedding," Hunter said. There were nods of agreement around the table.

After the cake was served and enjoyed, the crowd began to thin and soon it was announced that Eden and Theo were leaving. Everyone went to the front, where they were given small bags of petals to throw at the happy couple. Ryan took pictures first, then after the car was gone, stood behind her. Sheridan was very aware of how close he was, much closer than necessary.

As the lobby emptied and people made their way back into the party, Ryan leaned forward and whispered into her ear, "Come with me." Grabbing her hand, he walked them down a hall where there were rooms used for classes and smaller meetings. Finding an unlocked door, he opened it, stepped in, and pulled her in behind him. Her heart was racing. The only light was coming from the window in the door, and it kept the room dim. They'd been alone before, but there was no doubt this was different. Especially since he hadn't let go of her hand. He gave a small tug, bringing her body against his.

"There are two things you need to know," he said in her ear, his warm breath making her tingle. "First, I'm going to kiss you. And second, in case our location hasn't given it away, this has nothing to do with keeping up appearances for my mother. Tell me now if you don't want me to."

She couldn't have been happier to know this wasn't part of their act. She also liked that he gave her a choice, even though she didn't have one. "Kiss me."

His hand caressed her cheek before his mouth covered hers. Whatever zing she'd felt before was nothing compared to how her body lit up as they kissed. She'd been kissed before, but there was something wonderful about the way Ryan took control, threading his hands in her hair, keeping her close. And when his tongue teased her lips, she opened her mouth for him, enjoying the champagne-tinged taste of him.

He moved from her mouth to kiss along her jaw, then down her neck, awakening her senses and making her want more. Sheridan pressed herself against him, aching for his touch. He'd ditched the suit jacket hours before, and she could feel the warmth and muscles that were waiting for her under his shirt. As he kissed her, he teased the shell of her ear with the tip of his finger, stroked her arm, and ran his hands down her back. Tingles changed to shivers.

It had been forever since she'd felt like this. She knew when. And she knew who — and she refused to think about him. She was wiser now, and there were parameters and life choices that would keep her from being foolish. He wasn't staying. She wasn't going anywhere.

"I want you alone, Sheridan," he said.

She knew what he meant, but she wanted to hear it. "More alone than we are right now?"

"Much more. I swear, you've been driving me crazy from the first day we danced together." He kept kissing her between sentences, his lips teasing her skin. "I've been trying to behave because this wasn't a part of my initial dating suggestion, but I'm done holding back. Please tell me I'm not the only one feeling this attraction."

It was an easy answer. "You're not the only one."

"Tell me you're comfortable changing this part of our relationship."

She loved the demand in his voice, and hearing it coupled with a request made it more enticing. If she wanted him to stop, he would. But she didn't. "I'll be comfortable when we decide one last thing."

"And that is?" he asked, kissing her neck and making her body respond in ways it hadn't in so very long.

Oh, she was looking forward to losing herself in this man for a few weeks. "Your place or mine?"

Chapter Twelve

Ryan had no intention of anything physical happening between him and Sheridan when he asked her to pretend to be his girlfriend, but the more time he spent with her, the more he wanted to spend with her. And the more attracted he was to her.

It started the moment she stepped into the studio for the lesson and had grown with every interaction. There were so many occasions where he'd wanted to reach out and touch her, kiss her when they were alone, but he hadn't been sure of her interest. Today, however, with every smile she gave him, every time they had physical contact, he was more certain she was feeling the same way. And all he could think about was getting her alone.

And naked.

Now she was in his arms, and he didn't want to let her go. When she molded her body against his, when she opened her mouth to him — all he wanted was more. He cupped the back of her neck, the curls of her hair teasing his hand.

But she was right. They needed to get out of here. Sex in a room where they could be discovered was not what he wanted. No, he wanted privacy to explore her, space to discover everything that pleased her, and, if his hunger for her was any indication, time to do it all again. That meant getting out of here as quickly as possible.

"Either place is fine with me, assuming you don't have a twin bed." She hadn't included a tour of her bedroom when he came by her house.

"Queen size," she said. "But I don't have condoms."

That made the decision easy. "My place it is." He gave her one last kiss, then, still holding her hand, led them back to the lobby, where he stopped as scenarios ran through his head.

"Second thoughts?" she asked.

He turned to her. God, she was gorgeous. Especially with her lips slightly puffy from his kisses. Would anyone notice? "Hardly. But I've got my other camera in the reception room, and I assume you've got your keys and things in there."

"I do," she said with a nod.

"Which means we need to find a way to go back, grab our things, and get out of there before anyone tries to make us stay longer." And he needed his dick to settle down, or he'd be giving people something much more to talk about. Closing his eyes, he pictured his mom giving him the third degree and suggesting he buy the house next door.

That worked.

"Lucky for you, I come with a ready-made excuse. Early morning starts mean I rarely stay out late. I've already had two late nights in a row." She put the back of her hand up to her forehead, thickened her Southern accent, and said, "I don't think I can keep my eyes open much longer. I must be going."

"Perfect," he said. Damn, she was alluring, but he resisted the urge to kiss her again in favor of getting out of there faster.

As they returned to the reception, they ran into Martin and Millie. Ryan was grateful he'd gotten himself under control. "There you two are," Millie said. Was that a knowing look in her eyes? "For a second, we wondered if you left already."

"No, I was showing Sheridan where I took my first photography class." That wasn't exactly a lie. He had taken it at the community center. It may or may not have been in the room he'd brought her to. "Are you heading home?"

"We are. It's been a perfect day, but I want to get a good night's sleep before everyone comes over for brunch tomorrow." She gave them each a hug. "We'll see you both there, right? Sheridan, you don't have to work in the morning, do you?"

"No, I've got the day off. And I'm so exhausted after the last few days, I may sleep until eight." Ryan gave her a look he hoped told her she was not going to get much sleep tonight.

"Well, we're not expecting anyone until ten at the earliest, so you get all the rest you need. Ryan, you should get this girl home."

Nothing like being told to do exactly what he wanted to do in the first place. "Good idea. Why don't we get your things, and I'll see you to your car." Millie cleared her throat. "And follow you home to make sure you get there okay."

Sheridan gave him a smile that had him wondering if he'd be able to keep his composure and said, "That sounds lovely." Turning to Millie and Martin, she said, "Everything was incredible. You must be so very happy."

Millie's eyes filled with tears. Martin put an arm around her shoulders, gave her a squeeze, and answered for her, "We couldn't have imagined a better day for Theo and Eden. We can hardly wait for Cole and Mia's."

"Fortunately, you don't have to wait too long," Sheridan said. Four weeks, Ryan knew. Initially, he'd had mixed feelings about having to fly out again so soon. But if tonight went the way he was imagining, those four weeks were going to be longer than he wanted.

After waving his parents off, he said, "We need to grab our things and go."

"You're cute when you're in a hurry," she said as they made a beeline for their table.

He stopped walking so abruptly she almost bumped into him. He leaned close to her ear. "Wait until you see how cute I am when I take my time."

Her whispered, "Oh," had his blood heating again.

Somehow, they managed to say goodnight to everyone in under ten minutes. He figured no one felt the need for long goodbyes because they were seeing each other again in a few hours. Whatever the reason, he was glad he and Sheridan could get out quickly.

As they walked to her baby blue Bronco, he thought about the night to come and said, "Once I've got you with me, I am not going to want to let you go. So why don't you stay the night? Go home, change, and bring what you need for tomorrow. In the morning, we'll drive over to my folks' house together."

She took out her keys and said, "So sure I'm going to want to spend the night?"

He liked her teasing tone. Although he was looking forward to hearing her breathless gasps. Putting a hand under her chin, he turned her head to him and kissed her. "Hoping. And also hoping that you'll be too exhausted to get out of my bed."

"Cocky, aren't you?"

He took her hand and put it to his crotch. Finally having her alone and knowing the night was theirs had him excited again. "You tell me." She gave him a squeeze, and he hardened further, which earned him a slow grin.

"I'll change fast," she said, then gave him another kiss before getting in her car and driving away.

Soon he was walking into Dani's place, taking things off the bed where he'd thrown them before he left for the church. To fill the time and set the mood, he searched through cupboards and closets, looking for candles. Fortunately, Nick and Dani used this place as a vacation rental for tourists, so even though it took him opening every closet and cupboard in the place, he eventually found what he was looking for, along with an electric lighter.

He lit several to give the room a soft glow. He was a "lights on" kind of guy when it came to sex, but he'd had enough partners not ready for that kind of exposure the first time they got naked with someone, so he wouldn't assume. Whatever it took to keep Sheridan comfortable and in the mood, he was happy to do.

Going into the bathroom, he found the condoms he kept in his travel kit and put them by the bed. There should be enough for tonight and hopefully an extra few in case they had time tomorrow. Good thing he was leaving on Monday, or he'd have to drive out of town to get more. Well, not entirely a good thing. He made a mental note to bring more with him next time.

He shook his head. Nothing had happened yet, and he was already thinking about next time? Was that a problem? Letting everyone think they were dating was one thing, but this... was different.

Before the worry spiral could suck him under, there was a knock at the door. He looked at his watch. It took her less than a half hour later, and he smiled. She'd been quick. That told him she was as needy as he was. Good to know. He opened the door and pulled her inside, kissing her immediately, tangling his fingers in her hair and tasting the minty flavor of the toothpaste she must have used before she left the house. When they stopped, she said, "I feel underdressed."

He hadn't done more than drop his jacket over the couch. She was wearing a lavender shirt over a pair of jeans that hugged her curves and made her ass look sexy. He couldn't wait to get them off. "Don't worry. Neither of us is going to be wearing anything in a few minutes."

He reached under her shirt as she unbuttoned his and they shuffle walked to the bedroom. By the time they got there, they were both naked from the waist up and as much as he wanted to strip her the rest of the way, her breasts were too tempting not to give immediate attention.

Cupping them in his hands, he bent to take one nipple in his mouth. He teased the sensitive skin, then sucked deeply until she gasped, before moving to the other and doing the same. She arched into his touch, responsive. He wanted more.

They reached for each other's pants at the same time, fumbling with buttons and zippers until they managed to get things undone and off. Then he fell back onto the bed, his feet still on the floor, and pulled her on top. He loved the feel of her naked body covering him, his erection pressed against her stomach. "Hello up there," he said, pushing her hair out of her face so he could see her better.

She laughed. "Hello down there. Fancy seeing you here."

"Well, I don't come here often, but I am planning to come tonight." She laughed and leaned toward him, but he stopped her with a finger on her lips. "And I'm planning on seeing you come several times."

Her laughter died as her smile turned hungry. She was beautiful before, but it was nothing compared to this. Still, his earlier worries returned. "Before anything more happens — and in case you can't tell, I absolutely want it to — I think we should be open about this."

"We're going to have sex," she said and wiggled her hips. He was not going to last with this woman. She kissed his chest then continued, kissing him after each sentence. "Possibly more than once if the multiple condoms I see over there are any indication of your plans. And if we both enjoy it as much as I think we will, we'll have it again when you're here for the next weddings. But I know this is nothing more than a lovely addition to our friendship. Not something either of us intend to broadcast to the town."

He put his hands on the sides of her face and stared into her blue eyes, glad for the light of the candles. "Part of me wants to ask how it is you were available to say yes to me, but most of me is so damn glad, I'm going to shut up and thank my lucky stars later."

"Good plan," she said.

And then there was no more need for words. His hands roamed everywhere he could touch — shoulders, back, over the curve of her hips and to her luscious ass. Holding her against him, he flipped them over so she was under him. Then he stood, put his arms under her and lifted her to the center of the bed, where he could have full access to her.

He paused for a second to take her in. She was stunning. Full breasts with erect nipples. A small waist and rounded hips, soft stomach, and curls between her legs that he couldn't wait to touch. She wasn't tall, but her height was mostly leg, and he wanted them wrapped around him. Covering her with his body and settling between her legs, he could feel the wetness that was waiting for him. Trying to slow himself down, he kissed her, pulling her tongue into his mouth. Her nails raked down his back, and he hoped before the end of the night she'd leave scratch marks.

His hands caressed her breasts, down her stomach to her thighs, then between her legs, where he was able to touch her pussy. She gasped at the contact, and he kissed her harder as he slowly slid a finger inside. Her body tightened ever so slightly, then got wetter. He couldn't wait to slide his cock in her.

"I want more of you," he said. Could she hear the need in his voice?

"Any part in particular?" He liked that she could tease, even when she was as turned on as he was.

"These are quite lovely," he said, kissing her breasts, licking and sucking at her nipples. He kissed his way down her body, nibbling and listening for her responses. "And you have a gorgeous waist that I'm kind of happy people rarely see because of the way you dress. But this," he pulled her thighs apart, "is what I really want."

He gently spread the lips of her pussy with his fingers and slowly licked her from the bottom of her opening to the top, where he swirled his tongue around her hardened clit for the briefest of moments. He was rewarded with her lifting her hips as if to serve herself to him, and he pressed his mouth to take all she offered. God, she tasted wonderful. Better than any icing.

His mouth never left her sensitive flesh as he stroked her inner thighs with his hands, occasionally sliding a finger inside her.

"Ryan, that's... you're... yes...."

There were the breathless gasps he wanted to pull from her. He wanted her to not be able to speak or think — just feel. And enjoy everything he gave her. If she couldn't manage more than one word at a time, he was doing things right.

Savoring the taste of her, he felt the sheets pull around him. She was close, gripping them like a lifeline as her legs tightened around his shoulders. And while her moans were sweet, he wanted to make her shatter with bliss.

And he wanted to hear her need. "Tell me what you want." For a second, he thought she wouldn't answer. He used the tip of his tongue to barely touch her clit. She shivered. "Tell me."

"Make me come. Use your fingers, your mouth. Everything. Anything."

"With great pleasure," he said. He slid two fingers into her, curling them up to excite her more while he enjoyed every part of her pussy before focusing on her clit. Swirling, licking, sucking, taking the gentlest of bites. He did everything he could to excite her. And when her thighs pressed against his head and her hips lifted, he knew she was at the point of no return.

She gave up on the sheets and dug her fingers into his hair, calling out his name, the sound ringing off the walls of the small bedroom. "I'm... I'm..."

And then she came with a scream and a release that was exquisite.

Thrilled — and hard as fuck — from pleasing her, he continued to touch her, licking gently as she came down from her orgasm. He kissed the insides of her thighs, the skin above her pubic curls, then continued up her body. Before he got to her lips, she put her hands on the sides of his face. "Get. The. Condom. Now."

Damn, she was sexy when she was demanding. "Yes, ma'am," he said, which earned him a sound halfway between a laugh and a groan.

Chapter Thirteen

Sheridan had enjoyed orgasms with lovers before. One of her two previous partners had been pretty consistent about giving them to her, and she'd had some with Paul, but Ryan was different. Attentive and astute. And he hadn't tried to rush her, so it would be his "turn." It was clear from what he said and did that her satisfaction mattered to him.

And he had most definitely satisfied her.

Well, maybe not. Because she wanted more. If Ryan didn't fuck her, she was going to scream. It was the most intense and wonderful of reactions.

When he started licking her, she planned to return the favor after he stopped, but now she couldn't think of anything but having him inside of her. She couldn't recall if she'd ever been demanding with a lover in the past but decided it wasn't worth the brain power to remember. Fortunately, the condoms were waiting, and Ryan seemed only too happy to get one out and on. She'd please him orally another time.

As soon as he was sheathed, she grabbed his cock, stroking him, letting her pinky tickle his balls on the downstroke. “Careful or I’ll come too soon.”

She let go. “That’s a very serious threat.”

“No need to go to extremes,” he said and put her hand back on his erection as he moved between her legs again. “Show me you want me, Sheridan. Put me in you.”

At this point in the night, her consent and desire were obvious, but she loved this added measure. She opened herself wider and guided the tip of his cock to her entrance. She was so wet, he slid in easily. As he moved slowly, deliberately, letting her orgasm swollen pussy stretch to accommodate him, his moan of pleasure sent shivers through her. “God, Sheridan, you feel so good. So tight around me.”

For a split second, she worried if rarely having sex had changed her body. It had been so long it was probably the reason for her tightness, rather than her orgasm. Did it make her seem different from other lovers Ryan had? Would he notice?

Then Ryan slid out of her, and as he drove himself deep in her again, waves of delight coursed through her body and every worry left her head. He moved slowly at first and she matched his rhythm, swiveling her hips to increase his pleasure. His gasp told her it was the right thing to do.

The next time he pushed into her, he captured her mouth in a kiss, his tongue teasing hers, giving her a taste of her own pleasure. And his hands were everywhere. In her hair, teasing her collarbone, cupping her breasts. Sensation after sensation from every direction.

Wanting to please him as much, she mirrored what he did. Teasing the hair on his chest, lifting her head to lick and bite his nipples, then reaching over his shoulders and down his back to grab his ass. And every moan or sigh he couldn't control empowered her. It may have been years, but she had no doubt she was pleasing him.

She was caught up in how touching him was as exciting as being touched when he said, "I'm so close." He almost sounded like he was in pain. "Want you to come with me."

"Don't worry, just —" but her words stopped when his hand came between them, and he found her clit. She didn't realize how close she was to another climax until he circled the swollen nub with his finger and sent explosions of pleasure through her. She gasped and lifted her hips, wrapped her legs around him to take him deeper still.

"Yes, Sheridan. Yes." His back bowed as he surged into her, and his head fell back as he yelled his release. The sound sent her over the edge, and her second orgasm hit.

She was still reeling from the height when he took her mouth in a punishing kiss as she felt a final shudder run through his body. Seconds later, he collapsed on top of her. She wrapped her arms around him as he buried his face in her neck.

"Cinnamon and magnolias," he whispered.

They lay there, catching their breath for a few minutes longer until his softening cock slid from her body, and he rolled off of her. He found a box of tissues by the bed, took off the condom, and then brought her close. She found a cozy spot on his chest, a little above his heart.

"That was..." she started, but wasn't sure what to say, not only because she was rarely in this position, but because not all of her brain cells were online.

He kissed her softly. "Yes, it was. I've been wondering for days if what I saw in the kitchen would translate to the bedroom... and it did."

Confused, Sheridan said, "What do you mean? Cooking is about control. Right ingredients, right results." It was one of the things she liked best about it; the way you could count on the outcome.

"That may be true, but cooking for you is about passion, and that's what I saw here." He sat up on his elbow, and she looked at him, still off-kilter from being called passionate. "I know we discussed what this is and isn't between us, but I hope you know that when I asked you to pretend to be my girlfriend, it was not some smooth way to convince you to go to bed with me."

She laughed. "I promise, the thought never occurred to me." It honestly hadn't, but she wasn't going to explain why. To him, her attraction was normal, typical. He was the first lover who didn't know she was demi before they went to bed together. And while being demi didn't bother her, she was enjoying not having it be something her partner asked about. Leaning in, she kissed him below his ear and whispered, "However, a lot is occurring to me now." On impulse, she nibbled his lobe, then gave it a quick lick.

He gasped and grabbed her ass, pulling her on top of him. She was certain she'd done something wrong until he kissed her hard and said, "Damn, you found that fast."

"Found what?" She was glad he was smiling but was still confused.

"My ears are extremely sensitive. If you want me to lose all ability to think clearly, all you have to do is nibble my ears, and I'm a goner."

"Good to know. Filing that away for future use."

"Me and my big mouth," he said, still sounding playful.

"I like your mouth," she said, kissing him. "And your fingers." She brought his hand to her mouth and licked up his index finger, then slowly stroked his softened erection, enjoying how it jumped under her attention. "And your cock."

"As long as I'm here, they are yours."

As long as he was here. Most women would hate that idea, but for her, it was ideal. She could enjoy whatever time they had together and never worry that it was going to impact the life she'd built.

It might, she discovered after he fingered her another orgasm, have an impact on her sleep patterns. She was in a strange bed, and she wasn't used to having someone next to her. Although her body was completely sated, it took Sheridan longer than she expected to fall asleep. And when Ryan pressed against her back a few hours later, his hand stroking her breasts, she discovered she wasn't as sated as she believed.

Neither was he.

After that second round, she'd fallen asleep deeply. Maybe that was the trick. More sex.

As usual, she woke early, although if the light was any indication, it was later than her normal time. Thank goodness. She never wanted to inflict her business hours on a partner.

Turning, her eyes raked over Ryan, appreciating how sexy he looked, even in sleep. What would he think if she....

She was hesitant at first, then decided to give in to the desire to touch him. It was a new sensation, wanting and being wanted like this. And knowing it couldn't last, she intended to take advantage of every opportunity they had. She started with a kiss to his jaw, followed by one below his ear. He shifted, stretching his legs, and she continued. A kiss to his collarbone and his chest. Then she let her hand dive under the covers, sliding down his body. She kissed his lips as she teased his cock with a soft stroke.

He was fully awake — and erect — a moment later.

Which left them with very little time to get dressed and get to the Sinclairs for brunch.

Chapter Fourteen

Brunch at his parents' house was fun and relaxed, and Ryan suspected that was due in part to Sheridan being with him. He'd known asking her to be his girlfriend would make things easier because he wouldn't have to deal with Millie's matchmaking, but he didn't expect that having her to talk to and share in the experience would make him enjoy the time more. It did.

Of course, some of his ease might have to do with the three rounds of great sex they'd had.

Every time he looked at her and she smiled, all he could picture was how gorgeous she looked naked beneath him, calling his name as she came. He hadn't been sure if she'd be interested when he initiated sex in the middle of the night — he'd had lovers who were one-and-done — but her response had been immediate and welcoming. And waking up to her hands and mouth on him? Perfect.

However, it wouldn't do to have an erection around his family, so he did his best to keep his focus on the conversation rather than the woman sitting next to him. Unfortunately, his brothers were too observant.

Nick had been the first to notice. "Way to make this look real," he said under his breath shortly after they arrived and Dani pulled Sheridan away.

"Can't let Mom get suspicious," Ryan said. "I've got two more weddings to get through."

"I don't know... you've both got a look that is hard to fake," Cole said, pretending to be serious and failing miserably. "Anything you want to share with the rest of the class?"

"No," Ryan replied too quickly, but added nothing. They let the silence continue and Ryan was saved from answering by the arrival of the newlyweds. Later, he pulled Nick aside and told him the truth. Well, some of it. "There's a lot of chemistry which we may or may not be acting on, but it is not something I'm going to discuss, and, regardless, it doesn't matter." And he promptly ignored the small part of him disappointed in that truth.

At one o'clock, Theo and Eden left to do the last of their packing before heading out for their honeymoon. That was Ryan's cue to leave as well. During one of the planning calls, he'd offered to drive them to the airport so they could leave on their trip to Hawaii from Boston rather than Manchester and fly nonstop. When he'd first planned his visits, he expected to want to get out of town as quickly as possible after the wedding, and this seemed like an easy excuse. Now, he would have liked another day to linger.

In bed.

With Sheridan.

Instead, when he brought her back to Dani's house to get her car, he wrapped his arms around her waist, kissed her behind her ear and said, "I have an hour before I have to get my brother and one condom left."

"That's too bad," she said with an exaggerated sad face, "because I have to be... no, wait. I don't have to be anywhere." The pout changed into a radiant smile.

They were naked before they got to the bedroom.

He was inside her seconds later. And he came so fast that he had time to lick her to orgasm before he needed to get himself ready to leave.

With an ease he hadn't felt with a woman in... longer than he could remember, she helped him change the sheets, empty the refrigerator, and lock up the house.

He put his overstuffed luggage in the trunk, then walked her to her car. When she lowered the window after she got in, he said, "I've got a job booked that means I'm not going to be coming out for Cole's wedding until the day before, and I'm heading out the day after, but should I bring more condoms with me?" Was that hope he was feeling as he waited for an answer?

"Sounds like a plan," she said before leaning out the window to give him a lingering kiss that made him wish they had more time.

As he watched her drive away, he smiled. Best plan ever.

Soon, he was playing chauffeur with Theo and Eden in the back seat, lost in each other as he drove them south and maneuvered through Boston traffic. He dropped them at their terminal before returning his rental car and taking the shuttle to his gate. As he sat there waiting to board, he texted his parents to let them know everyone was where they were supposed to be, then sent one to Sheridan, too.

And he wasn't going to read anything into that.

Or the fact that he couldn't stop smiling when she sent back airplane and sun emojis with the words, *Safe travels.*

As much as the drive to Boston was a pain in the ass, Ryan was glad to have the non-stop flight back to California. And the first-class seat. It gave him room to work and catch up on the emails he'd ignored over the weekend. It also meant that when those were done, he was able to catch up on sleep.

Getting a pillow, blanket, and sleep mask from the flight attendant, he drifted off thinking of Sheridan and how the southern minx had worn him out.

After taking Monday off to get back on Pacific time, Ryan was ready to work on Tuesday. His newest job, which January had secured for him, was getting shots for a renovated movie theater that was reopening as an art house in the Hancock Park area of Los Angeles.

The affluent suburb, which was near Paramount Studios, was the perfect location for the theater. The area was famous for its pre-war architecture, elite shopping, and the La Brea Tar Pits. Ryan had been hesitant to take the job when he heard about Vance Brooks, the 'kid' who was in charge of the place. From his research, Ryan figured the guy was two years younger than him, and after their one talk when Ryan called to schedule the shoot, fairly disinterested. Ryan got the sense from both their phone conversation and his dealings with the PR firm managing the opening that this business venture was being funded by Vance's rich parents and their movie star friends to give him something to do.

The drive from his apartment in Northridge to the theater was twenty-five miles and, according to his GPS, would take almost an hour to get to because traffic was "lighter than usual". Typical. Another example of how he was a world away from New Hampshire. The only time it was hard to drive around Fable Notch was on Festival days. And even then, people could park and walk to where they wanted to go.

When he got to the theater, the front door was unlocked, and there was no one around. He found a sign marked "Office" and knocked.

"Yeah," said the voice on the other side. So welcoming. Ryan went in and found Vance staring at his computer. He didn't glance at Ryan. Trying not to sound annoyed, Ryan introduced himself. When Vance was still confused, Ryan reminded him of why he was there. "Oh right, that was today. Well, there's no one around, so feel free to go wherever you want."

Ryan had been sent a shot list and told to add any he wanted. Deciding to get the shots with his bored employer out of the way first, Ryan took pictures with Vance in front of the building, the lobby, and the bar area. He tried to engage the guy in conversation to add excitement to his expression, but nothing made him animated. Ryan couldn't help but compare him to the people he'd spent time with the week before.

Sheridan's passion for baking. Nick's love of turning old houses into homes people loved being in. Cole's commitment to teaching and writing music. Five minutes with them and he was caught up in what they did and why they did it. With this guy? There wasn't enough editing software in the world to make him look engaged, but Ryan would do what he could. He had a feeling most of the shots used would be of the property, not its manager.

For the final ones, he asked Vance to sit in a seat in the middle of the empty theater. They turned on the light in the projection room, which gave the whole set up a very old Hollywood look.

With a flash of inspiration, Ryan said, "You wouldn't happen to have a cigar, would you?"

"You can't smoke in here."

"It's for you."

"I can't smoke in here either."

Ryan held in the groan of exasperation and explained, "I was thinking of creating an effect of you sitting here in a dark room, smoke around your head making things hazy. It's an old place. That would give it an old look."

"Gotcha, man, that's a cool idea. I got something we can use for that." He ran out of the room, and Ryan used the time to take more pictures of the theater. It was stunning with its restored 1920s art deco grandeur. The kid might not care, but Ryan could see how the place would be an instant success, even without all the A-list names associated with it. When Vance came back, there was already a cloud around his head. And a familiar skunk smell. "Will this work?"

No one was going to know what he was smoking by looking at the pictures. Especially if Ryan could digitally add more smoke to obscure the joint in his hand. At least the guy was animated. He'd take what he could get. "Works for me."

When they were done, Vance offered Ryan a toke, which he passed on, explaining he still had another hour of pictures to take. Vance shrugged and left, saying he'd be in his office, and Ryan focused on getting the rest of the shots on the list. Shaking his head as Vance left, Ryan thought some people had no idea how good they had it.

Hoping to have photos he could send to January as part of his portfolio for the casino job, Ryan took the time to get extra images: artsy shots of the scroll work on the proscenium, stark yet beautiful pictures of the still empty concessions counter, closeups of the tile work on the lobby floor. After he had what he needed, he uploaded images to his laptop, did a touch of editing, and went in search of Vance to show him the results. The guy probably didn't have any say in what was used — and likely didn't care — but Ryan felt funny not sharing what he'd done and, hopefully, getting feedback.

He found Vance in his office, still smelling like skunk. "I've gotten what your PR company needs and a bunch more, so I'll be heading out shortly. Do you want to see what I'm sending them?"

"Sure." Could he sound any more disinterested? Ryan usually enjoyed revealing the images to his clients. Sitting in meetings discussing strategies and brand tag lines wasn't as much fun as looking at pictures and seeing a vision come to life. This was when they got excited.

For the first several pictures, Vance said nothing but "uh huh" as Ryan scrolled through. But when they got to the ones of Vance in the smoke, he perked up. "Fuck, that's sick. Never would have imagined I'd looked like that."

Ryan had used his computer software to blur the joint. It wouldn't be the final shot, but it was close. "Glad you like them," Ryan said, pleased he could get the guy interested. The picture broke the ice and as they continued, Ryan discovered Vance loved independent and experimental movies and had solid ideas for the theater, but he was feeling overwhelmed by the size of the project. "You need to get yourself some help. People who will be as excited as you are. Shouldn't be too hard to find around here."

Vance seemed to consider the recommendation. "Maybe you're right. It would be great if this took off. Do something I like and have my folks off my back. That'd be a win-win."

Was there anyone who didn't want to break away from their roots? "It would. Good luck," Ryan said, closing his computer and packing his things. He hoped the young man would find his way.

As they shook hands, Vance said, "You gotta come to the opening gala. It's going to rock. Everyone is going to be here."

"Sorry, I don't do red carpet work." Ryan made it a policy to never be a part of the paparazzi, regardless of the situation because of Cole. Long before he became a professional, Ryan heard the challenges they caused his brother, especially at the end. Once he had gone back on that commitment when a job had fallen through, and he'd needed rent. He'd hated every minute of it. The next time he'd had a tight month, he'd worked the overnight shift at a grocery store stocking shelves and hauling in deliveries to make the money. It was better work. "I could give you a referral or two if you want, but I'm sure you know plenty of folks."

"Nah, come as a guest. You seem cool."

There was a time when Ryan would have jumped at the chance, especially since it could be a good opportunity to mingle and find future clients, but after his time in Fable Notch surrounded by familiar faces, he couldn't bring himself to get excited for a party filled with strangers. Still, it wouldn't do to insult a client. "Thanks. I appreciate the invite. I'll check my schedule. In the meantime, I'll send the edited pictures to your PR person in the next couple of days, so you'll have them for your website and advertising."

"Yeah, whatever." Visibly bored by the conversation now that it wasn't about the party, Vance was on to whatever he wanted to do next.

Back in his car, he saw a missed message from January. He called her back and got the details of a job for the Canillos. They'd bought a restaurant in Los Angeles and had a big-name chef lined up to open for them. They were planning to launch the guy in California, then have him open branches of the restaurant in several of the casinos. The assignment included taking pictures of the restaurant coming together and the chef at work.

As soon as January mentioned the chef working, Ryan pictured Sheridan. Did she know she smiled as she baked? That her eyes sparkled as she talked to her customers and glowed when she noticed them enjoying themselves.

She also glowed after sex.

Shit.

Not good to have an erection while driving. Their time together had been so hot, but he hadn't considered the consequences. It had been two days, and he was already looking forward to seeing her again. And spending time with her.

Fine, taking her to bed. The woman was an amazing lover, responsive and exciting.

He hadn't told her that spending the night with someone was rare for him. It was usually months into a relationship before he considered it. With Sheridan, it had been days. From their first kiss, he wanted her to stay with him.

Must be because there was no danger of this becoming anything serious that he could let his guard down. He was sure by the time he arrived for Cole's wedding next month, time and distance would have calmed his libido.

Chapter Fifteen

"We need details," Laurel said when she and Dani invaded Sheridan's house for dinner Tuesday night. "Dani says you were glowing at the Sinclairs' on Sunday."

At least they'd brought food, though she was the one being grilled.

Part of Sheridan wanted to deny it. There would be fewer questions later, which would make it easier after Ryan was gone, but she was feeling wonderful, and her thoughts regularly drifted back to the weekend. And she trusted her friends. "We kissed. We kissed some more. Then we went to where Ryan was staying and fucked all night long." Both women looked at her, shocked. Yeah, she shocked herself. That wasn't a phrase she had ever used. As the silence stretched on, Sheridan said, "Fine, I'll back up and tell you everything." She left out several specifics, but gave them more than a basic idea of what she and Ryan shared. Talking about it made the tingles come back. Is that why women told their friends these things?

"Well," Dani said when Sheridan was done, "that bed was lucky for Nick and I."

Sheridan rolled her eyes.

"But the dating is still fake," Laurel confirmed, her practical streak showing.

"It is. We're not in a relationship or trying to build one. The sex between us was good. Really good. And I'm looking forward to more when he comes back."

"What about your heart?" Dani asked.

It was sweet the way her friends worried. "It shouldn't be in danger. My eyes are open and, unlike the two of you, Ryan isn't someone I already had a thing for." Laurel had a crush on Hunter for years before they got involved, and Dani had fallen in love with Nick when they were kids. "I may not have a lot of experience with relationships, but I'm pretty sure I can figure out how to avoid one."

As the weeks between the weddings went by, two unexpected things happened. First, Sheridan found she enjoyed hearing from Ryan. Most days, he'd send her texts and occasionally pictures. She'd reply with images of her own and customer stories customers — like the one who wanted their peanut butter and fluff sandwich on an English muffin. She'd laughed at the green-faced emoji he used as a reply. But looking forward to his texts didn't mean he was anything more than a friend.

That she wanted to have sex with again.

The second thing was being continually asked about Ryan. She'd known the rumors would spread and people would ask, but she wasn't used to her social life being interesting to anyone. The first time it happened at the café was a week after the wedding. As she handed a customer her order, the woman, whose name she didn't know but whose face was familiar, said, "I hear you and Ryan Sinclair are an item."

"I hear that, too," Sheridan said with what she hoped was a friendly but noncommittal smile. As the week went on, it happened more often. The questions about them being an item became questions about whether she'd heard from him, was it serious between them, and when was he coming back. One-word answers of yes, no, and June weren't always enough to satisfy the asker. By the second week, she was tempted to ask Wesley to switch places with her so she could hide in the kitchen. But when their server on Friday night at the brewery asked similar questions, Sheridan accepted there was no hiding in Fable Notch.

She was going to have to prepare herself for people commenting for the next four months and who knew how long after once they learned she and Ryan had "broken up." Good thing she wouldn't be interested in dating again too quickly or that would have people commenting, too.

They were halfway to Mia's wedding when she got the visit she'd been both expecting, and she had to admit, dreading.

"Millie Sinclair is here," said one of their afternoon servers coming into the kitchen where Sheridan was helping Wesley put together lunch orders. "She asked if you had a minute."

Sheridan was almost surprised Millie had waited so long. She visited the café occasionally, but Sheridan hadn't seen her since the day after the wedding. She wondered what prompted Millie to stop by today. "Tell her I'll be out as soon as I can."

"Gotta talk to the mother-in-law?" Wesley said.

"Shut up," she said, with no malice in her voice. Like her friends, she hadn't been able to hide from Wesley the fact that she and Ryan had slept together. Apparently, having few relationships made it next to impossible for her to cover her emotions. Maybe this was something she could use this fake relationship to learn. And there was no time like the present to practice. She hoped whatever Millie wanted to talk about had easy answers.

Sheridan finished slicing a tomato, washed her hands, and headed out. The café was busy, but she spotted Millie sitting at a window table with Valerie Stewart. At least she hadn't only come here as an excuse to talk to Sheridan. "Hello, ladies. It's lovely to see you both. But I feel I should ask — did you come for my grilled cheese or are you checking up on me?"

Millie gave an embarrassed smile that suggested Sheridan was right. "You know I love your sandwiches. That was true before you and Ryan started dating."

"I'm always glad to hear that," she said. Hopefully, it would still be true after their "relationship" ended. Ryan said he would make it out to be his fault, so Sheridan would get a few weeks of sympathy and sadness from Millie. With any luck, Millie would never learn the truth. As much as Sheridan understood why Ryan wanted to do this — and she had her own reasons for agreeing — this could still wind up being a very uncomfortable situation for everyone.

"How is he doing? Do you two have a chance to talk, what with your hours and the time difference between here and California?"

"We manage, and he's good. Always busy." She almost mentioned the international job, but not knowing if Ryan had told her, she kept quiet.

"He's a wonderful young man. Talented, smart. He'd be an excellent provider."

Sheridan kept her smile plastered on. This was what Ryan was trying to avoid. "I have no doubt. You raised a good man." Before Millie could "sell" Ryan more, the server arrived with their lunch. Sheridan took the plates and put them in front of the women. Millie had, indeed, ordered the grilled cheese, but she had a bag of potato chips rather than soup with her order. "Is there anything else I can get you?"

"No, but I wanted you to know Theo and Eden are coming back from their honeymoon on Friday, and we're having everyone over for dinner on Sunday. We'd love for you to join us." Before she could answer, Millie added, "And don't say no because Ryan won't be there."

Sheridan was torn. She'd love to see Eden, and with Dani and Mia there, it would be easy to fit in. Which was why she needed to decline. Because when September came and Dani and Nick were married, things with Ryan would be over and Millie would go back to being one of the many people Sheridan enjoyed seeing around town. And nothing more. "Thank you so much for the invitation," she said, "but I already have plans. Please tell

Eden and Theo 'welcome home' from me. Enjoy your meal. Don't want that grilled cheese getting cold."

She left as quickly as she could, so Millie wouldn't have time to ask what her plans were. There was no way Sheridan could come up with something believable fast enough. When she got to the counter, she plated two cookies and told Millie's server to bring them when she gave the women their check.

She felt bad turning down Millie's offer. She enjoyed any time she got to hang out with Dani, and it would be lovely to hear about Eden's trip, but that could wait until the next time Eden joined the group. Yes, her friends were her family, but that didn't mean she belonged at a family dinner with the brothers and their spouses.

And she would not dwell on the emotion that came to her with the thought.

That night, she was getting ready for bed when the phone rang. Looking at the time, she wondered if it might be Ryan checking in at the end of his day. He never called, but she couldn't imagine who else it might be.

Hope changed to concern when she saw *Mom* on the caller ID.

Hazel wasn't much for communication. Birthdays. Holidays. Sheridan and Paisley had called her together last month on Mother's Day. She couldn't help but be worried about Hazel reaching out unexpectedly, but she kept her voice bright and said what was expected of her. "Hi Momma. So lovely to hear from you. How are you?"

"I am as good as can be expected," said Hazel, her southern accent as thick as it had always been. Hazel had never lived anywhere other than Alabama. There was a pause, followed by a long dramatic sigh. "I'm sorry to tell you, but Gordon and I are getting a divorce."

Sheridan dropped onto her bed. After almost seven years with the same man, she hoped Hazel had found someone who made her happy, someone she could stay with. "I'm so sorry. What happened?" Which to Sheridan was code for, 'what did you do now?' because as far as she could tell it was always Hazel who found herself disinterested in keeping a marriage going.

"He decided to think with his pecker." That was unexpected. And more profane than Sheridan was used to from her mother. Hazel usually complained her husbands were too busy with work to pay attention to her or something as simple as, 'I just don't love him the way I should.' As if that was definable.

Curious, she asked, "And what, if you don't mind sharing, does his pecker think?" It was a weird thing to say about one's stepfather, but she rarely saw the man, and she'd been in her twenties when they married. It wasn't like he was a parent to her.

"That the twenty-something juice bar worker at the gym was what he wanted rather than a loving, devoted wife." Her mother gave another long sigh, and Sheridan piled her pillows at the head of the bed and made herself comfortable, knowing she would be listening for a while. "I thought the motorcycle was the only thing I had to worry about when his midlife crisis hit last year. Well, that and the beard, but I didn't mind that. Too much." Sheridan had a feeling Hazel's definition of 'too much' might be different from her husband's, but she didn't comment.

"Momma, that's awful. You don't deserve that," she said and meant it. Sheridan might not have a lot of experience in relationships, but when someone violated trust, that was hard to get past.

"You have no idea what I've put up with for the sake of a happy home." As her mother went on about how much she'd done for Gordon and how unfair all of this was, Sheridan zoned out. This part was the same every time. "Thank goodness I signed that prenuptial agreement. At least I'll be taken care of when all of this sordidness is over."

Sheridan was glad to know her mother could find an upside to the end of her fourth marriage. She didn't doubt Hazel would be on the hunt for husband number five sooner rather than later. Hazel was, after all, only in her mid-fifties and looked younger thanks to years of beauty treatments and a strict nighttime regimen. She had plenty of time to hook another one. Or two. After fifteen minutes of Hazel complaining about Gordon and how put upon she was, Sheridan asked Hazel if she wanted a call in a few days and her mother said, "Whatever for?"

Of course, why would Hazel want comfort or support? On some level, Sheridan thought, Hazel expected the marriage to end.

Almost immediately after Hazel had passed along her life update, the call ended. Sheridan's mother hadn't asked about her at all. Not her work or her friends. But Hazel never understood her daughters or their interests. Starting when Sheridan and Paisley were in their teens, Hazel pushed for both of her daughters to be married. She sent them pictures of wedding dresses, reception venues, starter homes for a 'young family', though neither of them was eager to get married after what they saw. Eventually, when Sheridan understood herself, she explained her demisexuality to Hazel, but it caused more confusion than understanding. In the end, Hazel stopped asking about her love life (or lack thereof), which was good enough.

Too wired to sleep, Sheridan went back to the living room, put the television volume on low, and scrolled through channels, ending up on reruns of shows she'd seen so many times she barely needed to hear them. And she pictured the other mothers she knew, specifically Millie Sinclair and Valerie Stewart. How they were both there for their children, how they knew everything going on in their lives — no small feat given the size of Valerie's family.

Yes, Sheridan appreciated Laurel and her brothers sometimes complained about familial interference, and Ryan had asked for their fake dating situation because of his mother's interest, but wasn't that better? Maybe talking to Millie had been a little uncomfortable, but she loved how effortlessly Millie welcomed Sheridan and wanted her to feel a part of things. She hoped that things between them wouldn't change too much after Dani's wedding, when her relationship with Ryan ended.

The week leading up to Cole and Mia's wedding was more hectic than usual. When Mia asked Sheridan to make a cinnamon roll wedding cake, Sheridan had given a tentative yes until she could figure out how it could be done. Ultimately, she gave Mia a few choices, including creating a cinnamon-flavored traditional cake. Mia had chosen a large cinnamon roll at the top and lots of individual ones that could be easily served. Sheridan now had the number of people attending — sixty — and how many rolls she'd be making. Also sixty. Okay, seventy-two. What was one more dozen when she was already making five? Mia said it wasn't necessary to make one for each attendee. They could be cut in half, but the more Sheridan considered it, the more she wanted everyone to have their own.

She already made two dozen on the weekdays and four on the weekends. Sure, this was more than doubling her normal output, but it wasn't difficult. It simply required planning. And timing, so she and Wesley could manage what the kitchen needed to do for their regular customers. She would never shortchange the people who came to her café.

As the week went on, Sheridan was at the café later and later, prepping ingredients both for the wedding and to have things done early so she could use the ovens as much as necessary on Saturday. The goal was to bake Saturday afternoon, leave everything to cool overnight while she went to Mia's for the movie night bachelorette party, then transport everything to the Sinclairs' on Sunday morning, where she would have help from the catering staff to ice everything.

When she left the café at seven on Friday night, she was exhausted. They'd had a busy day, selling out of nearly all of their baked goods, which meant doing more prep work than expected alongside the dough for the "cake". By the time she got home, she was grateful she'd brought chicken salad with her because she didn't have the energy to make more than a sandwich for dinner.

After she'd eaten, she changed into her nightshirt. She figured if she got into bed by nine, she could get at least eight solid hours of sleep. With an hour to relax, she made herself comfortable on the couch with a bowl of microwave popcorn and her favorite otter videos from a couple on YouTube, which always made her smile.

She had barely finished the first video when there was a knock at her door. She sat up so quickly she almost covered herself with popcorn. Who would stop by at this hour? Her friends would text if they needed something. And if it were Laurel or Dani, they would have knocked once and come in. It wasn't as if she never got visitors, but this wasn't the kind of town where random people came to your door at night.

With a touch of apprehension, she got up and went to the door, although she stopped in the kitchen to pull a knife out of the block. Just in case. Killers didn't knock, but no need to be dumb as a stump. She turned on the porch light and opened the door a crack so she could see who was there, hoping it wasn't someone who was going to kick their way in.

Short dark hair, hazel eyes that looked sleepy, and a sheepish smile.

She opened the door the rest of the way. "Ryan."

Suddenly, getting to bed early didn't seem so important.

Chapter Sixteen

As Ryan stood in front of Sheridan's house waiting for her to answer the door, he berated himself for making this choice. Sure, when he woke up this morning, heading to Fable Notch early and having more time with her felt like a good idea, but now that he was actually here, he wasn't as certain.

Over the last four weeks, he'd enjoyed getting to know her better. He'd enjoyed sharing his day with her, hearing about hers. He liked that she never expected him to call and that when she reached out to him, it was always a pleasant surprise.

But showing up a day early and unannounced? Was that saying more than he intended? Because even though he wanted to see her, it didn't mean anything else. The dating thing was still a performance to keep his mother from meddling. Would Sheridan assume his being here meant something more serious? Maybe he should have called first. Or gone to Dani's house and stopped by tomorrow when he was expected. He knew better than to be too forward with women. It gave them ideas that you wanted more.

But when she opened the door and smiled at him, the noise in his head disappeared. He couldn't help it. He was glad to see her. How long did he have to wait to kiss her? "I know there's a possibility I've lost track of the days, but weren't you supposed to be arriving tomorrow afternoon?"

"I was," he said, stepping in as she stepped back. "But the job I was on wrapped sooner than expected. I had nothing planned, so I checked the flights and made a change. I figured if I got in early…." He bent forward, cupped her chin, and gave her a lingering kiss that had her leaning into him. "I could get into you early." Shit, did he really say that?

She looked at him, then burst out laughing. "That was a terrible line."

He rubbed the spot between his eyes. "Yeah, it sounded a lot better in my head."

"I don't doubt it for a moment. And I know which head had the idea."

Now it was his turn to laugh. Thank goodness she had a sense of humor. "You could be right." Doubt jumped in again. Just because she responded to the kiss didn't mean she wanted him to stay. He'd had women in his life think dating meant they could get together whenever they wanted. It was usually the first sign to him that things needed to end. Maybe he had overplayed his hand or overestimated her desire for him? "I know it's late, and I should have called. If you want, I'll go to Dani's place for the night, and you'll see me tomorrow the way you expected."

"No need. Besides, I like both of your heads," she said. As she leaned in and kissed him again, her hand went to his crotch, and he groaned.

God, she made him smile. And need. He pulled her to him, trapping her hand between them, and grabbed her ass, breathing in the scent of flowers and cinnamon as they kissed. He'd missed her. He might not be ready to let anyone else know, but he could admit it to himself. "According to my watch, I've got two hours to enjoy you before you need to be asleep. I know it's important to keep to your schedule."

"Actually, I was hoping to get to sleep earlier tonight," she said.

"Then there's no time to wait." He bent and scooped her into his arms. That's when he noticed the weapon. "Do you usually answer the door with a knife in your hands?"

"No, but I don't usually get unexpected guests."

"Better safe than sorry." He walked them to the kitchen allowing her to put the knife back. "Where to?"

"Couch is close, but bed is better. Bedroom. Top of the stairs to the right. Light's already on."

He carried her easily to her room where the speed at which she undressed him suggested she didn't want to wait either. As soon as she was naked, he couldn't get enough of her. His hands covered her breasts as his fingers teased her nipples, his mouth moved to her jaw, then to nibble at her ear before he continued to kiss his way down her body, her sighs and moans all the encouragement he needed.

When his fingers moved to play with her pussy, he found her wet for him. Now he sighed. "Glad to know you're as ready as I am."

Her hands caressed his chest, then grabbed his ass. "I've been looking forward to this, and I admit I'm glad to not have to wait." He liked hearing that.

Kissing her shoulder, then licking and suck her hardened nipples, he asked, "Is there anything in particular you've missed? Anything you want?" He knew what he wanted to do, but he'd love to hear what she wanted so he could give it to her. But she was silent. He let go of her nipple and looked up at her. She didn't appear upset. More like hesitant. "Did I say something wrong?"

"No, it's not that. Not at all. I'm just... you're the first to..." Her voice trailed off, and she blushed, seemingly embarrassed by what she wanted to say.

He couldn't imagine what the rest of that sentence was, so he asked, "First to what?"

It was a second before she said, "To ask me what I wanted."

Her previous lovers must have been assholes, but he wasn't going to think about them. And he liked being different from the others and exciting her in a way they didn't. She deserved to have her pleasure put first, as soon as she told him what to do. "Are you going to answer me?"

"I'd like... I mean, if you wouldn't mind...." She covered her eyes with her hand.

He took her hand away from her face and kissed her palm. "Don't do that. I asked. Tell me." He was aching to know.

She stared at him for a moment, as if trying to decide if he meant what he was saying. She must have seen what she needed because she took a deep breath and said, "I want to take your cock in my mouth as you lick my pussy."

He didn't think his dick could get harder, but her words had the rest of his blood rushing between his legs. "And this is why it's worth asking." He kissed her. "Do you prefer top or bottom?"

"Who knew there would be so many questions? I thought we were just going to have sex." He was glad to hear the teasing in her voice, glad she'd relaxed.

"Oh, there's nothing 'just' about it. Top or bottom?"

"Top," she said. He rolled onto his back and gave her full access to his body. The hungry smile that slowly bloomed on her face was worth the flight in coach and the two layovers it took to get here.

Then her pussy was above him, ready for him to enjoy, and he wished he was staying longer. Deciding there would be time for regrets later, he licked her as her mouth surrounded the head of his cock. When they both moaned, he felt the vibrations in his cock and goosebumps covered his skin.

He'd missed this. The taste of her, the feel of her close, her responding to him. And, damn, she was good at sucking his cock. Her tongue swirled around the tip before her mouth enveloped him. When she pulled back, her hand was there to tease and touch him.

Unfortunately, because he'd been imagining being with her for days, his orgasm approached faster than he expected. "Sheridan," he said breathlessly, hoping she'd hear him and stop. He reached for her face and pulled her lips off of him.

"Did I do something wrong?" Her tongue swirled the crown of his cock, and he almost lost the ability to speak.

"God, no. You're doing everything right. Too right."

She cupped his balls, and one finger traced the sensitive skin beneath them. She was killing him. "How can it be too right?"

"Because at the rate you're going, I am going to come before I can be inside of you."

"Then I guess that will have to wait," she said and sucked him into her mouth again.

He groaned and grabbed the sheets. "Are... you... sure?" He could probably get hard for her again pretty fast, but it had been a long day, and he didn't want to disappoint her.

"Keep doing what you're doing," she said, lowering her pussy against his mouth.

He took her at her word. Fine, if she was going to send him over this way, she was going with him. He stroked his tongue from the bottom to the top of her opening before focusing it on her clit while driving one, then two fingers in her. She got wetter for him and took him deeper into her mouth, telling him he was pleasing her as much as she was pleasing him.

He couldn't tell who was reading whose responses but suddenly, they were both moving faster. Her mouth and her hands worked together to bring his climax to a peak as he curled his fingers inside her and sucked and swirled her clit. He shouted her name as his orgasm hit, and moments later, she did the same.

She rolled off of him, her body limp, as she caught her breath. He put one hand on her ankle as he reached for a tissue from the box next to her bed and dried his lips. Sitting up, he looked at her, lying in the soft light of the room, her body shiny with sweat, a grin on her face. "You seem rather satisfied," he said.

"I feel rather satisfied. Very satisfied," she said, and he noticed her accent was heavier. Apparently, pleasure brought it out. He'd have to remember that. After a moment, she turned herself around and pressed against him.

"This was definitely not the evening I had planned," she said as they lay there, his fingers caressing her back, hers playing with the hair on his chest.

"Really? It was almost exactly what I had planned."

"Almost?"

He kissed her. "I still want to bury my cock in you, but that can wait."

She hummed in approval, then rested her head on his chest and said, "When did you decide to change your arrival date?"

"Last night. I expected the client work I was doing would take me until I needed to leave, but we got the shots faster than I expected. Their copywriter was on-site with me, and she came up with ideas that allowed us to deliver exactly what the client wanted. I thought it would be fun to surprise you. You know I don't like to sit around and be bored."

"Well, it was a surprise." She kissed him. "And it was certainly fun," she added, finding the blanket and covering them. "And definitely not boring."

"Careful. Too much encouragement and you're going to either be late or exhausted tomorrow for work. Maybe both."

She put the back of her hand up to her head in a mock expression of drama and woe. "Too true. It's lights out for me. Well, it will be if you'd turn off the light." He reached for the bedside lamp, but she stopped his hand before he could. "I'm sorry. I shouldn't have assumed that you'd want to spend the night. You've been traveling for hours. Did you want to head to Dani's house? That way, you don't have to worry about me waking you in the morning."

Ever considerate and thinking of others. He'd noticed that about her. "I can always nap tomorrow if I need to or fall back to sleep after you leave, assuming you don't kick me out. For now, I'm good right where I am," he said and plunged them into darkness. "Besides, I might want to wake you before morning."

"Funny you should say that. I was thinking the same thing. You brought condoms, right?"

He kissed her softly. "Plenty."

"I love it when you're optimistic." She snuggled against him. "As surprises go, I have to say this one was wonderful."

Ryan held Sheridan in his arms, listening to the change in her breathing as she fell asleep against him, enjoying the fragrance of her shampoo mixed, as always, with the scent of cinnamon that clung to her. He'd never be able to smell it again without thinking of her. Fortunately, that wouldn't be a hardship. The more he got to know her, the more he liked her. She was as warm and inviting as the treats she made for her café.

And more delicious.

God, he'd loved having her spread for him, getting to feast on her pussy and drive her wild. Watching her lose control the way she did was gorgeous. So much the opposite of the way she was in the kitchen, where she had everything down to almost military precision. It didn't surprise him that she was a generous lover, making sure he was pleased. That was definitely part of her nature. He was glad she could receive as well.

Ryan had been with enough women to have experience with both giving and selfish lovers. Ones who were only too willing to please him as a way of showing their worth and hold on him. There was a neediness to the way they approached sex he found a turn off. And then there were those who wanted to be pleased and did little or nothing to please him in return. As if allowing him to have sex with them was enough. It wasn't. He didn't stay with either type for too long.

But Sheridan wasn't like that at all.

As sleep took him, he was glad he came out early and had this time with her. Fortunately, it didn't say anything about how he was feeling or change anything.

Chapter Seventeen

The next morning, Sheridan woke before her alarm and turned it off so the ring tone wouldn't disturb Ryan. If her moving around didn't wake him, she'd let him sleep and leave him a note. She didn't mind knowing he was still in her bed.

As she went into the bathroom to dress, she thought about last night. The moment she'd seen him on her porch, her body lit up with awareness and desire. They'd had fun through texts in the last month and she tried not to assume that what had happened after Eden's wedding would automatically happen again.

But she had hoped. He'd been a considerate and attentive lover, and she definitely wanted more. However, she also understood he was as committed to being free of relationship entanglements as she was, even if they had different reasons.

When she came out of the bathroom, Ryan whispered, "Good morning."

She squeaked in surprise. "Good morning. I'm sorry if I woke you."

In the early morning light, she saw him grin. "How sorry?"

"What do you mean?"

"Sorry enough to apologize by coming back here and riding me before you head to work?"

She smiled and hoped it hid her nerves. As someone who didn't have sex often, being on the bottom was easier for her. Her partner could set the pace, and she could match him. But on top? Would Ryan be able to tell that she wasn't as comfortable?

Deciding if she was going to risk it, it should be with someone she didn't need to make an impression on. She gave her watch a quick glance and said, "I suppose my boss won't mind if I'm late."

She took off her clothes and Ryan flipped back the covers. He was already hard. Nothing like a little encouragement. As soon as she was close, he pulled her onto the bed and kissed her, his hands going to her breasts, then between her legs. "Let me get you ready," he said as he teased her pussy, sliding a finger over her outer lips. He circled her clit, and she wrapped her hand around his cock, stroking it slowly and playing with the pre-cum that told her he was as aroused as she was.

Moments later, he was reaching for a condom. Deciding to be brave, she took it and covered him quickly. Straddling him, she held his cock to her opening. She paused, wondering if she should move slowly or quickly. "Minx," he said, not understanding her hesitation. He used his cock to tease her opening. As her pleasure increased at the unexpected sensations, she lowered herself slowly onto him, taking him inch by inch. "God, yes, Sheridan," he said with a sigh when he was fully inside her.

Picturing what she'd seen in movies, she rocked her hips forward and back, making them both gasp. He touched her everywhere as if he couldn't get enough, and she melted into the sensations. Following her own pleasure, she put her hands on his chest and raised her pussy, then pressed herself down again. When he moaned, she took it as a good sign and continued until they'd found a rhythm exciting for them both.

As they both got closer to their peak, Ryan lifted his hips to meet her thrusts and drive deeper into her. She cried out with pleasure and surprise. The last time she'd been on top, she'd done all the work as her partner laid there. This was different. And so much better.

"Oh God, Ryan, that's... that's..."

"Exactly," he said, sounding as breathless as she did. "I love feeling you gush all over me. Don't hold back."

As if she could. She let herself get carried away by everything she was feeling, allowing sensation to be her guide. If it felt good, she did it — and kept doing it. Until her body got to that moment where it climbed. "I'm so... Ryan... close. Don't...."

"I won't," he said as he grabbed her hips. Her climax hit her in a rush that felt like explosions going off throughout her body. She swiveled her hips, tightened her pussy, and raked her nails down his chest. "Yes, like that. Please... yes... I'm going to come, too."

Knowing she'd brought him to this point empowered her. She arched back and put her hands on his thighs, pumping herself up and down, taking him deeper until he screamed out her name. She loved watching the shudders of his orgasm run through his body.

Finally, he let go, his hands falling to the bed. She could see his rapid heartbeat and she bent forward to kiss his chest. Then she allowed herself to collapse on top of him.

His hands caressed her back in long, lazy strokes, which felt wonderful on her sensitized skin. But as they lay there in the silence, she thought of her inexperience being on top during sex. Before she could stop herself, Sheridan asked, "Was that okay for you?" When he didn't answer, she asked what she was really concerned about. "Was I okay?"

He shifted in the bed, and she pulled away, allowing him to sit up. He looked at her as though she'd suggested going on a non-carb diet. "Which part of my screaming your name and coming so hard I think I saw stars wasn't clear?" She dropped her eyes. "Sheridan?"

It was time for her to trust him with the truth. She didn't know how it might change things between them, but she wanted him to know this part of her. "There's something I need to tell you, but I'm not sure what you're going to think." With a deep breath, she plunged forward. "I don't have a lot of sexual experience. You're only my third partner."

His eyebrows went up. "You've got to be kidding. You're gorgeous and sexy. There's got to be plenty of men who've been interested in you."

"Interested in me, yes, but I almost never return the feeling." She looked away, but he cupped her face in his hands and turned her head back. She had no choice but to meet his eyes when she said, "I'm demisexual."

As he took his hand back, she assumed he was confused, but before she could explain, he said, "That means you're rarely sexually attracted to someone, right?"

It was a relief that he was familiar with the term. "That's part of it. More accurately, I don't experience a sexual attraction to someone unless I've formed an emotional bond with them first. My attraction to you happened after I got to know you more."

"So, lust at first sight is out for you," he said. She nodded. "I hope you don't mind, but that's what happened for me. I thought you were hot from that first Zoom call and when I first saw you at the dance studio...." His eyes raked over her naked body. "Well, wow."

Her cheeks warmed. "Thanks," she said. It was flattering to know.

"If you don't mind my asking, when did things change for you?"

"I zinged the day we were making cookies at the café."

He gave her a half smile. "Zinged?

Funny how that was going to be harder to explain than being demi. "I don't know how else to describe what it felt like. One moment you were a nice guy I was helping, someone I was glad to have as a new friend, and the next I was wondering what it would be like to kiss you."

"I hope I didn't disappoint," he said.

She chuckled. "Not at all. But as you now know, that's usually my concern since I have so little experience. I'm always worried the person I kiss will be able to tell."

"Let me check," he said and kissed her, teasing her mouth with his tongue and letting them both get carried away. When he pulled back, he said, "Nope. Perfect."

As he leaned to kiss her again, he stopped. “Wait, you agreed to the fake dating thing even though you weren’t attracted to me? Why?”

She was wondering if that would occur to him. “First, to help out. You did seem truly desperate. But also, to keep myself safe. Big social events can get uncomfortable for me when there’s a possibility of being flirted with and no possibility of me returning the interest.”

“Like what I saw at Flurry.”

“Exactly. You needed me to keep Millie off your back. By saying yes, I got to keep every man off of mine. Win-win.” She leaned in to kiss him and noticed her bedside clock. “Shit,” she said, jumping out of bed.

“Okay, maybe I’m the bad kisser,” he said, but she could hear in his tone he was joking.

“I hate to come and go, but I need to get to the café.”

He laughed and watched her dress. “Not quite as sexy as seeing you take your clothes off, but still not a bad view. Are you busy later?”

“I’m doing all the baking for the wedding cake today, so I’ll be at the café late.” She was still nervous about getting that all together, but once she got going, she hoped to relax. He told her he’d stop by and see if she was free for dinner. In the meantime, he was going to Dani’s and to get more sleep before letting people know he’d arrived. “And we’re supposed to be having movie nights for the bride and groom.”

“That’s right. Almost forgot,” he said with a yawn.

“Sorry to have woken you so early.”

He grabbed her hand, pulled her to him, and kissed her thoroughly. “I am not sorry in the least.”

Chapter Eighteen

After Sheridan left for work Saturday — the best early morning he could remember in a while — Ryan did as he said. He went to Dani's, slept for a few more hours, then went to his parents' for lunch. When he stopped by the café later, she was too busy to take a break and his help would probably slow her down, so he kissed her, licked sugar off her fingers, and said he'd see her later.

She seemed nervous with him and although that could be because she was stressed about the cake prep, he wondered if it had something to do with sharing her sexuality with him. She'd been so responsive and passionate; it was nothing he would have guessed. It didn't change his attraction to her, and he was glad she'd "zinged" with him.

That night, he got to Nick's early for the movie night, which gave him a chance to see Dani before she needed to leave and to play with Nick's dogs.

"Guess pets aren't an option for you," Nick said while Ryan was on the floor happily losing at tug-of-war with Otis and Lola.

"Not unless there's one who doesn't mind being alone for several days at a time. Maybe a lizard. You seem to enjoy having them around." When Ryan arrived, he'd passed Nick out jogging with the unleashed dogs, which included tossing a ball so they could bring it back.

"I love it. They're the best coworkers I've ever had. They never let me work too long," he said, joining Ryan on the floor and giving the pups attention. Although Nick went to New York to consult occasionally, Second Chance Houses was a home-based business.

"And this place," Ryan said, gesturing to the house. "It's like the ones you used to draw."

"It's amazing to me I built my dream house before I knew what my dream life would look like. And now I have it."

There was no mistaking the deep joy Nick had for what he'd created. Ryan wondered if he'd ever have that feeling, but before he could dwell on it, Cole and Dean arrived with some of Dean's school friends, and they got ready for the party.

Like the night at the Varnum, Ryan enjoyed hanging out with everyone. He always thought of the town as being filled with people his parents' age, but Nick's house was filled with guys their age. In addition to the two male members of Cole's band, all of the Stewart brothers were in town, so they'd come — which instantly made for a crowd — along with Hunter, Derek, and Ashton Royce. He hadn't had much of a chance to meet Ash at the last event, but Ash had heard about Ryan. When the two of them were in the kitchen getting more pizza, Ash said, "I know you're not here for long this visit, but if you wouldn't mind, I would like your input on what I could do better with the way we're presenting Fluid." Fluid was the non-binary clothing line and store Ash had opened in a refurbished mill. "I think it looks too much like all the other Royce lines. It needs... something."

He was flattered by the request. "I'm happy to see what you've got and give you feedback."

"And are you available to hire?"

Ryan's eyebrows went up. He'd never worked with anyone locally. He'd never considered searching for jobs in the area. It was an intriguing idea. If Ash hired him, he could come back, see his brothers. See Sheridan. The idea had appeal. "I suppose. Let me look first, and I'll let you know."

At ten, they were starting a third movie when he got a text from Sheridan. *Going to bed early. Exhausted. See you at the wedding.*

As much as he would have liked to be in bed with her, he had no idea when they were going to be done, and she'd had a busy day. *Sweet dreams. Save me a dance,* he texted back and rejoined the group.

The first thing Ryan did after he was dressed on Sunday morning was head to Mia's to take pictures of her getting ready. He got several beautiful shots of her with her close friend, Casey, putting on her wedding dress and fixing her hair, as well as ones of her with Dean. When they were done, Dean grabbed what he needed so he could go with Ryan to the Sinclairs' house, where they were joining Cole and his brothers.

"Do you have the ring?" Mia asked as they headed out, mother and bride mixing together effortlessly.

Dean patted his vest pocket. "Right here. Do you have the other one?" he asked Casey.

She picked up a box by the bouquet she'd be carrying. "I'm all set."

"Then I'll see you at the altar, Mama Mia," Dean said and gave her a hug. Dean may have meant it to be quick, but Mia held on. Ryan lifted his camera to capture the touching moment. When they pulled apart, their eyes were bright with unshed tears. "I'm so happy for you and Cole."

"I'm happy for us all," she said and gave him another quick squeeze before she waved them both off.

"Man, this is going to be a great day," Dean said as they drove to the Sinclairs. "Mom and Cole? They're amazing together. They make you believe in love."

"I saw something similar with my parents," Ryan said. He watched Martin and Millie weather the storms life threw at them, growing closer and stronger in good times and tough ones. It was special.

"Yeah, but you don't believe in it, do you?" Ryan glanced at Dean then back at the road, not that there was much traffic. "I mean, that's what I heard."

"What have you heard?" Ryan was curious what was said about him in his absence.

"Nothing bad," Dean said quickly. "Millie brings you up occasionally when we're over there, and Cole is quick to remind her that not everyone settles in one place or with one person. That you're happy, and she should be happy for you."

The boy's tone told Ryan he was leaving something out. "And?" he prompted.

Dean seemed to think about it before continuing. "I did hear Cole say something to Theo once about you changing women more often than you changed cities."

Ryan couldn't stop the bark of laughter. "He's not wrong." Dean looked a little uncomfortable, so Ryan said, "Hey, don't sweat it. No one knows me better than those guys. I could say I haven't met the right woman yet, but that's the flip answer. Maybe it's because I watched Cole, Theo, and Nick go through so much with the women they loved before getting their happy endings that I'm not willing to risk giving my heart to anyone. Or maybe because I saw how great real love can be, I don't want to settle for anything less than awesome." He'd never said that before — or considered it — but he heard the truth of it.

As they pulled into the Sinclairs' driveway, early enough to have gotten one of the few spaces, Dean said, "That makes sense. Mom went through a lot when Cole came back — and they told me some of what happened when they split years ago. She never let anyone get that close again because it hurt so much. And because she never got over him. Gotta be careful when it comes to love, I guess."

The boy was wise. "Careful and smart. Assuming that's possible with love." Ryan grabbed his cameras from the back of the car and walked with Dean into the house. As they stepped into the chaos that was his parents' living room, all thoughts of love fled. On a table in one corner, centerpieces were being given a final touch. In the kitchen, there was a small army of people preparing food. Plates and silverware were piled on the dining room table. It reminded him of Sheridan and the orderly way she and Wesley moved through their space.

As Ryan tried to find any member of his family, Devon Tremont came in with her clipboard in one hand, a pen in another, so focused on what she was looking at, she nearly bumped into them. "Oh, sorry. Just trying to keep things going here. We've got a schedule. If you're looking for your brothers, they're down the hall. Your folks are upstairs." At least she knew where people were, but before he could thank her, she was off to whatever needed her attention next.

Ryan stopped to take pictures of the mayhem. He'd seen his parents' house busy before — Thanksgivings when he was here frequently had a full house — but this was beyond anything. After almost getting knocked into a few more times, he surrendered and put the camera away. He and Dean found the Hansons in his mother's music room at the back of the house, as far away from the confusion as possible. They all looked relaxed and happy.

"One best man, delivered as requested," Ryan said as they entered. Cole's face lit with warmth and love at the sight of the teen. Ryan was bummed he didn't catch the expression on camera. Just as Martin and Millie considered the three boys they took in to be their sons, Cole felt the same way about Dean.

Not wanting to miss anything else, Ryan took out his camera again, this time putting it over his neck where it was going to stay for the rest of the event. It bugged the shit out of him when he didn't catch a moment.

They were sitting around drinking coffee and juice from a tray service that had been set up when Millie came in with muffins. "Didn't want you boys to forget to eat."

"When have we ever forgotten that, Mom?" Theo teased. One of the first changes Ryan noticed after the Hansons started coming around regularly was how much more food was in the house. Ryan had grown up in the rarefied situation of not lacking for anything — whether love or food. The Hansons' father had left years before then, and heard people talk in hushed tones about Susan Hanson, but it wasn't until she died and Theo and Nick came to live with them when Ryan was in high school that he understood the bigger truth of their difficult home life.

With his mouth full, Nick said, "You didn't have to do this. We had breakfast."

"Yes, I can see that." As she left, she called out, "Don't get crumbs all over yourselves."

"Will she ever stop mothering us?" Cole asked with no malice in his voice.

No one responded because they all knew the answer — nope. Never.

Finishing the bite in his mouth, Ryan brushed himself off — his mom had been right about the crumbs — and said, "I'm going to get shots of things outside before people arrive. See you under the big top." He gave the group a salute and headed out.

The day was warm and sunny, everything a bride could hope for when she planned a June wedding. When Ryan had been at his parents' the day before, he had seen the two tents going up. But today, with the addition of a flowered arch, and chairs arranged for the ceremony as well as tables being set for the reception, it had been transformed.

He walked around, taking close ups of centerpieces as well as the entire property from a distance, with the mountains in the background. It was the perfect time to do this, while no one needed him for other things. After the ceremony, Cole and Mia asked for a couple of formal shots, and as with any client, he was more than happy to give them what they wanted.

He hadn't done weddings since he first became a photographer. The money was good, but the clients were often difficult. As soon as he could make more strategic decisions with his career, he'd dropped them. But it was different watching this come together for people he cared about. As he worked and did his best to keep out of Devon's way — and the people she was directing with near military expertise — he was startled by the screech of an amplifier.

Turning around, he saw a familiar face plugging a microphone into a speaker. Familiar, but not someone he'd ever met — Paxton Jones. The woman had become famous as the lead singer for Cole's band, Emporium, and was now enjoying a wildly successful solo career after the band's breakup. Next to her were Brian Flemming and Hugh Walker, the other band members. He knew they'd be here as guests, but he hadn't expected her to be singing.

He was going to grab candids of the three of them talking and laughing, but decided not to do so without permission. "Hi, I'm Ryan Sinclair," he said, holding out a hand which each of them shook. They, unnecessarily, offered their names in return. "Mind if I take photos as you're getting ready?"

"Not at all," Paxton said, then recognition and a smile lit her face, transforming it from beautiful to breathtaking. He'd seen her in videos and pictures, but in person she was lovelier. She could have had a modeling career if she didn't have such an amazing voice. He supposed the two together were part of what made her a star. "You're Cole's youngest brother, aren't you?"

Ryan couldn't help it. He loved that Cole had shared enough about him and their family that Paxton recognized him as a brother. "I am, but today I'm also the official photographer."

"Then snap away," she said. "We shouldn't be too long. We wanted to make sure all the equipment is working before the guests arrived so there are no surprises come the ceremony."

Yeah, nothing like tech failures to ruin a plan. It was why he had back up cameras and extras of everything. "Pretend I'm not here."

Paxton gave him a curious look and said, "I never pretend anyone isn't there."

Interesting. And kind. He'd never read anything negative about Paxton in gossip columns, but there was a generosity in her words he didn't expect. "What I meant was, I'll do my best not to interfere with your work while I do mine."

The smile returned. "I'd expect nothing less from a professional."

He clicked a quick shot while she was still looking at him, and she laughed and shook her head. Glancing at the camera screen, he saw an image of Paxton like none he'd ever seen before. She looked like the rock star everyone knew... but different. He made a mental note to send her a copy of the photo later and hoped she'd like it.

It took the band less than fifteen minutes to finish setting up, and their timing was great, because shortly after, the guests arrived. From the number of chairs, Ryan would guess that Cole and Mia were expecting the same numbers as Theo and Eden had, under a hundred, but that still meant people would be parking all over the neighborhood.

Fortunately, all the neighbors were in attendance as well. Millie didn't want to leave anyone out.

Unfortunately, that included Caroline Osgood, his prom date. He'd forgotten she would likely be there since, according to Millie, Caroline had never left the area and moved into her parents' house when they left for Arizona.

"Ryan, it is *so* good to see you," she said and gave him an uninvited hug. He didn't move the camera away from between them and, thankfully, she let go quickly. "I'd been hoping you'd be here."

"Well, Cole is my brother." She seemed to wait for him to ask her a question to keep the conversation going, but he had no interest in talking to her, so he let the uncomfortable silence stretch out.

Finally, she said, "I'm sorry I missed you when you were here for the first wedding. I heard it was wonderful."

"It was."

This time she anticipated his unenthusiastic response and launched into a monologue on her work as a dental hygienist and what she was doing to update her parents' home.

Ryan had heard the expression 'sensing someone in the room,' but he'd never experienced it. He wasn't facing the entrance and yet he knew the moment Sheridan arrived. When he turned, he spotted her immediately, stepping into the tent with Laurel and Hunter.

And looking lovely. She was wearing an off-the-shoulder, calf length, floral dress in shades of peach. Her curls were wild and free, and Ryan couldn't stop himself from remembering how they looked framing her face while she was on her back.

Beneath him.

In bed.

"Ryan, are you listening to me?" Caroline said, the tone of her voice grating on his nerves as it had years ago.

Before he could respond with an attitude his mother would not have approved of, Sheridan was by his side. Grateful for her appearance, he put his arm around her waist and gave her a lingering kiss. He brought his hand to her cheek, and she pressed against him, making it obvious they were more than friends. When the kiss ended, he looked into Sheridan's eyes and smiled as he said, "No, Caroline, I'm not."

Sheridan gave him another kiss, this one below his ear, and said in a quiet voice, "You looked like you needed saving."

"I need more than that," he said and enjoyed her blushing response. He hadn't expected this fake-dating to help him out of other awkward situations, but it was effective. Turning and seeing Caroline still there, he said, “Sorry, I got distracted. Caroline, you must know Sheridan Behr. We started dating when I came in for Theo’s wedding.”

Sheridan leaned in and whispered, “We started doing much more than that.”

“And we keep doing it,” he responded, but this time in a voice loud enough for Caroline to hear.

She got the message. “Yes, I know Sheridan, and yes, I heard. I see someone I need to say hi to. I’ll see you around. Have a nice time.”

“I expect to have a very nice time,” he said. As Caroline walked away, Ryan put a second arm around Sheridan’s waist so they were face to face. And he pushed the camera out of the way. “How about you?”

“Sounds good to me, but first… the wedding.”

Chapter Nineteen

Ryan grabbed his camera bag, and they walked to the chairs set up for the ceremony, joining his brothers in the second row.

Leaning across Sheridan, Nick said, "We saved you the aisle seat so you can get up as necessary."

"Many thanks." He left his second camera with Sheridan, then positioned himself in the best location to see everything.

A few minutes later, everyone took their seats, and the officiant stepped into her place, front and center. Cole and Dean appeared to the right. Like Theo, Cole never looked happier. Dean appeared nervous, but Ryan suspected that was about not forgetting his role. As the space grew quiet, Paxton and the other former members of Emporium started "There Is Love" by Peter, Paul, and Mary. Ryan grabbed shots of their performance before moving to the top of the aisle.

First, Casey appeared in a lilac-colored dress that matched the flowers she was carrying. As she walked, Ryan noticed her smile and wink at someone. Looking at where her eyes had gone, he saw Derek returning the smile, his adoration lighting his face.

Ryan gave a silent chuckle. Another Fable Notch love story.

Once Casey was in position, Ryan kept his camera directed at Cole. There would be plenty of time to get pictures of Mia walking with her father, but there was one moment Ryan was determined to get.

And he did.

While everyone watched the bride's arrival, Ryan captured the second when Cole first saw Mia. His face was lit with joy, love, and wonder, as if he could hardly believe this was his life. As he had when he watched Eden join Theo, Ryan felt an emotional lump in his throat. He couldn't have been happier for his brother, and he was beyond glad to be here to share this day.

Mia was nearly halfway to Cole when Ryan turned to take pictures of her. She walked on the arm of her father, who was using a cane, so they moved slowly. She looked lovely in a simple A-line dress that gave off Greek goddess vibes. And if he stood directly in front of her, she wouldn't have seen him. She had eyes only for Cole.

As it should be, Ryan thought.

Moments later, the bride and groom were face to face. Ryan was about to take his seat when he turned and saw his parents. They were holding hands, his mother's head on his father's shoulder, tears in both of their eyes, their expression filled with a love that Ryan could sense was both for the couple and for each other. He'd never doubted their connection and commitment, yet seeing it so transparent rocked him. His gut clenched; his breath caught.

He snapped a series of pictures he could already imagine printing and giving to them as a gift. He might make copies for the whole family. It was an image he was not likely to forget, and his brothers would appreciate it as well. A staggering wave of gratitude overcame him, and he gave them each a quick but strong hug before returning to his seat.

He sat next to Sheridan but didn't spend much time there because minutes later he was back in the aisle getting shots of Cole and Mia exchanging vows and rings, then heading to the other side so he could get them walking back down the aisle.

When the ceremony was officially over, everyone moved directly to the reception, which was in a second tent. The bar was open, and the first glasses of champagne were poured for Cole and Mia, who toasted each other and then their guests. Staff removed the ceremony chairs, and Jeremy Stewart set himself up to start the music and DJ the event. That gave Ryan the time he needed to do formals with the bride and groom.

Once the music was ready, Cole and Mia danced to a female singer's cover of "Can't Help Falling In Love With You" that was magical. Ryan took picture after picture, glad as he often was he did this work in the digital age and didn't have to worry about running out of film. When the song ended, Cole kissed Mia, and Jeremy let the couple stand in silence, surrounded by their love and that of the people around them.

It was perfect.

When they looked up from each other, Jeremy called everyone to the dance floor, started the music again, and the party began. Ryan put down his camera and took

Sheridan's hand. He liked how easily she moved with him, fit in his arms.

"You smell like icing," he said as he danced close to her.

"That's because I spent the morning covering cinnamon rolls."

"I can think of fun things to do with any leftovers." He gave her a mischievous grin, and she laughed. It was so easy with her.

They danced for several songs before returning to their seats. Looking around the table, he noticed he was with most of the same folks as last time. Laurel and Hunter, Dani and Nick. This time, Gabriel Stewart, the oldest of Laurel's brothers and Hunter's closest friend, was at their table, along with Zoe and baby Stella. He liked the familiarity. He could see how much bigger Stella had grown in the last few weeks, enjoyed listening to Laurel and Hunter talk about plans for the fall batch of hard cider she would make using the apples from his orchard, and heard about the dog therapy program Dani wanted to create.

It was comfortable. Welcoming. Unfortunately, the feeling didn't last.

After lunch was served, Ryan went to work, walking from table to table taking pictures both casual and posed. At every stop, he fielded questions and comments on his work, his parents, Sheridan, and when he was moving back. He smiled and offered noncommittal answers, trying to hide his growing discomfort. He was relieved to arrive at Theo's table, where he knew he wouldn't be interrogated.

Before he could take a picture, Theo pulled him aside. "Dude, you okay? You look like a mouse cornered by a gang of cats."

He didn't want to bring anyone down. This was a happy occasion, and he was happy. Just frustrated. "Thought I was hiding it."

"Not from anyone who grew up with you."

Ryan was suddenly worried. "Shit, you don't think Cole noticed, do you?"

Theo gave Ryan's shoulder a reassuring squeeze. "Cole is noticing nothing but Mia. You're good there. Talk to me."

He took a deep breath. "I got Mom off my back by saying Sheridan and I were dating, but I feel like everyone in town has commented on our relationship and keeps asking when I'm moving home. Maybe I should print a handout so I don't have to keep giving the same answers: Yes, we are. Yes, she's terrific. No, not anytime soon."

"I had the reverse issue. Everyone wondering how long before I'd leave again." Ryan was still amazed Theo had made Fable Notch home. "But I get the challenge of uncomfortable questions. Anything I can do?"

Ryan appreciated the offer, but this was an easy one to answer. "Nope. Just needed to wallow in self-pity for a bit. I'm fine."

Theo didn't look like he believed Ryan, but for whatever reason, he chose not to say anything. At least, as Ryan took pictures of Theo's table, there were no awkward questions. And, he reminded himself, he was leaving tomorrow. Interest in him would die down over the next few months while he was away.

When he was done, he went to the bar to grab a beer. He was looking forward to getting some peace at his table, but as he started toward his seat, the space got quiet.

"Can I have your attention, please?" Cole said, standing at the microphone.

"Time to work," Ryan said, putting his beer down and positioning himself where he could get the best shot of Cole.

"When I came back to Fable Notch, I was in a rough place both personally and professionally." Ryan saw Cole give a quick nod to his former bandmates. Brian gave him a thumbs up. "It took a deadly crash to help me wake up and see what I wanted, what I was missing. That was you, Mia. I cannot tell you what it meant to me that you were willing to give me — us — one more chance."

He held out his hand, and she joined him. She gave him a kiss and was near enough to the microphone for everyone to hear her say, "Two."

Everyone laughed. "You're right. It was two more. I almost blew that first one. And given that I'm planning on a lifetime with you, I'll probably need more." He kissed her hand. Ryan snapped picture after picture, hoping at least one would capture the love flowing between them. "Back then, one of the things I was struggling with was writing new songs. While we were together, I started a new one, the first I'd written in months. I promised you the song was yours, that I would never share it. Well, I'm going to break part of that promise, because the song is done, and if you don't mind, I want to share it with you, and everyone, now."

Mia nodded, tears in her eyes. As Brian and Hugh sat behind their instruments, Cole took his place at the keyboard. Jeremy brought over a stool for Mia, and when she was ready, Cole said, "This is called 'Kiss You Forever.'"

He sang, *"Too many years I lived without you.*
Too many years we lived apart.
But you always had my love.
You always had my heart."

Ryan lowered the camera, wanting to experience part of the moment without his lens. The song was beautiful, of course, but it was so much more. It not only unfolded the story of Cole's love for Mia and how he'd lost her, but the truth of what he went through, what it took for him to learn what he needed so he could have the life he wanted. Anyone who knew their history could hear the power and raw emotion Cole poured into the lyrics.

Ryan couldn't imagine what it might be like to love like that, to have someone love him so deeply. It seemed simultaneously wonderful and terrifying. He looked back to where Sheridan was sitting with Nick and Dani, all eyes on Cole.

As if she sensed him, Sheridan glanced at him and gave him a smile, which he returned. If he had any interest in settling down, she was the type of woman he'd choose. Caring, generous, understanding. But she didn't want a relationship either, and that was a good thing.

Wasn't it?

He returned his focus to Cole, who was repeating the chorus, and this time Mia joined him, their voices blending perfectly.

"And I've never been able to decide,
If you're more beautiful in the sunset or the moonlight.
If I prefer your smiles or your sighs.
But I know your laughter is my favorite sound.
And I want to kiss you forever.
Let me into your heart.
Let me into your life.
Let me be the last one you kiss."

As the music stopped, there wasn't a dry eye in the house. Ryan took a quick picture of the crowd sitting there in stunned silence, then returned his focus to Cole and Mia as the place erupted in cheers and applause. He caught their smiles and their kiss. He never thought he'd describe love as beautiful, but after the last two weddings, he couldn't help but see that it was.

Sheridan listened as Cole sang to Mia, getting as emotional as everyone around her. But it wasn't only witnessing the deep love these two people shared — which was breathtaking — it was realizing this was something she'd never seen and didn't believe was possible.

From what she remembered, her parents had been in love, but she'd been young, and she hadn't concerned herself with it. After her father died and Hazel started her string of marriages, Sheridan saw how impermanent love could be and how foolish it was to base your happiness on someone else. Hazel was so certain the right man would make her happy, she repeatedly jumped on the relationship roller coaster. There would be the climb of joyous infatuation when Hazel met someone new, followed by the rush of what she claimed was love, only to have it quickly descend into frustration and anger.

But what Sheridan saw around her was different.

Laurel and Dani had found love rooted in friendship, support, and no small amount of sexual attraction. Both of them had been through serious bumps to be with the men in their lives and were, she knew, willing to go through more. Their happiness wasn't dependent on the person they were with — they had full lives without the men they loved — but their relationships made their lives better, gave them each something special and a combination of comfort and support that was enviable.

Sheridan wasn't certain if it was something she wanted for herself, but her faith in love and marriage was restored by the joy she saw around her.

The event moved from Cole's song to the presentation of the "cake." Sheridan watched nervously as Cole and Mia sliced into the oversized cinnamon roll that had been moved from the top of the cake stand. After they'd each had a bite, Mia shot her a thumbs up, and Sheridan relaxed.

A few minutes later, Ryan joined them at the table again. He sat down heavily on the folding chair, tottered for a second, then righted himself. "That was almost very embarrassing." He looked at Sheridan and asked, "What's a southern expression for clumsy?"

"Clumsy as a cow on board pile," she said. "Or he could trip over a flat surface."

Zoe held up a finger. "That would be me. Hopefully Stella will be more graceful. Maybe I'll put her in one of Eden's toddler dance classes when she's ready." She took a bite of her dessert as soon as it was served and sighed. "Then again, maybe I should go to one of those classes now. Burn off some of this yumminess before it goes to my ass."

"You look fine," Gabriel said, and Zoe smiled at him. Was something happening there? Sheridan supposed it was a possibility, although Laurel had said Gabriel was firmly against having children of his own, and Zoe was a single mom.

Before anyone could comment on his response, Paxton Jones interrupted them, coming to their table in a rush. "Excuse me, who is Sheridan?" Everyone pointed to her as she tentatively raised her hand. "You're responsible for these cinnamon rolls?"

"I am."

"I'm sure you hear this all the time, but they are amazing! I'm going to have to come by your café tomorrow and buy a bunch before I leave. Do you ship? Can I order online?"

"No, sorry, not at this time," Sheridan said. She loved it when people liked her cooking, but she wasn't used to attention from someone so famous.

"Guess I'm going to have to pace myself, so I don't eat them all in one sitting."

"They won't be as good if you freeze them, but it will help them last longer. Take one out the night before to defrost and give it a few seconds in the microwave to warm it up."

Paxton beamed. "Perfect. That gives me an excuse to buy more."

Sheridan usually made fewer rolls on Mondays since it was their slowest day, but she made a mental note to plan for more. "Would you like me to put some aside for you?"

"Oh yes, a half dozen. Thank you for letting me barge in like this. See you tomorrow." She gave them a wave and went back to her table.

They all sat in stunned silence before Dani said, "Well, it's not every day a rock star raves about your best-selling product."

"Thank goodness, because that was intense," Sheridan said, putting her hand to her chest as if to calm her fluttering heart.

"It's totally deserved," Ryan said as he took a bite of the one left on his plate. Then he leaned over and said, "And I can't wait to get to the sweet center."

She turned to him, his lips close enough to kiss, his smile telling her he meant the innuendo. "Later."

With a grin, he said, "Promise?"

"Yes." She'd never been good at flirting or banter, but with him it was easy. And she was looking forward to being alone with him. She'd been sorry they hadn't been able to see each other the night before.

Throughout dessert, Sheridan fielded compliments as people came to their table to comment on how much they loved the cinnamon rolls and how original the "cake" was. "Worth all the stress and work?" Ryan asked as another satisfied guest left.

"It was," she said. "But I'm happiest that Cole and Mia are pleased."

A few minutes later, Ryan asked if she wanted to dance, but before they could stand, Mayor Keller stopped by putting a hand on both of their shoulders. "Sheridan, what a surprise to have your cinnamon rolls here. I'd been so disappointed I couldn't come to the café this morning because of the wedding, but it turns out I got to have my weekend treat after all."

"I'm so glad you enjoyed it, Mayor," she said and explained to Ryan how Brenda regularly came to Just Right.

"And I couldn't let today go by without saying hello to you, Ryan," the mayor continued. "It's great to see you. What a special time for you and your family."

"It is, ma'am."

"I spoke with your father recently, and he said how pleased he and Millie are to have you here for the weddings. And I heard you're dating our Sheridan. Perhaps that means we'll get to see more of you. Your parents would love that, I'm sure." Ryan smiled, but Sheridan could see the tightness in his jaw. As the mayor's husband came over to pull her onto the dance floor, she called, "You'll be next."

"I will *not* be next," Ryan said under his breath. Sheridan looked at him, fairly certain she was the only one who heard. Before she could say anything, he stood and managed an "excuse me" before walking to the bar. Considering he hadn't finished his beer from earlier, she didn't think he wanted another drink. She toyed with the idea of giving him space, then decided her friend might need her. As soon as she was next to him, he started talking. "I knew this was going to happen. People asking me about my life, about us, but it's...." He trailed off as he raked a hand through his hair.

"Not what you want to discuss."

"Why can't people accept I'm happy with my life the way it is? I don't want to change it. Sure, I want to see my folks and my brothers, but don't want to move back. I want to get this new job, travel, have fun."

She took his hand in hers. "I get it. And the people who care about you most? They get it too — even your folks," she added before he could interrupt. "Millie and Martin want you happy. Sure, they'd prefer it if you were happy where they could see you more. They love you, but they'd rather you be out in the world enjoying yourself than here and miserable."

"I suppose." He blew out a breath and shook his head as if to release the thoughts racing through it. When he met her eyes again, he attempted a smile. "How is it you understand?"

"Because *I'm* happy with my life. I'm running a business I love in a place I've made my home. But I also know that just because my choices make me happy, doesn't mean the same ones will give you the same results." As they stood there, she had an idea. She didn't love it, but it could help him. "There aren't any wedding-related events you have to be at tomorrow, right?"

"No, Cole and Mia are leaving for the airport tonight. They're staying at a hotel and flying out first thing in the morning. Dean is staying with my folks for the week."

"Then there's nothing keeping you here." She ignored the pang that came with the words. She had no problem with things hurting because it meant Ryan would get what he needed. "Don't wait. Leave tonight, take an earlier flight."

His look of surprise was almost comical. "You wouldn't mind if I left early?"

"Would I like more time with you? Of course. But besides you being the man I enjoy going to bed with, we're friends. And my friend looks like he needs a break."

"I do." She heard the relief in his voice and was glad she'd said what she did. Looking down, he seemed to notice they were still holding hands. He brought hers to his lips and gave it a kiss. "Thank you. This was not the help I expected."

"A lot that wasn't expected has happened between us." His dimple appeared. A good sign.

"Does that mean I can still have a few hours to devour you after we're done here?"

She leaned in and kissed the spot at the edge of his ear. As he shivered, she whispered, "Absolutely," and allowed herself to enjoy a rare but more than pleasant moment of sexual empowerment.

Ryan was as good as his word, and soon after he was done taking pictures of Cole and Mia leaving, they said their goodbyes and went to her house. He didn't wait for her to undress. Just put her on the bed, pulled off her underwear, and licked her until she came screaming his name and begging him to fuck her.

An hour later, after her legs stopped feeling like jelly, she got out of bed, put on her robe, and went downstairs to make him coffee. There wasn't much she could do for him, but she figured caffeine to go would be helpful.

When she came upstairs, he was in front of her closet door. From the stiff way he was standing, she could tell something was wrong, but couldn't imagine what. She'd only been gone a few minutes. "Your coffee, sir." She held out the mug, and he turned slowly toward her.

That's when she saw what he'd been staring at. The wedding dress.

In a low voice that bordered on a growl, he said, "Why do you have that?"

Chapter Twenty

He thought everything between them was fine. Better than fine. When she went to the kitchen, he changed his flight, and texted his family that he needed to leave earlier — blaming it on the airlines. He received responses of disappointment but acceptance.

Looking at the clothes they'd tossed everywhere, he decided to be a gentleman and hang up the dress she'd worn to the wedding. When he opened the closet door, he saw the long white gown on the back.

He knew what it was. It might not have been as flowing as Mia's or as poofy as Eden's, but he recognized a wedding dress when he saw one. And Sheridan hadn't been in any relationships recently. She had to have bought this because of him.

How had he missed the signs? Didn't she tell him she understood his choices and why he wanted to leave? How could she say that and still buy this?

"Marriage seemed like the obvious next step and the dress was gorgeous." Her tone was so calm, like she was telling him the lunch specials. He was ready to shout that it most certainly *wasn't* the next step when she said, "Six years ago."

What was she talking about? "What was six years ago?"

"When I bought the dress."

He stood there as more of his brain cells came back online. He gave her credit for staying silent as he figured out what she was telling him. His shoulders dropped as the tension left his body. "You didn't buy it because of me, because of us."

She gave him a soft smile, put the coffee mug in his hand, then led him to the bed, where they sat next to each other. Taking a deep breath, she said, "No, I didn't. Six years ago, I was involved in what I thought was a serious relationship. I loved him. He said he loved me. I was wrong."

He ran a hand through his hair. "You must think I'm an ass for jumping to conclusions. Or I think so highly of myself that after a few days together, you can't wait to make things permanent."

"Actually, I think someone must have done a number on you, too, the way you panicked. What happened?"

It wasn't a story he told anyone, mostly because he wasn't proud of how he'd handled it, but given what he'd accused Sheridan of, she deserved the truth. "I was involved with someone when I lived in New Mexico. We'd been together four months when there was a pregnancy scare. Two weeks of her going on and on about how excited she was, how I had plenty of time to find a more permanent job in Phoenix before the baby came." Two weeks where he felt as though he was having an ongoing anxiety attack and considered not coming home on several nights. "She even bought two little outfits, one for a boy and one for a girl. I tried to be gentle. Told her it was too soon, that I didn't think it was the right time, but she didn't hear me."

Sheridan winced. "And I thought I jumped the gun, thinking Paul wanted a future with me. We'd been together over a year and been friends for longer."

"When her period came, I didn't hide my relief well." He shook his head, remembering. "No, I didn't hide it at all. I was more excited we'd dodged the bullet than she'd been about the pregnancy. She was furious. Said I was immature and commitment phobic, and I should have told her I didn't want a baby."

"Sounds like you did, though, and she didn't listen or want to listen." Sheridan gave a slow nod, as if something occurred to her. "And you assumed I'd done the same thing."

He took her hand in his, coming back to the present. "I'm sorry. I should have known better."

"Well, as you pointed out, we have only been together a few days, even if it's spread over a longer period. And you have good reasons to be hesitant about trusting. In many ways, we're still getting to know each other."

Putting the coffee down, he cupped her face in his hands and kissed her. "I still should have known. You're nothing like her."

"No, I don't think I am," she agreed, "but I can see where a wedding dress in the closet of a woman you know hasn't been dating could be a red flag."

He chuckled. "That's an understatement. I almost went full on bull-charging-a-red-cape."

"I noticed that," she said and gave him a kiss. "But we talked it out. I think that puts a tally firmly in the mature column."

He hadn't noticed that, and he appreciated her pointing it out. The immature accusation was one that continually stung. "Want to see what I do know about you?" he asked, peeling off her robe, the dress forgotten.

He stayed as long as he could, then gave her a lingering kiss, got dressed, and headed for the airport. And if Sheridan was sorry to see him go, she was glad to be someone who didn't hold him back.

The next day was a busier Monday than usual with people who'd stayed after the wedding coming in for cinnamon rolls, including Paxton, but it was on Wednesday when Sheridan noticed a bigger change. Midweek, they didn't typically run out of cinnamon rolls until around nine, but they were wiped out by eight-thirty.

After the cinnamon rolls were gone, there were grumbles from people who had to be directed to a different choice. For the first time since she opened, Sheridan ran out of muffins and scones on a weekday. Odder was people asking for cinnamon rolls all day. People who knew her café, knew those didn't last past the morning hours, no matter what day of the week it was.

Sheridan prided herself on knowing what her business needed and when. She'd tracked sales vigilantly for her first two years and still regularly checked their records to make sure things hadn't changed. She was aware of how much she sold daily, as well as how that varied from season to season. She knew when there would be an overall increase in customers — fall and ski season especially — and when things would be slower — like in January when people went on new diets and stayed away from the temptations her place offered for a few weeks.

But by the time she flipped the sign to "Closed" at three o'clock, the baked goods case held two lonely cookies and one peanut butter brownie, and the only reason there was anything at all was because as soon as her afternoon help arrived, she ran to the back and made more.

"What the hell is going on?" Wesley had asked as he made sandwiches while she put two trays in the oven, grateful she kept ahead on dough.

It was a good question. "I have no idea. Maybe there's something going on at the Castle on the Hill." Sometimes conferences at the hotel resulted in an unexpected uptick in business because the attendees were given recommendations for places to see in town.

For the last hour they were open, most people had come and gone without buying anything because there were so few choices. A few of her regulars said they'd wait and come back tomorrow. She didn't like not having what they wanted, but it couldn't be helped.

After turning off the lights, she went into the kitchen, exhausted. She'd never had a busier Wednesday. She wanted to review the day's receipts, but there was too much to do to make sure they had enough to open tomorrow. Wesley stayed with her to do as much prep as possible without going overboard in case business was back to normal the next day. She didn't expect the day would be as busy, but Sheridan was determined to be prepared.

But she wasn't prepared.

The next day, there were customers waiting when she turned the sign to "Open" and before eight, there was a line out the door of people she didn't recognize. It wasn't as though she'd never had a line, but it usually only happened during festivals. Wesley had to join her at the front counter frequently to keep the line moving, and the cinnamon rolls were gone earlier than the day before. After disappointing a half dozen customers in a row, Wesley made up a sign that read, "NO CINNAMON ROLLS LEFT" and put it in the window. That shortened the wait considerably, but plenty of people stayed and purchased what was available.

At least because it was June, her patrons weren't standing outside freezing. Every seat in the place, as well as the ones outside, was filled.

At ten, Sheridan made some quick calls to her serving staff, asking if any of them could come in earlier and breathed a sigh of relief when two said yes. She wished she could call Laurel and ask her to reach out to her servers for additional help, but Laurel wouldn't be awake. Still, she sent a text with an SOS.

She got unexpected, and very welcome, help when Laurel appeared shortly after eleven. As she stepped out from the kitchen tying an apron around her waist, she said, "How can I help?" Sheridan was so stunned she couldn't say anything. Laurel explained, "Dani saw the line out the door on her way to work. She called me. Sorry I didn't see the message sooner."

There wasn't time to give her friend a hug. "If you can help me at the counter, I can let Wesley stay in the back to make sandwiches."

"Let's do it," Laurel said.

If it weren't for the stress of keeping up with the demand, Sheridan might have enjoyed working with her friend again. It hadn't happened since Sheridan started her own place. Fortunately, they fell into it easily, moving around each other efficiently, helping customer after customer. Wesley kept the kitchen running and had more baked goods ready when their first servers arrived at eleven-thirty.

When Sheridan went to pick up an order, she asked if he thought she should put together another batch of cinnamon rolls — she had dough in the refrigerator for tomorrow — but he nixed the idea. "We don't want people who come later to get what the early arrivals couldn't." Instead, they made more brownies, bars, and cookies.

At lunch, the line was still long, but Sheridan got another surprise from a neighbor. Megan Boyle, who ran Pie in the Sky, had six quiches sent over — three broccoli and cheese and three asparagus, ricotta, and prosciutto. They immediately added them to the specials board with a note stating where they were from. They cut them in quarters, added a salad and chips on the side, and had twenty-four more lunch offerings. Sheridan would have cried if she wasn't concerned it would slow her down. She owed Megan a huge thank you.

Most days, Sheridan didn't change the sign to "Closed" until closer to three thirty, letting people linger as long as they wanted, but today, as soon as the clock hit three, the sign flipped. She locked the door and told the people who were finishing to let her know when they were ready to leave so she could let them out.

After being shooed out of the kitchen by Wesley who said he could handle the clean-up with help from the remaining servers, Sheridan poured herself a huge glass of sweet tea before dropping into a chair across from Laurel who was sitting at one of the recently vacated tables. "I don't think I've ever had a more exhausting day," Sheridan said. "Not since the week after you opened and there was that flood in the kitchen just before the Friday dinner rush."

Laurel shuddered. "That is easily on my top five worst nights. I remember thinking our college needed to add a Master Class on disaster management."

"This wasn't a disaster, but it certainly wasn't the norm." She let her head fall back for a moment and let out a sigh. What had happened? "I don't want to complain about having a lot of business, because that sends the wrong message to the Restaurant Gods, but why have we suddenly become the most popular place in town?"

"You've gone viral," said a voice from the kitchen. Sheridan looked up as Chris Farrel, her web designer, walked in. He must have used the back door rather than try to get in the front. "Sorry to barge in. When I saw the line out your door and later noticed your website crashed, I did some searching. The cake you made for the wedding this past weekend is news."

Sheridan didn't understand. "How is that possible?" Had Ryan posted about her on his social media the way he'd said he would when they first met? Because she might have to kill him if this was the result, and Millie would definitely not forgive her for that.

Chapter Twenty-One

"Paxton Jones," Chris said, as if that answered everything. Sheridan must have looked confused, because he continued. "The day after the wedding, she posted pictures of the cake you made as well as the cinnamon rolls she bought before she left town. She tagged her photo with your location and social media information and added the hashtag #justrightrolls. Like a lot of celebrities, she has a very active fan base who like baked goods as much as her songs. The result? Instant popularity."

"You mean instant problem." Social media hadn't been something Sheridan concerned herself with in her personal life or in her business. When she'd first opened the store, she managed the business's Facebook and Instagram accounts, but it had never been anything much. She'd post a picture of the day's specials or a new menu item so people could check what was available before coming over. Occasionally, she'd add a reel of something coming out of the oven, but once sales were consistent, she'd stopped. Chris used her photos on the website and added a page that said, 'Daily specials might include...'.

She hadn't given it a thought in forever. Still trying to wrap her head around what happened and what it might mean, she asked, "How long does going viral last?"

"You'll have to reach out to Janelle and Ash for that," Laurel said. "Remember when #ash-hole trended while they were on *Seams Impossible* together?"

Sheridan groaned. That had only lasted a few weeks, but Sheridan suspected that was because of show ending and Janelle and Ash not winning. She loved that people were talking about her shop, and more business was good business, but if she couldn't keep up with what customers wanted, she was going to let a lot of folks down and that tore her up. "What am I going to do?"

"I may have recommendations," Wesley said as he came from the kitchen, holding a notepad and joining them. "I took a quick inventory of what we have, and what we're expecting to receive with deliveries this week. Then I called Megan to see if she can send us more quiches for the next few days. She's happy to lend a hand. We have the funds available to order more from our suppliers—of food and non-food inventory—and put a rush on shipping. We may need to limit our menu if there are things we can't get."

Laurel raised a finger and said, "I can call my servers, see if any of them can come in to help so you two can be in the back. I'd offer you my kitchen, but you know I'm a lousy baker, so there wouldn't be anyone to run it."

It sounded helpful, but Sheridan wasn't sure it was going to be enough. "Tomorrow is Friday. I can't ask this of you and your team with the weekend starting. No matter what, I am going to be runnin' all over hell's half acre."

Laurel smiled. "I know you're flustered when your southern-isms pop out. Although 'one legged man at an ass kicking conference' remains my favorite for this situation."

"I don't know what either means," Chris said.

With a sigh, Sheridan said, "Busy, Sugar. It means very busy."

Laurel reached out and took Sheridan's hand. "Besides, you're not asking. We're offering. You've got friends here. We're going to help you through this."

Help started with Wesley staying to prep more food than ever for the next day while Laurel sat nearby with her phone on speaker and called around to see where it might be possible to get what they needed. She also reached out to Zoe and Janice at the Davis Market, explaining the situation and telling them there wouldn't be sandwich deliveries from the café for a while.

By the time Sheridan got to her house several hours later, she was exhausted. She fell onto her couch, uninterested in doing anything but sitting in the quiet. Her body was sore from the marathon day she'd had, her back especially tight. Her mind, however, wouldn't calm. Time for otter videos. Anything to make her smile and take her away from her worries.

A half hour passed before her stomach rumbled so loudly it startled her. Had she eaten at all today? She couldn't remember. She shuffled to the kitchen. Peanut butter and fluff were all she could manage, but the comfort food was exactly right. She ate half while standing at the sink, then went back to the living room to finish.

As she sat down, she took out her phone to see if there was anything she might have missed from Wesley and was surprised to see two texts, a missed call, and a voicemail from Ryan. The texts told her he'd heard the news about her sudden popularity. On the voicemail he said, "Whatever time you get in tonight, call me."

She appreciated him reaching out, but after the day she had, wasn't sure she had the energy to talk to anyone. Before she could decide, however, the phone buzzed with his name on the caller ID. Deciding it was fate, she answered it. "Guess the Fable Notch grapevine was hard at work today," she said by way of a greeting. "Who told you?"

"Who didn't?" he said with a laugh, and the sound helped her relax. She couldn't say why, but it felt good to hear his voice. "Nick reached out to me first."

"Probably because of Dani." She explained how Dani had contacted Laurel, too.

"Next, Mom messaged me because she saw the lines out front later in the day. Apparently, that's not a typical time for you to be busy."

"No, we get a bigger rush in the mornings." She'd considered the idea of opening earlier so her regulars could get what they wanted, but there was no reason to assume they'd want to get out of bed at the crack of dawn for muffins. She explained Paxton's post and the results. "We don't get low on baked goods until one. Now we're running out by eleven."

"Cinnamon rolls not included," he said.

"Those are disappearing as fast as I can put them out, which I suppose isn't a surprise, considering that's what went viral in the first place." She stretched out on the couch and though it wasn't cold, she covered herself with a blanket, wanting the comfort. "I thought going viral was supposed to be a good thing. Don't people usually want that?"

"They think they do, but sustained popularity and steady growth is what you want, and that's different. As you're discovering, most businesses don't have the infrastructure necessary for going viral."

He sounded so serious and knowledgeable. It was cute. "You're sexy when you talk business. How do you know about this?"

"When I started, I had clients who said they were hoping for a product to go viral. They explained all the influencers and marketing professionals they were partnering with to make it happen. It rarely worked, but as long as they could see growth, they were happy, and I'd get hired again for the next campaign. Then one of my clients did it. They sent their product to a reality star who used it, loved it, and shared it several times on her social media."

Sheridan could imagine. "It backfired, didn't it?"

"Completely. Trying to keep up with production wasn't possible, the negative reviews on customer service and delivery piled up, and they had to stop offering the product until they could build up inventory and figure out how to manage sales. When they came back, the demand was never as high again because people had stopped wanting it." That sounded horrible. She would hate it if she had to stop offering something her customers loved. But what if they couldn't keep up with demand? What would have to change? Before she could voice her concerns, a yawn overtook her. "Sounds like you need to get to sleep. I assume you're going to be waking up earlier than usual tomorrow."

"I am." She stood and folded the blanket. "I'm going to get in bed with a book and hope my mind shuts down and sleep comes quickly."

His voice dropped, and he said, "Can I say I wish I were there to get in bed with you and help you relax?"

The idea made her shiver. A better distraction than otters. "You know you've made me pleasantly exhausted in the past, but I think I'd disappoint you tonight. I don't have the energy for much of anything."

"I could find a way to not be disappointed. I'd give you a massage," he said. She let out an involuntary moan. Maybe she'd book a session at the spa at the Castle on the Hill once things got back to normal. "Okay, if you're going to make happy sounds like that, someday I'm definitely giving you a massage."

"I may take you up on that," she said, heading to her bedroom. When she got there, she said, "Give me a second," and put the phone on the bed while she changed into an oversized T-shirt. As she picked up the phone again, she laughed, hearing him humming the theme from Jeopardy. "I'm back. Love the musical accompaniment."

"What is 'Are you getting into your nightgown'?" he said.

"It's a T-shirt, but the judges will accept that answer for $200." Now it was his turn to moan. "Want to know what the daily double is?"

"Only if it's a video clue," he said. Oh, he could charm the dew of a honeysuckle, she thought. "But I'm going to stop flirting — and try not to think of you in bed — and let you get to sleep."

"I appreciate that," she said, although she couldn't help but wish she had the time and energy to talk longer. "Hopefully we'll make it through the next few days and people will find something new to be obsessed with."

"Attention is pretty fickle these days. Whatever happens, I'm sure you'll figure it out," Ryan said. "How bad could it be?"

Two days later, Sheridan had her answer.

Bad.

Even with help, it was overwhelming. She could hardly keep the coffee pots filled, let alone the food. And not only were they busy all day, but because they were running out of things, customers were nasty and abrupt. Dealing with the moods of the public was a part of being in the food service industry, but it was so rare for her to have people annoyed. For the first time, customers shouted at her and her staff. It had been awful.

Of course, none of this came from people she knew, but that was its own type of upsetting. Everyone local was kind and understanding. It stung each time Sheridan didn't have what they asked for, and she felt as though she were disappointing them. She hated it.

By the time they closed on Saturday, when they were low on everything, Wesley agreed they needed to make immediate changes until the furor around their business died down. On Sunday morning, they put up a sign with their new hours, which told customers they would close two hours earlier than usual. The sign also showed they would be open for coffee only on Mondays and Tuesdays. Wesley wanted to be closed on both days. They needed the time to rebuild their inventory — and their strength — but Sheridan couldn't bear to let down her

Coffee Club members. Chris updated her website and made it a single page with their store hours as the only information. Then he shut down their social media sites to discourage more attention and negative reviews from people who weren't able to get what they wanted.

Sheridan hoped it would help, but by Thursday, it hadn't made a noticeable difference, and after two weeks of mayhem, she couldn't hold it together anymore.

"We need to close," she said to Wesley on Sunday.

"We did. It's you and me and almost no one in the place until Wednesday," he said. Did he think she forgot their new hours? Given how exhausted she was, that was a possibility. He put his arm around her and gave her a hug.

"No, we need to shut the café. I can't keep doing this. You can't keep doing this. Maybe if we close for two or three weeks, people will forget, and when we reopen, things will be back to normal." Tears she'd been holding back for days as she tried to be strong, broke through. She turned into his chest and sobbed. All her hard work, building a stable life she loved, and it was slipping through her fingers. If the café closed, would it be able to reopen successfully? What would she lose beyond customers? She couldn't bring herself to think about that.

She didn't notice he'd walked them to a table in the dining area until they were seated side by side. And she had no idea where he'd gotten the glass of sweet tea he handed her. When she calmed a little, she took a sip and continued, "Unless we can magically double our physical size and capacity in the next few days, there's no way to sustain this. I've been considering this all week, and I don't see another solution. But this is your business, too, so if you have another idea, I'd love to hear it."

He was silent, focused on their dilemma. Finally, he said, "We have two and a half days before we open again, and a very large delivery scheduled to arrive on Tuesday. Let's see if we can't come up with some ideas by then. But I will say this — you're right. Something has to change, one way or another. Are you okay with that?"

Sheridan's heart was hammering. She appreciated that he knew her well enough to ask. It also meant he knew the answer. And so did she. "No, not particularly."

Over the next two days, Laurel and Dani came by bringing food, movies, and words of encouragement, but every night, she was left alone with her racing thoughts and increased worries. Ryan tried to help by sending funny pictures, but she'd reply with nothing more than an emoji. The fact that he didn't call told her he understood she didn't want to talk.

Even otter videos weren't soothing.

On Tuesday, Sheridan was padding around her house in her bathrobe and slippers, lists running through her head of what had to be done. She'd need to get dressed eventually and go to the café, receive the supply delivery, and prep for the next day. But for the first time, the thought of going to the café brought a sinking feeling in her stomach. Sitting on the couch for the last day and a half hadn't done anything to revive her energy or help her find a solution. Knowing all that needed to be done kept her brain reeling and her body exhausted. She couldn't come up with a way to get them through their new popularity that didn't involve burning out, burning every bridge, or both.

As she drank her coffee, a car pulled up in her driveway. Figuring it was Dani on her way to work, she went to get another mug and was surprised when Wesley walked in. "Breakfast is served." He held up a white bag with the Just Right bear logo stamped on the front.

She appreciated the gesture, especially since she hadn't eaten much in the last few days. Worry kept her appetite down. "I hope no one saw you go into the café or people will think we're open and a line will instantly form."

"No danger of that," he said cryptically. He went to her cabinets, grabbed two plates, and put the sausage, egg, and cheese sandwiches on them. Lifting the top piece of bread, he added a dollop of sausage gravy from a container before covering them again. He joined her at the table, and they each took a bite.

Sheridan sighed as the flavors exploded in her mouth. It was no surprise this was their most popular breakfast choice. "Thank you. I needed this."

"I thought you might." He paused, and she braced herself for whatever bad news he was going to tell her. "I figured out what the business needs. A second location."

Her hands stopped before she could take the next bite, and she looked at him as though he'd suggested growing cotton in the backyard. It wasn't as if she never wanted to expand, but it wasn't in her business plan for at least a few more years. Thinking she must have heard him wrong, she said, "How are we supposed to open another location?"

A grin lit up his face. "We're going to use one that already exists. I didn't make these at the café," he said, motioning to the sandwiches with his chin before taking another bite. She put the food down and waited for him to continue. "I made them in the kitchen at the Davis Market."

That wasn't a total surprise. They'd been using the Market's ovens for some of their overflow baking in the last few weeks. Sheridan baked at the café, Wesley at the Market. Janice was an angel for making room for them. "Isn't that what we've been doing?"

"Yes, and no. I kept remembering what you said. How we needed to magically double our size and capacity to keep up with business. Then I had an idea. I went to the Market yesterday, sat down with Janice and Zoe, and suggested something almost exactly like that." As Sheridan ate her sandwich, Wesley explained how he talked with the two women about improving things for both businesses. He looked at his watch. "And as soon as you're done with your sandwich — and get out of your pajamas — we're heading over there for a meeting."

Although not sure she was fit for talking to anyone, Sheridan nodded, finished her breakfast, and headed upstairs. She got dressed, threw her hair in a messy bun and got into the car with Wesley, all the while uncertain about what he had in mind.

Soon they were seated in the dining area of the Market with Janice and Hunter Davis. Zoe came out, baby Stella wrapped in yards of cloth around her back, and presented them with a plate of cinnamon rolls. "Ta-da," she said with a flourish as she placed them on the table.

Sheridan was confused. There wasn't any chilled dough as far as she knew. That was their task for this afternoon, assuming she was opening tomorrow. She put one on her plate and took a bite. When it tasted as good as hers, her throat closed. Guess her place wasn't the only one who could make these. "They're excellent."

"Of course they are," Zoe said. "It's your recipe. Wesley gave it to me. Your recipe, our oven, made entirely in our kitchen. Welcome to Just Right at the Market."

"Okay, I'm as lost as last year's Easter egg," Sheridan said, and the expression made everyone smile.

Janice explained, "Wesley came by and told us how you were struggling. He suggested we become your secondary breakfast place."

"But you serve breakfast," Sheridan said. She didn't think of the Market as competition any more than she thought of the Kinsman that way.

Zoe shrugged. "Mostly muffins and coffee. Apple cider donuts in season. We figured if we expanded our morning offerings with your menu, it would take some of the traffic pressure off of you while increasing ours at the beginning of the day. We're pretty quiet before eleven. This would give people a reason to come earlier."

As she sat there taking in the idea, Hunter said, "Our plan is Wesley would manage the kitchen for the breakfast crowd in the morning. This frees Zoe and Janice to do other things for the Market, like our direct sales."

"And it would give me some mornings to sleep in," Zoe added, pleased at the idea.

Hunter continued. "Business is strong, and we were looking into buying another oven and refrigerator. Wesley said you might be willing to split the cost. If you like the idea, we need to decide if you'd rather set this up as renting space from us or if Davis would get a percentage of the profits. Either way, I think it would support us both. What do you think?"

She didn't have to think, but she did burst into tears. Everyone looked worried until she said, "It sounds amazing. Thank you."

Zoe jumped up and came around to hug her. "Welcome to the family," she said, and that's how it felt, as though her family had gotten bigger.

She took a deep breath — the first easy one she'd taken since this started — and said, "Let's get this figured out."

For the next two hours, they worked through the details, working through what they needed, creating a timetable, and making an appointment with a lawyer to draw up a final contract.

As they walked to Wesley's car when they were done, she asked, "What about tomorrow? Do we open? Or wait?"

"My vote is to wait. I think we could both use the time off, but no more than a week."

Sheridan agreed. And this time she might be able to relax enough to have the time off do her some good. That night, she called Laurel and Dani and told them what was happening, although Laurel had heard most of it from Hunter already. Deciding this was an ideal time, they both changed their schedules so the three of them could go away to a bed-and-breakfast in Maine for a long weekend, where they did nothing but hang out, laugh, and read.

"A second site, that's fabulous," Ryan said when she shared the news with him. "How are you feeling?"

"Hopeful, scared. A bit overwhelmed," she told him honestly. "Part of me still can't believe this happened."

But it had. And before she knew it, it was their first Tuesday with two locations. On Mondays, both sites were closed. Wesley planned to split his time between the kitchens and join her at noon for the lunch crowd. She hired counter help for the morning rush so she could manage the back. Chris had reactivated their social media and done a posting blast telling people they could enjoy the Just Right breakfast menu at the Davis Market. They'd also posted signage so everyone who walked by while they were closed would be aware of the new option.

Two hours after opening, Sheridan could see their plan was successful. There was a solid crowd at the café, but it was manageable. Quick calls to Wesley told her people were showing up at the Market. They had done it.

As she was closing for the day, Laurel and Dani arrived with champagne. "We have got to celebrate this," Dani said.

"You're a chain," Laurel cheered.

Sheridan laughed and hugged her friends. "Not exactly, but close enough." For the first time she could remember, change hadn't ruined her world.

Chapter Twenty-Two

Ryan hated that there was nothing he could do to help Sheridan through her viral status. Not only would he be in the way if he went to Fable Notch, but he was too busy to leave California. Since he'd been back, he'd been working non-stop. Typically, he planned a day or two off between jobs — it gave him time to relax, stay on top of invoicing, reach out to contacts, and put finishing touches on client work — but from what he could see, he was going to be flat out almost until Nick's wedding in September.

He had jobs coming in from previous contacts referring him to new clients, and January was getting more work for him as well. Probably to help grow his portfolio for the Canillos. He wouldn't complain. He'd had enough dry spells when he was starting out to never consider having work a problem.

During his infrequent downtime, his thoughts strayed to Fable Notch. He went out to a local burger place to grab dinner and their fries weren't as good as the Varnum's. The book he was reading had a bookmark from the Thousand Lives Bookstore. The radio played songs by Emporium. And every now and then he caught a whiff of cinnamon, which had him longing for a woman more tempting than icing.

Which was why he noticed the panties in a store's window display as he walked by. Along with several others, there was a pink pair with two cinnamon rolls on the ass with the phrase, "Nice buns." He walked in, figured out what he hoped was the right size for Sheridan and bought three pairs which the store was happy to ship. He added a card, "Thinking of you" and hoped they'd make her smile when they arrived.

A few days later, he got a text from her with a picture of her ass reflected in the mirror wearing the underwear. He responded with a heart eyed emoji. And an erection he didn't take a picture of. Now that she and Wesley had opened their second location, they'd been able to chat more often, but they were both so busy their schedules didn't always match well.

On a free night, Ryan got around to sorting and editing the pictures he'd taken for Theo and Eden's wedding. There was one main folder with the ones he liked best and a second which had extras — shots that were similar, but not as good. There was also a junk folder of ones which were blurred, had people with their eyes closed, or where the lighting and composition were all wrong. Those he never sent. He transferred the folders to a flash drive and put it in an envelope to mail the next day.

Deciding to let Theo know the package would be coming soon, he gave his brother a call. "What's wrong?" Theo said by way of a greeting.

"Nothing. Do I call so rarely you automatically assume something's wrong when I reach out?"

"Yes," Theo said matter-of-factly. "We only hear from you in texts."

"That's not true."

"Then tell me the last time you called to chat?" Ryan thought. And thought. Shit. His brother was right. "So, I repeat, what's wrong?"

"Nothing. Honestly. I'm mailing you the pictures from your wedding, and I wanted to call so you can watch for it." That's all it was, right?

"In that case, it's good to hear from you. What are you up to?"

Ryan filled Theo in on work and what he was putting together for the Canillos. He asked — casually, of course — how Sheridan's business was doing, and what was doing with their folks. "How's married life treating you?"

"At the moment, less than great."

That was unexpected. What could have gone wrong so quickly? "Did you and Eden have a fight?"

Theo laughed. "No, nothing like that. I'm in the Syracuse area for the next week or so on a case. Maybe longer. Depends on what Harlow and I find."

"And Eden's okay with that?"

"Why wouldn't she be? I mean, would she prefer I was home with her every night? I hope so. I know I'd rather be. But this is my work, and she accepts it along with the rest of me." Theo stopped and Ryan could almost hear him consider what he wanted to say next. "You do know you can accept someone and not like everything that goes along with the package, right?"

"Yeah, of course," Ryan said quickly. But did he? Theo's comment made him curious. "There are things you don't like about Eden?"

"I still don't like her father, although Patrick and I have found a way to tolerate each other, and that's an improvement. She keeps the house too warm in the winter, and I don't like the way she uses all the hot water when she showers. And we had a few tense discussions about money after we started living together. Turns out she's not the best at managing a budget, although she's getting better since opening her own business."

"Those seem pretty minor."

Theo laughed and said, "Not when the shower's cold. But they're minor because the things I love about her are so much bigger. And don't forget, she has to put up with worse from me. Not just my travel schedule, but my nightmares." Ryan knew Theo had PTSD symptoms from his time in the army. "And my asshole brothers."

"Very funny," Ryan said, knowing he was included and, as always, loving it. It was time, he decided, to ask the question pinging around in his head since his brothers got engaged. "Aren't you worried about being confined by the choices you've made?"

"What choice doesn't confine you? If you choose chicken for dinner, you can't have steak. But what does that matter if chicken is what you want?" It was a good point. Ryan didn't have an answer and let the silence stretch out. "Yes, every choice comes with consequences, some known and some a total surprise. Choosing to help Martin came with a lot of discomfort around facing who I was as a kid and what I thought of this town, but it was more important to be here, so I agreed. The total surprise? Well, that's obvious."

"Weren't you worried you'd let him down?" That was Ryan's other nagging concern. How could he put himself in a position where he might disappoint someone? It was one of the reasons he asked Sheridan for help. He couldn't let his mother down if she assumed he was dating.

"Are you kidding? I was petrified. Actually, I was positive I would screw it up. Martin and Millie were the only ones who believed I could do it."

"And you still went."

"You know what it's like saying no to them." Theo had a point. His parents were very hard to turn down. "And I guess part of me hoped maybe this time things would be different, that I could show people I'd changed. What was better was showing myself I'd changed. I think, as we get older, we're better able to make choices in line with what matters to us and, hopefully, we get better at accepting any unforeseen consequences. We know what's important, where we're willing to bend, and where we can't. This job you're up for — are you sure you can give them what they want?"

"Fuck yeah." For all the added stress of additional work, he loved the possibilities that would come with this contract. "I don't mean to sound cocky. I know it's also a big risk. The bigger you play, the bigger the impact if it doesn't go well." That wasn't something he had to worry too much about. It wasn't like anyone else would be impacted if he failed.

"Sometimes the only way to find out is to leap. Damn, I sound smart, don't I?"

Ryan laughed. "You do."

"And you know how I got that way?" When he said nothing, Theo continued. "Making mistakes." Ryan didn't like the sound of that. There was too much truth in it. But he could accept it. "Aren't you glad you called?"

Smiling to himself, he said, "Absolutely."

By the middle of August, Sheridan was thrilled with how things were going. The café's lines remained longer than before they went viral, but not as bad as they had been those first weeks. Their business at the Market was strong, and Hunter and Janice could not have been happier with the results. And with the increase in her income, she ordered the stuffed bears wearing tiny Just Right Café T-shirts she'd always wanted. They'd become very popular. Life had found a new stability, and Sheridan was back to looking forward to work every day.

Until two days after the Dog Days of Summer Festival.

The Festival had been exhausting, which was to be expected, and wonderful because her new blueberry rolls had won first place. Laurel, who had won the year before, said she was happy to lose to something that was so incredible. Sheridan had beamed with pride. But it had been an exhausting few days, and she'd let herself get rundown.

On Tuesday, she woke up hours before her alarm. She was hot and cold at the same time, and her body felt achy, her head heavy. She hadn't had a bout of the flu in years, but she recognized it immediately. Falling back on her pillows, she moaned, both from how lousy she felt and what was coming.

The next three to four days were going to be hell. And Wesley would need to call in more help. She rolled out of bed, keeping her blanket wrapped around her, and padded to the bathroom. It was too dark to see anything, so she reluctantly turned on the light, squinting when the room brightened and hoping it wouldn't make it hard to go back to sleep.

She found painkillers, and one dose of decongestant that hadn't expired. She took both, then got back into bed. Grabbing her phone, she texted Wesley and Michelle, their new morning hire, to let them know. She trusted Michelle would get it early enough to open on time.

As she lay there hoping to drift off, her mind touched on what needed to be done by others with her out for the week. There were cinnamon rolls for at least the first two days — their increased business had her keeping more inventory on hand — and enough biscuits to get them through until she returned.

She also needed to get more cold medicine, and maybe ask Wesley if he would leave soups on her doorstep. Would the pharmacy deliver? That was something to decide after more sleep.

It was afternoon when she woke again, which told her how long the cold medicine lasted. She had a sore throat, the aches were back, and she was feeling too warm. She also had texts waiting for her from Wesley, telling her to get in touch when she could. He picked up on the first ring, which told her he'd been watching for her call. "What can I do?" he said instead of a greeting.

"Soup?" she croaked, her throat scratchy and dry. "Medicine."

"Will do. Who should I tell?"

"No. One." It wasn't like they could do anything, and she didn't want to get anyone sick. She could handle this.

An hour after they got off the phone, he'd brought by chicken soup and minestrone, a container of orange juice, a quiche from Pie in the Sky, and a shelf of medicines. He insisted on coming in to put things away and make sure she took what she needed. To appease her, he wore a mask. After he unpacked what he brought while she stayed on the couch, he handed her an extra bag. "Cookies. I always crave sweets when I'm sick."

"You didn't have to do all of this," she said, and he gave her a look. "What? The soup and medicine would have been enough."

Saying nothing, he turned away. When he finished what he was doing, he brought over a big glass of orange juice and sat on the other end of the couch. His stern expression had her concerned. "Sheridan, I've noticed that a lot of people in the food service industry choose this work because it's a way for us to give. We enjoy taking care of others. But I've also noticed we tend to be lopsided and don't let others take care of us."

Her first reaction was to deny it, but he was right. Despite being bundled in blankets, she felt completely exposed. She'd learned to cook to take care of her sister while their mother grieved the death of their father. When her cooking made Hazel happy, she continued. And every time she started a new school, bringing in the cookies she baked might not have made her true friends, but it made fitting in easier. She took a sip of juice, then simply said, "Thank you."

His eyes crinkled, and she knew he was smiling under the mask. "You're very welcome." He went to the kitchen to warm up a bowl of soup and brought it to her. "Seems like you're good for now. Eat this while it's hot. I'll be back tomorrow to check on you."

Pushing down the immediate response to argue, she gave him a nod. As she lay under a blanket watching television, she sent a wave of thanks to Wesley for every spoonful of soup. And for the Snickerdoodle cookies, which were exactly what she wanted a few hours later.

After her next dose of medicine, she crawled back into bed and snuggled under the covers with a book. Unable to focus, she gave up and switched to watching cute animal videos on her phone, which was why she saw the reminder alarm: Attendants Call.

Shit. She'd completely forgotten they were scheduled to have those with Dani's wedding so close. Dani was having the most formal of the weddings, and Devon wanted everyone certain on what was happening and when.

She could do this. It wasn't as if anyone could catch what she had over Zoom. And if she was worried about her appearance, she could keep her camera off for the night. She got out of bed to get her computer and swayed on her feet. Dropping back to the mattress, she closed her eyes to get her balance, only to zone out for a minute. Sleeping sitting up? Not a good sign. Yeah, there was no way she was staying up for another hour until they started and then for the duration of the call.

She managed a quick text to Dani explaining why she wouldn't be there and fell asleep moments after Dani replied with, *No problem. Take care of yourself.*

The next morning, she was still feeling like the north end of a southbound pig. She dosed herself again and got comfortable on the couch. There were texts from Dani and Laurel checking in, both offering to come by. Remembering what Wesley said, she told them she'd be happy to have things dropped off, but not to come in so they wouldn't get sick. Knocks on her door later in the day told her when they'd dropped off her care packages. Laurel brought beef tips and waffle fries — Sheridan's favorite from the Seven Brothers Brewery — and Dani, who didn't cook, brought three adventure thriller books by Chris Niles, which looked exciting. She hoped she could concentrate enough to read later.

Thank you, she texted them, along with a heart.

Dani responded. *Just want you better. More deliveries available anytime.*

Maybe it was because she was sick, but Sheridan's eyes filled with tears. Having her friends do this for her... mattered. And it felt good to accept help.

The food from Laurel fortified her — as did her next dose of medication — and she was able to stay awake until nearly eight before she headed to bed, not much earlier than on her usual workdays. She opened one of her new books and managed one chapter before she drifted off to sleep.

On Thursday, her fever stayed down, and she managed a short walk and a long shower, both of which felt great but took what little energy she had. It seemed like she'd barely gotten to bed that night when she woke with a start, sure there was someone in her house.

Listening, she heard nothing. The cold medication must be making her imagine things. Or the sinister action of the book she was reading gave her odd dreams. No one broke into a house in Fable Notch. Especially at eight in the morning.

Then she heard it again.

Noise. Downstairs.

Not imagined.

She looked around her room for a weapon she could use to defend herself, but there was nothing. Maybe the crystal vase would be good, but only if he got close. It was better than nothing, so she grabbed it.

As she got out of bed, she wondered if she should call the police. All of her book heroines were more than capable of taking care of themselves in dangerous situations, but Sheridan had never been in one. Carrying her phone in addition to the vase, and ready to hit send on 911, she quietly went to the top of the staircase to listen.

And heard humming.

Serial killers and robbers didn't hum, did they? She was pretty certain they didn't or wouldn't. Unless there was a Humming Killer out there. If she weren't more than a little scared, she would have laughed at the directions of her thoughts. It couldn't be Laurel. The woman was never awake at this time, but maybe Dani had an early appointment and stopped by to drop things off rather than leave them outside. Sheridan took a few steps down the stairs, listening carefully.

"Bridge Over Troubled Waters."

That's what the voice was humming. And it definitely wasn't Laurel or Dani because the voice was male. It must be Wesley. She turned the corner to greet him and almost dropped both the phone and the vase. It wasn't Wesley.

It was Ryan.

Chapter Twenty-Three

The red-eye from California got Ryan into Boston shortly after six. Priority ticketing had him off the plane and into his rental car in record time. Going against rush hour traffic — and maybe driving faster than the speed limit — had him pulling up to Sheridan's house a little more than two hours later. He stopped at the Market where, thanks to a phone call when he was a half hour away, Wesley greeted him with two breakfast sandwiches and a large orange juice for Sheridan.

He'd knocked on her front door, but when he got no response, he checked the door, and finding it unlocked — of course — let himself in. The place was silent and dark, so he assumed she was still sleeping. He tried to be quiet as he put his luggage in the living room, then unpacked the food, but he must have woken her because as he was putting the juice in the refrigerator, she stepped into the room.

"Ryan?" She looked tired, rumpled, and surprised.

And absolutely beautiful.

God, he wanted to take her in his arms, but since she wasn't herself, he settled for saying, "Good morning, sunshine."

Her glazed expression suggested that sunshine was not what she was feeling. "What are you doing here?"

"Well, now that you're awake, I'm going to make you tea." He opened a cabinet, then a second one, before he found what he wanted. He took out two boxes and showed them to her. "Berry Zinger or Sinus Soother?"

She still appeared confused. "Am I going to have to repeat myself?" He waited. First things first. "Sinus Soother. It helps."

He pulled out a chair for her at the little table. After she sat, he filled a kettle with water and turned the burner on under it. As he poured the orange juice into a glass, he said, "You weren't on the Attendants call on Tuesday night. Dani said you were sick. Then my mom called me to tell me you weren't at the café when she stopped by. She said in all the time she's known you, she's never heard of you missing work. So, I… I came to see if I could, you know, help." Suddenly, he realized how odd this sounded.

Sheridan was looking at him as though he'd suggested taking her on a carriage ride on the moon. Rubbing her eyes as if that might make things clearer, she said, "You flew out here from California to make me tea?"

Okay, when she put it like that, it sounded strange, but in the moment when he'd heard she was sick and on her own, he couldn't seem to stop himself. He'd been looking at his schedule, then buying his ticket while he was still on the phone with his mother. "And anything else you might need." He handed her the glass of orange juice, and she took a sip.

"You got this from my place," she said and drank more.

"I did. I can't believe you can tell. It's just orange juice."

"We add ginger and honey. Something my grandmother used to do," she explained.

He took out another glass, poured himself some, and tasted it. "That is terrific. I stopped at the café at the Market on my way here to get you — well, us — breakfast, and Wesley insisted on including it. Now I understand why." He looked inside the bag and found something other than the sandwiches. "Looks likes he added something else to my order." He pulled out a parchment paper wrapped bundle and opened it. "Are these frosted peanut butter cookies?"

"Marshmallow frosted peanut butter cookies," she said. His eyes went wide, and she laughed. Good, he'd made her smile. "Remember the peanut butter and fluff sandwiches on the menu? Well, the week after we talked about them, I was making our peanut butter cookies and I thought, wouldn't it be great to add fluff to them?"

He took a bite, not caring that he hadn't had breakfast yet. "Ohmfkggd," he said with his mouth full. "These are unbelievable. I could eat a dozen."

"Thank you," she said, and he noticed a blush. "That's the best thing you can say to cook."

When the water came to a boil, he made her tea, warmed up the food and joined her at the table. "So, how are you feeling?"

She took a bite, then a sip of her tea before answering. "Better, but I went for a walk yesterday, and it wiped me out. I'd hoped to go back to work tomorrow or Sunday, but I think it's going to be Tuesday." He could hear her frustration. She loved her work so much, which he understood.

After they were done eating, they moved into the living room and snuggled on the couch. She curled against him and said, "I appreciate you being here. Don't tell anyone, but I was getting a bit lonely and bored."

"No one will hear it from me," he said, giving her a squeeze. He also wasn't going to share he'd been lonely, too.

They sat in silence for a while, and he liked how comfortable it was. Even though he hadn't seen her in a while, they didn't need to talk. They could simply be together, and it was enough. She pulled a blanket over her and said, "Not that I don't appreciate the breakfast delivery and the tea, but this is going overboard to make a lie believable. What did Millie say when you told her you were coming to help?"

Yeah, that was the oddest part of all, and he wondered what Sheridan was going to think. "I didn't tell her. No one knows I'm here. I was worried about you. The job I was on finished the day Millie mentioned you were still out sick and the work I have to do next can be done remotely—"

"So you flew across the country to babysit me?"

She didn't sound annoyed, just surprised. "Not babysit. I know you're perfectly capable of taking care of yourself. But I called Dani to see how you were doing, and she said you hadn't let her or Laurel do anything other than drop off supplies. That meant you were sick and on your own. I figured maybe you could use some TLC."

"I didn't know TLC could be delivered."

He kissed the top of her head. "Sometimes it can." He'd missed her, missed feeling her close. He didn't want to dwell on it too much — his desire to come out and help her — but he wasn't sorry to have done it, and that was enough. "How were you planning to pass the time today?" he asked. Now that he was here, he didn't actually know what they were going to do. Maybe he should have thought this through, not given into impulse. Then she snuggled closer, and he stopped caring.

"Reading mostly. Maybe watch movies or cute animal videos. I like the otter ones."

Remembering what Cole said about the choices from Mia's bachelorette party, he said, "I could do that. What are you in the mood for? *Notting Hill*? *Legally Blonde*?" He tried to think of other rom-coms but was drawing a blank.

"Those actually aren't my style," she said with a laugh. "I'm more of an action movie lover. How do you feel about John Wick?"

He blinked at her. "Seriously?" She nodded. "I love those. I've seen all but the last one."

"Then you're in luck. I own them all," she said with a hint of pride in her voice. "How about a marathon?"

They stretched out, side by side, and by dinner they'd watched the first three. Wesley messaged that he was dropping food off at the front door — enough for them both, smart man — and when they were done, they returned to the couch for the last installment.

An hour in, Sheridan fell asleep in his arms. He was tempted to carry her to bed, but he was comfortable, and the movie was good, so he didn't move.

Half an hour before the movie ended, she stirred and whispered, "What did I miss?"

"Everything, but we're up to the good part," he said, and they watched the rest together.

As the credits rolled, she said, "Guess I'm still not up to full energy."

"Let's get you to bed so I can give you a massage like I promised a few weeks ago. I bet you still need one."

As she got up, she protested. "I do, but—"

He held up his hand. "Nope. This is included in the Ryan Sinclair TLC package."

"Didn't know I was getting the VIP package," she said with a smile. Once they were upstairs, he went into the bathroom and went through her cabinets until he found a bottle of lotion. Then he sat next to her and said, "Take your shirt off, turn over, and let me help you."

"You're cute when you're bossy."

And she was cute without her shirt, but he wasn't going to comment on that. She did as he said, getting naked from the waist up, then lying on her stomach. He lotioned his hands and got to work on her tired muscles. Every moan and happy sigh sent a surge of blood to his cock, but he kept his focus on her until she was liquid beneath him. When he was done, he helped her get her shirt on, then, wearing only his briefs, he got into bed next to her.

She immediately turned and curled against him. "I'm glad you're here," she said before she fell asleep.

Me too, said a voice in his head. Part of him still couldn't believe he'd done this. Maybe it was because she didn't expect anything, didn't ask. He'd come because he couldn't help himself. But he was glad no one else knew he was here because the pull to come to her was something he didn't want to think about.

Chapter Twenty-Four

Sheridan woke feeling better than she had in days. More rested. And she had no doubt the man sleeping next to her was part of the reason. She still couldn't quite believe he was there. Ryan was a kind and thoughtful person, but she knew how he felt about relationships — and what they shared wasn't supposed to be that. But in the quiet of the morning, she acknowledged she'd missed him.

The realization triggered a small alarm in her head, but it was too lovely to have him here to worry about what might be happening to her feelings. After Dani's wedding, he'd be back on the west coast, and she'd have memories to keep her company.

Which was why she decided more memories couldn't hurt. Pressing against him, she stroked his naked chest, teasing the hairs until she heard his breathing change, then she kissed him behind the ear and licked at the shell. "Someone has more energy today," he said with a breathy chuckle.

"Definitely," she said. "And I've heard rumors that sex has healing properties, so this could be very good for me."

"And where did you hear that?" he asked, turning towards her and pulling her nightshirt over her head.

She traced a finger up, then down his cock, and he hissed in response. She loved the way he was ready for her, wanted her. Especially because she felt the same way. "Does it matter?"

"Absolutely not," he said and kissed her softly, then with more passion as she responded.

She pressed against him, and his hands roamed down her back to her ass. She shivered at the contact and let herself relax and enjoy what he was doing to her.

And there was so much to enjoy as Ryan reached inside her panties and gently caressed her pussy. She was already wet for him — had been, probably, since he joined her in bed last night. Before long, they were both naked, touching each other, remembering and reconnecting, coming close to that moment of tipping over, only to pull back from the edge. And then they had to stop because the condoms were with his luggage. "Don't move." He scrambled out of bed.

"Wouldn't dream of it." She offered a whistle at his cute naked ass.

"As if I needed encouragement to go quickly," he called, and she heard him race down the stairs and back. He threw open his suitcase, tossed his clothes on the floor, got the condom, then practically jumped into bed with her again. She was laughing as they fumbled with the wrapper, giggling as they both tried to put it on him, and gasping when he sank deep inside her.

She'd missed this, the physical connection that was heightened by the emotional one. The familiarity that increased her excitement because he knew what pleased her. This time, they didn't slow until they'd both climaxed.

After he rolled off her, she wrapped a leg over him and kissed his chest, relishing in the floaty post-sex feeling. "Yup, I definitely feel better. But I think we need to do that a few more times. To make sure I'm fully healed."

"Well, I did come here to take care of you, so how can I say no?"

"How indeed." She was so blissfully comfortable with this man. There may not be anything lasting between them, but damned if they weren't great in bed together.

They lay there, warm and content. She was enjoying feel of him close and the late morning sun coming through her bedroom windows, something she rarely saw, when she heard a car pull up. She looked at the time. Ten thirty. Running through the list of people it might be, she said, "Maybe Dani had a late morning and wanted to stop by. You better stay put while she's here. Unless you want Nick to know you're in town."

"No, I want this to be just the two of us. Dani shouldn't have to lie. I'll keep the bed warm."

Sheridan was still putting on her robe when there was a knock, and the front door opened. "Don't be alarmed, Sheridan." That was not Dani. She turned and could see from his wide eyes he recognized the voice, too.

Millie.

"Oh fuck," Ryan whispered and ducked under the covers as if his mother could see through walls. It was silly, but she understood the reaction. She wanted to dive back under them herself. Sheridan tied her robe tightly, found her slippers, then went to greet Millie, closing the door behind her.

"Good morning," she said when she got to the bottom of the steps. She ran a hand through her hair and hoped she looked as though she'd been sleeping, not like she'd been having sex. "What a lovely surprise."

"Oh no. Did I wake you?" Millie said, sounding worried.

Shaking her head, Sheridan said, "I was resting." It was partially true.

"I'm sure your friends are bringing food, but I couldn't help myself. So even though yours is better, I brought you chicken soup and my chicken salad sandwiches. I know, it's a lot of chicken," she said, waving a hand and bustling into the kitchen, where she put things into the refrigerator, "but you need protein when you're sick. Turkey is better, but I didn't have a chance to make one." She turned to Sheridan, who'd taken a seat at the kitchen table. "Do you want me to make you turkey?"

Sheridan had no doubt that if she said yes, Millie would run out to the store and get the biggest bird she could find. "No, that's not necessary. Chicken is great. I appreciate it. Let me make us some tea," she said as she stood, automatically extending hospitality to her guest. *Shit, Sheridan. Ryan is in your bed. You need her out of here, not settling in for a conversation.*

"Stop. Sit," Millie said, putting a gentle hand on Sheridan's shoulder and pushing her back into the chair. "I promised Martin I wouldn't stay any longer than necessary, so you're going to tell me where I can find things so I can make you tea." Why did everyone want to make her tea? "Then we'll get you settled back in bed before I'm on my way."

"The couch," Sheridan said immediately, and Millie gave her a strange look. "I'm staying out of bed unless I intend to sleep. I'm trying to increase my energy." Her visitor was quite helpful in the energy department, but Sheridan wasn't going to say that.

"Don't push yourself too hard, dear," Millie said. "You don't want a relapse. Those are worse. I'm sure the cafés and Wesley can manage if you need to take care of yourself."

Ryan certainly knew how to take care of her. Oops, no. She needed to keep her thoughts away from the sexy man who was waiting for her as long as his mother was in her kitchen.

Ryan aside, Sheridan enjoyed Millie's company. It was nice to listen to Millie share about her new students at the music school, where Cole insisted she come on as a piano instructor, and wondering if by Christmas Theo and Eden would have an announcement about starting a family.

"Don't you think it's a little soon for that?" Sheridan asked. "They only got married three months ago."

Millie shrugged. "They were engaged for over a year and in love for nearly their entire lives. Why wait? They are going to be such marvelous parents."

Sheridan had to laugh. Ryan said his mother was single-minded when it came to family. Apparently, that included babies as well as marriages.

Millie was as good as her word, and as soon as the tea was ready, she walked Sheridan to the couch, made sure she was comfortable, then gave her a kiss on the forehead before saying goodbye and making Sheridan promise both to rest and to call her if she needed anything.

Seconds after the car pulled away, Ryan came down the stairs. Dressed. Unfortunately. "She didn't notice the extra car in front of your house?"

That hadn't occurred to Sheridan. "She didn't mention it, so I guess not."

"We'll have to be thankful for small things. Including her not staying long." He joined her on the couch, and as she curled against him, Sheridan explained Millie's promise to Martin and laughed. "My dad knows her all too well. What did she bring?"

"Chicken soup and sandwiches."

He checked his watch. "It's not quite eleven, but you haven't eaten. Are you hungry?" The look she gave him must have said what she was hungry for, because he wiggled his eyebrows at her. "Plenty of time for that later, I promise, but you need to keep your strength up, so let's feed you." He stood, held out a hand, and pulled her up.

They went to the kitchen, and, as they unpacked the food Millie brought, she asked, "How much time do we have? When is your flight back to California?"

"Sunday morning, although my flight is to Washington. I have an assignment starting Monday."

She asked about his newest job, as they danced around each other in her small kitchen, brushing shoulders, putting arms around each other's waists. They didn't need to touch as much as they did, but the area was small, and it made it easy. "How long will you be there?"

"I'm officially booked for four days, but I'll stay until the end of the week. I always build in extra time, especially if any of the work needs to be done outdoors, which is the case for this client. I won't leave until I get the shots I want and know that the client is happy."

She liked how dedicated he was to the quality of his work, and she told him that. When they were done eating, they settled back on the couch, her laying between his legs, which he wrapped around her. "I don't think I realized how much you travel," she said.

He nodded. "Not as much as I used to because there's so much work in California, but I get calls and referrals from clients all over the country, so I'm away several times a quarter. It will be a lot more if I get the casino job. I'll let go of my lease and manage with short-term rentals, even when I'm back in the States. Makes for lots of bonus miles on my airline credit card."

"Ooh, upgrades," she said. "Bet that comes in handy when you take a vacation. Assuming you take vacations."

"I do, occasionally, but I admit, they usually end up being working ones in one way or another." She turned to look at him, confused. "How can I go somewhere beautiful or exciting and not take pictures? And after I take them, I have to share them."

"A vicious cycle," she said with a laugh. "I don't think that happens to us restaurant owners. We can't exactly jump into someone else's kitchen."

"No, but I'll bet every time you eat someplace new, you're aware of the service, menu choices, and quality."

"I do. It's hard when you want to go out with friends, but your profession keeps sneaking in. Laurel is in the same boat, and she's as picky as I am."

"Not to mention the added challenge when you know you can make things better than other places." It pleased her that he liked her cooking. "Do you *ever* order cinnamon rolls anywhere?"

"If they have a good reputation, and I can see the quality when I look at it. Then, yes, I get competitive. I'm objective, I swear. But definitely competitive."

"Have you ever found one that compares to yours? Because yours are ah-mazing." She liked the sigh in his voice.

"One. At this diner in New Jersey. They do all their own baking. Someday I've got to get back there."

"What were you doing at a New Jersey diner?"

"When Laurel asked if I would come to help her while she opened the brewery, I decided to drive up slowly, see a few places I'd never seen, like DC and New York. College friends told me I should check out the Jersey Shore, so I added that as a stop. That's where I found the Sea Garden Diner. It's a fourth-generation family business, started by the great-grandparents. There are five kids in the current generation and most of them work there in one way or another. The oldest son is their baker."

"You learned all of that from one visit?"

"Occupational hazard." She shrugged. "I got to talking with my server about the food, and she sent out one of the sisters who was in the kitchen. I didn't leave for three hours and spent most of that sitting in the kitchen chatting. One of the best diners I've ever been to."

"You better not let Rosie hear you."

"She knows." At Ryan's surprised look, Sheridan laughed. "On my first visit to the Kinsman, I mentioned that the place reminded me of a spot I'd been to in Jersey. Rosie guessed it on the first try. She knows the parents."

"Great, New Jersey is as small as Fable Notch."

"Or at least the diner world is. Six-degrees of Rosie," Sheridan said. "That woman knows everything."

Ryan nodded. "Which I suppose is why my mother does. They've been best friends since grade school."

As the day went on, Ryan told her stories about Millie and growing up in Fable Notch. It was fun to hear about Cole, Theo, and Nick from his perspective. In return, she told him about her family, her father's death, and her mother's perpetual remarriages, how she and Laurel became friends and what it was like the first time she saw snow.

But strangely, the best part was the long stretches they sat on the couch and said nothing. She read while he worked on editing photos from his last job, showing her before and afters when he finished them. She especially loved the shots he'd taken of the area when he'd come for Theo's wedding. It was like looking at the White Mountains for the first time.

They watched more movies and went upstairs early. They didn't bother with nightclothes, just got into bed naked.

And when he left early the next day, Sheridan tried to convince herself that nothing had changed between them.

Chapter Twenty-Five

On Tuesday, Sheridan was back at work. Her energy wasn't a hundred percent, but she was close enough that sitting at home was making her feel more useless than soggy potato chips at a fifth Sunday potluck.

And leaving her too much time to think about Ryan. How much she enjoyed having him around, talking about everything and nothing, sharing movies. Sharing her bed.

Her customers gave her a very warm welcome back. But unlike when she'd had to close after their time in the viral-zone, people were glad to see her, not the business, which felt special. Usually, she preferred only her food to be noticed. Now she was happy to be someone people connected with.

For the next few weeks, she focused on her business, shared texts and calls with Ryan, and helped Dani get ready for her wedding. A week before the event, Ryan was unexpectedly hit with an assignment connected to his potential big job and had to fly to the Bahamas. Ryan knew the company was getting down to the wire on their decision, but he was concerned because this job had him working until the Thursday before the wedding.

He'd called on Saturday as he was packing and leaving for the airport, worry apparent in the breathlessness of his voice. "If anything goes wrong or if the flight's delayed, I'm going to be cutting it close."

"You'll be here and that's what matters," she'd said, hoping she sounded reassuring. "Go, show them how brilliant you are, and we'll see you soon. And good luck."

After that, they only connected through texts. From what he wrote, it seemed like he was doing well, but it was hard to tell without hearing him.

Then on Wednesday, Sheridan was home making herself a BLT for dinner when there was a quick double knock on her door, and Dani burst in. She closed the door and leaned on it as though she expected the devil to burst in behind her. "Do I want to know?"

With a pitiful wail, she said, "Hide me."

Not what Sheridan was expecting. She opened her arms and Dani came in for a hug. Still holding her friend, she said, "I'm guessing this doesn't have to do with Nick."

"Nope," Dani said, letting go and walking to the living room. She sat down heavily on the couch, covered her face with a pillow, and screamed. Sheridan waited for her to finish and put the pillow down. "As Janelle likes to say, 'If it's not one thing, it's my mother.' If she tries to get me to drink one more glass of lemon water, I'm going to toss it in her face." Dani's mother had long been a source of aggravation, and the wedding was bringing out the worst in the other woman.

Sheridan reached into her refrigerator, pulled out a pitcher, and poured her friend a drink. She put two snickerdoodle cookies on a plate, split the BLT, then joined her in the living room. Handing Dani the glass and plate, she said, "The only way to drink lemon water is like this — iced with tea and sugar." Dani took the glass, and they both took long drinks. "And don't worry, it's decaf. Wouldn't want you to have any sleepless nights so close to your big day. Unless you'd rather I make you hot chocolate. The nights are getting cool."

"This is perfect, thank you." Dani took a bite of the sandwich and sighed happily. With her mouth still full, she said, "I am trying not to overdo the sugar and carbs. Janelle has done a perfect job tailoring my dress."

"You are going to look stunning." Sheridan and Laurel had been with Dani when she chose her wedding dress, and Sheridan had gone with her to Tailor Thrift during one of the fittings.

Dani closed her eyes and let her head drop back. "I know you're not planning to marry, but should you change your mind, my best advice is to not have your mother arrive until the day of the ceremony."

Sheridan had to laugh. "Sugar, my mother has more expertise planning weddings than Devon. If I ever get married, I'm turning the whole thing over to her, and I'm the one who won't show up until the last possible moment."

"I didn't think she'd be able to get to me anymore. Things between us have been better since her last visit. And she adores Nick." Cynthia had come after Dani had a car accident nearly two years before. Ostensibly it was to help, but it had been more of an aggravation. It had also been less than a year after she'd started working at the veterinary clinic and weeks after Nick had come back into her life. Dani had been in a challenging place, but before Cynthia left, she'd managed to convince her mother that she was happy where she was and with her choices. In the process of standing up for herself, she'd changed their relationship.

Or at least some of it.

"And thank goodness for him," Dani went on as she continued to eat the sandwich. "I'm working through tomorrow, so Nick's been taking her to lunch and having her over to the house. I'm not sure how he's getting anything done. Or why he hasn't started drinking heavily. Or called off the wedding."

"I can answer that last one for you easily. Because he loves you completely. You're his everything." Dani was still tense over the situation with her mother, so Sheridan scooted next to her friend and put an arm around her. "You've only got a few more days until the wedding. We've got our spa night bachelorette party tomorrow — your mother's got to approve of that — and the rehearsal dinner at the Kinsman on Friday. Is there anything any of us can do to keep you from strangling her or locking her in a closet somewhere? I don't think you want to recite your vows from prison."

"I really don't. And I look terrible in orange. I'm looking forward to this so much. Not the dress and the party, although you know how much I love the gown, but making it official. Standing up in front of the people I care about most in the world and telling the man I love that I want to be with him for the rest of our lives." She took a shuddering breath and put her head on Sheridan's shoulder. "Oh my god, I'm marrying Nick in three days."

"That you are, my dear."

"I know it doesn't change anything, but in some ways… it changes everything." Sheridan liked the awe in Dani's voice. It showed that her friend understood the commitment she was making and took it seriously. Unlike Sheridan's mom, whose vows should be 'to love and honor until I don't feel like it anymore.'

"Where is your brother in all of this?" Xander had arrived from Seattle two days earlier both to get on east coast time and, supposedly, to help Dani manage her mother. "Can't he help?"

Dani gave a sarcastic laugh. "The golden boy who can do no wrong? Please. All she does with me is sing his praises. All she does with him is, probably, complain about me."

Sheridan had a feeling that wasn't entirely true, but it was what Dani believed, and that mattered more. "Can't you call him? Ask him to keep her occupied?"

"I suppose I can ask him to help more, but I can't imagine what they would do. Mom is totally focused on me and this wedding. She doesn't want to be distracted." Dani let out a heartfelt sigh. "That's why I'm still working — which is one of the things she's complaining about. She won't set foot in the clinic, so I'm safe there. But the minute I'm done, she's calling or sending texts and when we talk, it's how I should be focused on the wedding. I mean, how much can one person discuss floral arrangements? She was appalled to learn I hadn't had a hair rehearsal or been regularly having facials for the last few months."

"Okay, I'm from the south and hair, as you know, is a big deal there, but even I don't know what a hair rehearsal is."

Dani fluttered a hand through her hair. "That's not what's she called it, but it's something about going to the hairdresser and having them do your hair well before the wedding so you and they both know what to do."

"Is that necessary?" It sounded like a waste of time to Sheridan, but what did she know?

"I have no idea," Dani said, not hiding her exasperation. "Bryn has been doing my hair since I moved back. I told her I want a partial up-do. I showed her a picture of my veil, she showed me pictures in a magazine. Who knew I was supposed to have a practice run?"

"I don't think you're supposed to do anything you don't want to do."

"I know that. I do. Except every time my mother starts talking and suggesting things, I find my stomach in knots. How is it she can do that to me? And why does part of me still care what she thinks?" The last question came out as a wail.

Sheridan took the remaining half of the cookie and handed it to Dani. "Mommas and daughters are a complicated thing. I think deep down, there's no one we want to please more, even once we become our own women," she said. She almost laughed at how wise she sounded. "And no matter if we don't agree with them and their choices, for some reason we want them to understand and approve of ours."

Dani looked at her friend and nodded as her eyes filled with tears. "I feel like I'm twelve all over again. And I can tell you the only time I was truly happy at that age was when I was here for the summers. Three weeks into the school year, I started counting the days until I could come back."

Sheridan thought about her conversation with Ryan back before Eden's wedding, how he and the Hanson brothers all wanted to get out of Fable Notch, yet here was Dani talking about how much this place meant to her. Maybe you couldn't understand the value of something unless you either lost it or had to work for it. Her café had certainly become more precious to her after going viral and having to make hard – although ultimately beneficial – decisions. "I'm glad you've made your home here," Sheridan said.

"Me too," Dani said with a happy sigh.

After Dani left — taking some cookies Sheridan packed for her — Sheridan considered mothers and marriage. She felt sorry that her mother's most recent one was ending. With her terrible track record and repeatedly broken heart, Sheridan had to wonder why Hazel kept getting married. Wouldn't she be better off with a dog and several close friends?

Unable to shake the questions running through her head, she called Hazel. "Sheri-blossom," her mother said, answering the phone in a bright voice, and Sheridan smiled. A nickname from her childhood her mother hadn't used in years. Guess that meant Mom wasn't sitting around pining for her most recent husband. "To what do I owe the pleasure of your call?"

Sheridan wasn't sure how to broach the subject, so she jumped in. "My good friend Dani is getting married."

"Well, if you're looking for advice, I know you think I'm the wrong one to ask." Sheridan had been quite vocal about her exasperation the last time Hazel had called to tell her she was getting married. "Although I do have plenty of experience making mistakes. Maybe I can tell you — or her — what not to do."

"I'm not looking for advice so much as feeling curious. Why do you keep getting married?"

Hazel answered immediately. "I don't want to be alone." Sheridan thought maybe it was that simple for Hazel, for a lot of people.

"But you don't stay married, and no, I'm not saying you should try to make it work with Gordon after what he did." Everyone had their limits.

"As if he'd want to," her mother said, annoyance clear. "Last I heard, he's planning to marry the pageant princess."

Ouch. That had to sting. But not wanting to be distracted, Sheridan continued. "And yet you stay open to finding love again, knowing you can get hurt."

"What's wrong with getting hurt?" Sheridan sat there in silence. That wasn't the response she was expecting, and she didn't have an answer. Her mother continued, "My sweet child, if your father's passing taught me anything, it's that loss can't be avoided, so why avoid the things that are good? And loving someone and being loved? That's heaven on Earth."

She'd seen that in her friends, even if it hadn't been true for her. Her only experience was loving someone then discovering it wasn't returned. Between that and her mother's marital failures, she'd convinced herself romantic love was a foolish choice she wasn't going to make again. Instead, she poured her love into her food and her friendships, and while it had brought her a life she adored, it had also kept her very safe.

And then Ryan had barged into her life with his playful energy and generous understanding, coupled with his passion for his work and his oh so amazing way with her body. Without intending to, he'd upended her heart. There was definitely going to be pain when he left after Dani's wedding, but after all they'd shared, she couldn't bring herself to be sorry.

Chapter Twenty-Six

When January called Ryan and told him she had another job for him connected to the Canillo's, he was thrilled. Until she told him he needed to fly immediately to the Bahamas to get shots on the site where the casino was being built. It was closer to the wedding than he'd like, but he agreed to make it work. He was determined to show them what he could do and land this job.

For the first few days, things went well. He reviewed and made recommendations to the shot list they gave him, got great images, and spent time off-site and explore the area. He discovered out of the way shops and restaurants recommended by locals, small gardens, and old buildings which he posted on social media.

Then on Tuesday, they lost most of the day to dark gray skies, wind, and thunderstorms, which was a problem because most of the work was being done outdoors. He tried to manage with the available lighting, but his options and equipment were limited. This was the downside of shoots in locations he couldn't drive to. No way to pack all of his gear. He'd come with the basics and not much more, so he wasn't as prepared as he liked to be.

"We could order whatever you need, Mr. Sinclair," said one of the assistants he'd been assigned, sounding optimistic as Ryan got annoyed when another shot didn't work. She scrolled through her tablet and smiled at him. "It can be here by Saturday."

He smiled back, and from the way she grimaced, he knew he looked menacing. "Terrific. Except *I'm* not going to be here Saturday, so it doesn't do me any good, does it?"

She swallowed visibly and said, "No, sir," before scampering off.

It was the first time someone called him sir. It wasn't a milestone to be proud of. He apologized to her as soon as he saw her again.

Back in his hotel room on Wednesday, he called Sheridan and poured out his frustration. "What the fuck am I supposed to do? An unexpected front moved in, and weather is supposed to be shitty most of tomorrow, too."

"Not to sound cliché, but do the best you can with what you have," she'd answered. "No one expects you to do more than that. Even you can't control the weather."

"When I have my usual gear, I can." But there'd been no way to bring all of it with him. He scrubbed his hand over his face. "This sucks. The most important client I've ever had, and I can't give them what they want. So much for making a good impression."

"This isn't the only work of yours they've seen, right?" He mumbled an agreement. "Then they'll understand. They're not judging you on this one trip. As someone who recently went through a situation out of my control, I recommend looking for help. Are there any other departments or businesses that might have something you can use? That's what we did."

It was a good question. Some of the area hotels held big events. They might have lighting that was transportable. If it was too stark, he could find something to put over it or have an assistant hold a cloth near it to soften the brightness. He and Sheridan brainstormed more ideas, and before long, he was feeling better. "Thank you. I needed this." *I needed you,* he thought, but didn't say. He wasn't sure what to do with the realization, although he knew it was true.

Finally feeling calmer, Ryan kept her on the phone, reluctant to say goodnight. As he listened to her talk about life back home and how Dani was stressing, he let her accent flow over and soothe him further. By the time they said goodnight, he was grateful he called her, and not only for her help.

The next day, he put his plan for extra lighting into place. The assistant was thrilled to help again as they got lights and portable rigging from two of the hotels. He remained upbeat with everyone he was working with, and it was, fortunately, a better day. But by the time they wrapped, it was plain there was no way he was getting off of the island before late on Thursday at best, not without leaving too much of the work undone, and that was unacceptable.

The staff in charge of changing flights said it wasn't a problem. They thought he was concerned about the cost, which was the furthest thing from his mind. If he wasn't on a plane by Friday afternoon, he'd be late for the wedding. He texted Nick to say he wasn't going to make the ceremony rehearsal or rehearsal dinner and sent messages to Devon, Sheridan, Cole, and Theo, asking them to take pictures of the events on their phones. Damn it, he hated letting them down. And while they assured him they understood and he shouldn't worry, he couldn't help it. It was bad enough he wasn't certain he was giving the client what they wanted — something he never allowed — but letting down the people he loved?

That, he believed, should never happen.

Friday morning, Sheridan woke feeling more relaxed than she had in ages. The spa day she'd enjoyed for Dani's bachelorette party had been glorious. They'd been pampered from top to bottom. Literally, she thought, looking at her red manicured fingers and toes.

And after spending several hours in the same room as Cynthia, she understood why Dani came running over to avoid her mother. The woman definitely had specific ideas about what was right for Dani and the wedding. For all the choices Hazel made, Sheridan didn't agree with, at least her mother never tried to interfere with her life. Maybe being hands off wasn't so bad.

At work on Friday, Sheridan couldn't stop checking her phone. Ryan had been leaving text after text, stressing about getting to Fable Notch in time. The weather forecast was so good, he'd chosen to stay in the Bahamas until Friday morning. He was due to fly out at three thirty, and after a stop in New York, he was landing in

Boston around ten. Once he had his car, he'd have a two-hour drive, so he wouldn't be arriving before one in the morning. As much as they wanted to see each other, they agreed he'd go directly to Dani's, get some sleep, and see her tomorrow.

She was leaving the café to get changed for the ceremony rehearsal at the church when her phone rang. It was Ryan. She understood his concern, so she answered with, "Don't worry, we'll take plenty of pictures at the rehearsal and at the diner later. They may not be as good as you would take — okay, they definitely won't be — but it will be fine."

"No, it won't. My flight is delayed. At least two hours, possibly more. I have no fucking idea why, and they won't give us any information. I'm going to miss my connection at this rate. I'm standing around this airport, and I am seconds away from becoming apoplectic."

Shit, shit, shit. She tried to do the math in her head to figure out when he'd be arriving, but couldn't do it. "I'm so sorry, and I know there's nothing I can say or do to help." She hated how upset he sounded and how helpless they both were to fix it. Neither of them were good at not having options.

"I can't bring myself to call anyone else and hear the disappointment in their voices." From his tone, he was equally disappointed. And from the way the background noise kept changing, she had the feeling he was pacing. "Will you tell everyone I'll be there as soon as I possibly can? Hell, I'd start driving if there was a fucking bridge."

"I will. And try not to worry." He started to interrupt her, but she went on. "I know it's ridiculous to say, but I'm required by friendship law to say it. The wedding isn't until five thirty tomorrow. If you're here by then, that's all that matters."

There was silence. She braced for his outburst. Years of dealing with the public helped her know if he yelled, it was at the situation, not her. "Being there is all that matters," he repeated. "I've got twenty-seven hours. I'll be there."

"Yes, you will," she said and added a silent prayer that it was the truth. He'd hate himself if he didn't make it.

He let out a sigh. "Thank God I put my suit in my carry-on this time. Didn't want to take a chance."

Ah, he found a bright side. "I'll tell Janelle to have her steamer at the ready, so you'll be freshly pressed." She heard him chuckle. Another good sign.

"Thank you," he said softly. "For being there. For being positive. For... I don't know. Just being you."

Thickening her accent, she said, "It's what I'm best at, Darlin'." It earned her another laugh.

"You're good at quite a bit," he said with a suggestive hint in his voice.

Now it was her turn to laugh. "Look at that. Another reason to get your cute ass home."

"You think my ass is cute?"

What do you know — she could distract a man with sexual banter. That was a first. "I think a lot of you is cute, and the sooner you get here, the sooner I can show you."

"Okay, I'm off to steal a plane. Wish me luck."

"Good luck. Don't get caught."

When they hung up, she stared at the phone as if she could pull him through it. *Get here soon*, she thought.

The rehearsal went smoothly, although everyone was concerned when she explained Ryan's delay. She reassured them the same way she had him, but when there still wasn't a text at the end of the rehearsal telling her he'd boarded, she couldn't help worrying. Putting on her public smile so no one could tell she was nervous, they headed to the diner.

Sheridan had been looking forward to Friday's dinner all week. She didn't go to the Kinsman Diner often since they were open almost the same hours as the café. Sadly, Rosie wasn't serving breakfast, which was any diner's best meal as far as Sheridan was concerned, but the options were still amazing. Like Sheridan had done for Eden, Dani and Nick had chosen their comfort food favorites. There was meatloaf and mashed potatoes, sliced turkey with stuffing and gravy, and a mac and cheese so creamy it made any hardening of the arteries worth it.

Sheridan stood at the buffet and decided it was impossible to choose one entrée and put a serving of everything on her plate.

"The salad is for my mother," Dani said quietly, coming up behind her.

"And for you, too." Sheridan nodded at Dani's plate, which was more than half filled with greens. "You have almost no room for the good stuff on there."

"I'd rather have the salad and silence than Aunt Rosie's food tonight. Trust me, after the honeymoon, I am coming here every day for a week to make up for what I missed."

"Good," Sheridan said, putting her arm around Dani's waist and giving her a squeeze. Since their talk, Dani had been calmer, and Sheridan heard Xander had, indeed, kept their mother occupied. At the spa the night before, however, lemon juice had been pushed on all of them except Eden, who Cynthia considered slender enough. They all ignored her and drank champagne instead.

At seven, she got a text from Ryan. *Got a flight to Philly. Layover in Atlanta. Arriving at one. Rented a car. Will drive from there. Hopefully, I'll be there by ten tomorrow morning.*

Driving? He was going to drive from Philadelphia to Fable Notch? Sheridan did a quick map search. After a six-hour flight, he was going to have a seven-hour drive. Crap on a cupcake. But he didn't need her to fret, so she responded with, *That will give you time to nap. Keep me posted.*

She watched the three dots until he responded with, *Will do.*

She let everyone know he was on his way and what his plan was to get there. Millie was immediately frantic. "But that's such a long drive," she said, rubbing the knuckles of her hand. "He shouldn't have been working so close to the wedding. He should have known better."

Millie's frustration was a mixture of concern and love, but Sheridan felt the need to defend Ryan. "He does, but this is potentially a huge job opportunity for him, and there was no way he was going to turn down the assignment. He's doing everything he can to be here."

Millie looked confused. "What job?"

Damn it, Ryan, didn't you tell her? No way out of this. "He's being considered for a big international job. I don't know all the details, but I know it's important."

"So is family," Millie muttered.

Before Sheridan could say anything else, all of the Hansons chimed in with support for their brother until Martin said, "Ryan knows that. It's why he's driving seven hours after flying all day. And when he gets here, you will be happy to see him and not say a word about his being late." Millie opened her mouth to protest, but Martin put a finger to her lips. "Not a word."

The dinner finished an hour later, and Sheridan headed home, still full. Rosie had put out as many desserts as Sheridan had for Eden, and Sheridan wondered if the lemon meringue pie was a snide comment on all the lemon water Rosie's sister insisted on.

As she got into bed, she sent Ryan a text, which he'd get when he got off the plane, telling him to drive safely. Then she made plans for how to manage her time the next day.

She slept until seven since she was off for the weekend and woke to a text from Ryan. At three a.m. he'd sent: *In the car. ETA 10:30.*

That gave her plenty of time. She took a long, hot shower, got dressed, and let her hair air dry. There was going to be enough styling product and heat on it later. She got everything together she needed for when she headed to the hotel at noon.

The elegant gown she was wearing was the nicest dress she'd ever owned. More lovely than the wedding dress. They'd had a lot of fun when they looked for the gowns. They'd found a store which was more than happy to have them try on everything from short cocktail dresses that were not appropriate for a wedding to ones that would have been perfect if Dani chose a Bridgerton theme. The piles of dresses reminded Sheridan of the scene in the movie *27 Dresses* when the lead character shows the reporter all the bridesmaid outfits she'd been forced to wear. There had been a lot of laughter and groans, but they eventually found what they were looking for.

Dani, fortunately, was a kind bride, and while she didn't suggest anyone was going to want to wear the gowns again, she had wanted the four of them to wear styles they felt were flattering. So, while she wanted them to all wear the same color and length — black and to the floor — the cuts were different to suit each woman's figure. Sheridan thought they were going to look lovely, but not as stunning as Dani.

At nine thirty, she received another text. *An hour to go.* She sent back a smiley face so he wouldn't have to read anything. Then at ten, not wanting to be late, she put everything she'd been told to bring into her car and headed out.

To Dani's old house.

Chapter Twenty-Seven

The drive had been long but, other than morning rush hour traffic outside of Albany, uneventful. Ryan fantasized about Sheridan on and off the entire trip, hoping no one on the plane noticed his erection and finding it hard to drive occasionally. And he assumed he'd have to wait until after the wedding to see her. Instead, she was waiting for him.

When he saw her light blue car parked in front of Dani's, his heart gave a leap, and suddenly he wasn't as exhausted as he'd been moments ago. He still planned to go directly to bed, but sleep could wait. She was at the car door by the time he got out. He left everything in the back, picked her up, and kissed her. He didn't even manage a 'hello' before she wrapped her legs around him, and he carried her into the house.

Within seconds, they were naked. He couldn't get enough of her. Her mouth, her breasts, her hands all over him. He was hard, and when he slid a finger between her legs, he found her just as ready. "Shit," he said with a moment of clarity. "Condoms in the car."

"Condoms by the bed." He looked at the nightstand where a strip waited. "Remember, right ingredients, right results," she said with a smile.

"Damn, I like a woman who knows what she wants."

"I do. You." She grabbed one of the condoms, opened it and sheathed him, stroking his balls as she did. "I think we've waited long enough."

"Agreed," he said and sank into her body. She gasped and arched her back, taking him fully. A few hours ago, he would have told anyone who asked he was too tired for this. He'd been wrong. "You feel perfect."

Instead of answering, she tightened her pussy around him, making him moan. He crushed his lips to hers, kissing her with a need that had been building since he'd left her in August. He pulled her tongue into his mouth, tasting her, taking her. Wanting her. God, how he wanted her.

And now she was here, beneath him, calling his name, raking his back with her nails, driving him wild, and as needy for him as he was for her. As his climax neared, he reached between them to tease her clit, wanting her to come with him. It wasn't long before her orgasm hit, and he followed moments after.

He might have fallen asleep that way, but she gently rolled him onto his back, took the condom off, and covered them both. He wanted to say something. Tell her how incredible she was, how glad he was that she was here, but between one breath and the next he was asleep.

He woke hours later, alone, and checked his phone for the time. Two thirty. He was due at the hotel to take pictures of Dani and her wedding party in an hour.

No problem. He'd managed with less sleep. He went to the kitchen, made coffee, then found his luggage and cameras waiting on the living room coffee table with a note: *Good morning again. Lunch in the fridge. Brought your suit to Janelle's. She'll have it at the church by four. Welcome home. S*

Welcome home indeed.

Sheridan could have pounded dough in the kitchen and Ryan wouldn't have heard her when she left. She didn't think she'd ever seen someone fall asleep so fast. For a second while she waited for him to arrive, she wondered if she'd made a mistake. Maybe she should have let him get right to bed. But as soon as he smiled at her, she was glad she came.

And then I came again, she thought with a pleased smile.

Yup, it had been the right choice.

She had brought what she needed and went straight to the hotel after leaving Ryan. Dani had stayed in the bridal suite overnight and the wedding party was having lunch together before getting ready.

Sheridan had never been part of a wedding that required so much time together before the ceremony. First, there was a luncheon hosted by Dani's mother. Today's food was nothing like the night before. Broiled salmon, asparagus, and, of course, salad, everything served on plates as small as what Sheridan used for a single cookie. She wished she'd smuggled food in with her.

After the meal, Millie left to get ready while Sheridan, Laurel, Eden and Mia — and Cynthia — were descended on by a team of makeup and hair professionals. Brynn insisted on doing Sheridan's hair in addition to Dani's because she knew how to manage curls. It took a while, but eventually, with enough product and pins, she tamed Sheridan's mane into a gorgeous upsweep. Everyone was impressed. After, Sheridan had her first professional makeup session and when the woman was done, she almost didn't recognize herself.

She was still staring in the mirror when a familiar voice said, "Wow."

Turning, she saw Ryan, camera in hand, and as she smiled, he snapped a picture. "Why thank you, kind sir. Is it three thirty already?"

"Almost." He'd told her he was coming by to take candids of Dani and everyone getting ready. Over the next half hour, Sheridan had a feeling these photos were the ones she was going to like the best. While the formal ones would be lovely, these would capture the laughter and silliness they shared.

And although Ryan was as unobtrusive as possible, Sheridan found herself very aware of him. His hair was still damp, and she could smell soap and shampoo whenever he was near. She couldn't stop thinking of the warmth of his skin; the way he seemed to know how to touch her clit to bring her to climax; how he called out her name when he....

No. That was for later.

When it was time for her and Laurel to help Dani into her gown, Sheridan forgot everything else. The white ball gown was covered in lace, sparkling beads, and pearls. With its sweetheart neckline, cap sleeves, and aisle-worthy train, Dani was transformed into a princess. And happier than Sheridan had ever seen, which was saying something considering how joyous Dani had been since falling back in love with Nick.

As they added the comb veil to the back of her hair, the three of them looked in the mirror together, unable to stop smiling. They turned when they heard a sniffle, and Dani went to hug her mother. Sheridan couldn't stop tearing at the special moment.

After everyone was dressed, Devon ushered them to a location outside the hotel so Ryan could get formal shots with Dani's side of the wedding party, as well as ones with her and Cynthia. When they finished with the pictures, Dani's mother and stepfather headed to the church, while Dani and her friends waited for the limousine, which would take them together.

The ceremony was scheduled for five thirty, and they arrived an hour before. Ryan took more pictures in the waiting room before leaving to get dressed and join the groomsmen.

"It's so unfair that he can look dashing in fifteen minutes, and it took us hours," Mia said. There was agreement all around.

Ten minutes before the ceremony, there was a knock at the door, and Devon came in. "It's time," she said and escorted them to the back of the church where the doors had been closed. Sheridan could hear soft music playing on the other side. Devon handed bouquets to Mia and Eden and a basket of petals to Samantha Ahern, who was the flower girl, while Laurel helped Dani arrange her train, and Sheridan tended to the curls around her face.

"You look perfect," she said to her friend. She did. And it wasn't all the spa treatments and makeup that were making Dani glow. It was love.

"I am so ready for this."

"I know you are, Sugar." Devon stepped up and gave them their bouquets. As Sheridan took hers, she felt something on the underside. Turning the flowers over, she saw a piece of material tucked into the stems. "What's this?"

"Handkerchief. Just in case," Devon said with a wink, and lined everyone up.

Moments later, the doors opened, and Samantha stepped through. Sheridan could hear the murmured "aw's". Next were Mia and Eden, side by side. Dani had trouble deciding who should go first, Laurel or Sheridan — even though Sheridan had said it should be Laurel who walked in front of Dani because they'd known each other for so long. Devon suggested the women come out in pairs. Problem solved.

As they entered the sanctuary, Sheridan kept her eyes forward, smiling occasionally at all the familiar faces. When they got to the front, she saw Ryan taking pictures of their arrival. He put the camera down for a second to look at her directly and wink. She smiled at him, and her heart skipped a beat.

I'm in love with him.

She didn't know where the thought came from, but as soon as it occurred to her, she knew it was true. Amid all this wedding hoopla, she'd opened her heart to this special, considerate, funny man and fallen in love.

Whoops.

Oh, her friends were going to laugh when she told them she'd gone and done what they did — fall for a man who wasn't staying.

But this wasn't the time or place to think about it. For now, she would focus on Dani and Nick and enjoy whatever time she had with Ryan.

As Nick came forward to take Dani's hand, Ryan handed his camera to Devon and joined his brothers and Xander to stand by the groom.

The minister welcomed them and said some opening prayers. Millie and Cynthia each did a reading, and Sheridan was blinking back tears in no time.

When the minister spoke again, he said, "Nick and Dani have written vows to share with each other. Nick, will you begin?"

Dani handed her bouquet to Laurel, then Nick took her hands in his and said, "It's been almost two years since you agreed to marry me, and I can hardly believe we're here. There was a time when I couldn't imagine living in this town and now... I can't imagine what I was thinking." As the guests chuckled, Nick paused to kiss Dani's fingers. "Your strength and love carried me through some of the worst times in my life. It made me a better, stronger man. I promise to love you, support you, listen to you, and comfort you. I will be here for you and our family — furry members and future human ones — in every way you need me. You are my heart's home, and I couldn't be happier or more grateful to be your husband."

Blinking wasn't enough. Sheridan was glad to have the handkerchief.

Dani took a deep breath. "No one meets their soul mate at fifteen, but that's how old I was when I first knew I loved you. Of course, it was after years of friendship which made it better." Friendship before love. Sheridan understood that. "There's no one here who doesn't know our story — how we lost each other and found one another again — and as difficult as some chapters were, they were worth it to be here with you today. There was so much we both needed to learn, and I don't know if that would have happened if we'd stayed together. And because of what I've learned — about myself, about you, and about love — I know our lives are going to be amazing. I loved you then. I love you now. I love you always."

Nick let go of Dani's hand to wipe his tears away. Cole handed him a handkerchief, and Sheridan wondered if Devon had given them to the men, too.

"Do you, Danielle Amelia Vaughn, take Nicholas James Hanson as your husband?"

"I do."

"And do you, Nicholas James Hanson, take Danielle Amelia Vaughn as your wife?"

"I do."

Rings were exchanged, followed by a kiss that had Sheridan tearing up again, then they followed Dani and Nick out of the church. Ryan hooked his arm through hers as they made their way out. When they got to the door, he gave her a quick kiss and said, "I need to grab my camera and get back to work. See you at the reception?"

“See you there.”

Seeing him go, she was reminded this was how Ryan loved living his life. Running off to what he needed to do next. Excited about what he’d discover. Not wanting anyone to get in his way. It actually made him more interesting to her, and possibly what made her zing in the first place. Part of what she loved about him was his passion and drive. She was the same. Too bad the lives they’d chosen didn’t match.

Chapter Twenty-Eight

After Ryan got shots of Nick and Dani leaving the church and everyone cheering for them as they left, he jumped into his car and drove to the hotel. When he got there, he went into the reception hall to take pictures of the room with no one in it. Artsy images of the centerpieces and the bride and groom's table with crystal champagne glasses. By the time he stepped into the reception area, people had arrived, and he took candids of groups before looking for the woman he wanted to be with.

It didn't take long to spot her, even with her curls pulled into an unfamiliar, formal twist. Unfortunately, she was standing with Xander, Laurel, and Hunter, and he was aching to get her alone. He joined the group and put an arm around Sheridan's waist. She turned and gave him a smile that made him want to kiss her, but he held off. But he couldn't stop the grateful sigh when she reached for his neck and took off the tie. "I'm on a break until the bride and groom arrive for the reception," he told the group, then to Sheridan said, "Can I get you anything?"

"Food," she said, putting a hand on her stomach, and he gave her a strange look. Sheridan explained the tiny luncheon they were served and laughed at the horrified expression on his face.

"I'm on it. Be right back." He kissed her forehead and dashed back to where dinner would be served and grabbed the breadbasket from the first table he came to. Some wait staff member was going to get a surprise when the guests sat down, but his lady was hungry, and he was on a mission. When he returned, he held out the basket like a prize. With a flourish and a bow, he said, "Behold, I bring you bread."

Sheridan and Laurel both grabbed for it and took rolls. The men stepped back as if to create a safe distance. Ryan laughed, and Hunter looked over Laurel's head and said, "Never get between a woman and her carbs."

With her mouth full and a roll in each hand, Laurel said, "Wise man."

For the next few minutes, Ryan and Hunter made sure every passing server stopped so the women could eat. When an announcement came for people to come in for dinner, Ryan said, "That's my cue. I assume we're at the same table?"

Sheridan held up two place cards. "Table four. See you there."

"As soon as I can." And this time he didn't care. He kissed her.

He was ready when Dani and Nick took the floor and took pictures throughout their first dance to "Endless

Love," not only of them, but the happy faces of their parents and friends as two people deeply in love started the next part of their lives together.

Once again, Ryan felt what was becoming a familiar twinge as he thought about love and relationships. And Sheridan. What they'd shared had been unexpectedly wonderful, and he felt closer to her than he'd ever expected. And although Ryan didn't think that after a few days together he'd found his soul mate, he couldn't stop himself from wondering what it might be like to have someone in his life the way his brothers did.

No, he thought, shaking his head as if to loosen the idea. That was for the future. There would be time for settling down later. He still had too much to do.

Bringing his attention back to the event, he watched as Dani and Nick finished their dance wrapped in each other's arms, seeing only one another. It was beautiful.

When the music changed, Dani went to get her father, and Nick brought Millie to the dance floor. Ryan took more pictures as they danced with their parents to "My Wish" by Rascal Flatts. The lyrics were perfect, about wanting your dreams to stay big and worries to stay small. Yes, that was definitely what Millie wanted for her sons. All of them. Even him, the one who wasn't ready to settle down.

With the next song, everyone joined in the dancing. Ryan put his camera down and led Sheridan onto the dance floor. As he pulled her into his arms, he said, "You look lovely, but I cannot wait to take your hair out of that tight bun."

She laughed, "It's called a chignon and after you get the pins out, it still might not move. I think an entire can of hairspray was used to keep it in place."

He leaned in and said, "In that case, I'll drag you into the shower first." When she shivered, he said, "I like that reaction. Now I'm definitely going to do that."

The night was more hectic for him than the last two weddings since there were more guests. Getting pictures at the tables took longer, but he managed to get them done, and eat dinner, before Nick and Dani cut the cake. After, he was free to spend time with his friends and brothers.

While they waited for dessert to be served, Ryan stood talking with Cole and Theo. Cole said, "It's been great to have you around so much. I can't believe we're not going to see you again for... wait, when will we see you again?".

"Thanksgiving," Theo suggested. "Or you'll come at the end of the year for the holidays, right?"

"You two sound like Mom." And for the first time, he didn't hate that. "I will if I can, but it depends on this job. If I get it, it changes everything." And it would. He'd be traveling for years. Who knew when he'd be able to visit?

There was silence.

Ryan understood. He was feeling it, too. "Yeah, I know. It means a lot of time and being on someone else's schedule. I haven't had an employer situation like that in years. But it's going to get my work in front of a lot of important people and open doors for me."

"As long as they're doors you want opened," Cole said.

Before they could discuss it more, Nick came over and hugged them. Looking at Theo and Cole, he said, "Why didn't you two tell me I could be happier?"

Theo laughed, "Because you wouldn't have believed us."

"Thanks, Glinda," Nick said with a roll of his eyes. "But I suppose you're right. I would definitely not have thought it possible." He saluted them with the glass he was holding. "To us. Brothers forever."

Glasses clicked, and Ryan swallowed over the lump in his throat.

"Oh, I have to get a picture of the four of you." Ryan looked from their group to see Sheridan standing in front of them, Dani next to her. "Gimme the camera and show me how to use it."

He did, and she took several shots of them. Then everyone handed her their phones so she could take more. Nick had Dani join them, and they lifted her so they were each carrying her length-wise, as Sheridan snapped away. He had a feeling these pictures were going to be his favorites.

After they put her down, Dani held out her hand for Sheridan's phone and said, "Let me get a picture of the two of you." He and Sheridan gave Dani their phones. As Dani lined up the shot, she said, "Ryan, you're too stiff. Lighten up."

Sheridan leaned in and whispered, "There's a time and place for stiff, Sugar."

He looked at her and smiled at the twinkle in her eye. "I know what you're thinking."

"Yes, you do," she said. "What I'm thinking. What I'm picturing."

Oh hell, he was going to have an erection in these pictures if he wasn't careful.

"I'm still here, you know," Dani said, and they turned to look at her. She held up the phones, and the flash went off. "Perfect."

At ten, Nick and Dani had their last dance to Mary Chapin Carpenter's "Grow Old Along With Me" and everyone cheered as the couple departed for the night. No limo was necessary since they were staying in the bridal suite.

Shortly after, his parents came over to him and Sheridan before they headed home. After hugging them both, Millie said, "I'm so glad you made it. You gave us a scare."

"I know, Ma. I'm sorry." He'd been pretty worried himself. "But it all worked out. We'll see you tomorrow at brunch."

Like they'd done for Theo and Eden, his folks were having close friends and family over to the house the next day. "Get some sleep," she said, putting a hand on his cheek.

As they watched his parents leave, Sheridan said, "But not too much sleep."

When he looked at her, he wondered if the hunger in her eyes matched his. "Time to go."

Chapter Twenty-Nine

As they had after the first wedding, Ryan suggested they spend the night at his place. She told him she'd meet him at Dani's, but as soon as he was in his car, he changed his mind. He followed her to her house, went in with her as she changed — and ravaged her.

He undid her bra, and she playfully swatted him away. "Can't you wait until—"

"No," he said honestly, and he kissed her to silence any more protests. He'd wanted to be with her since waking alone that afternoon. He wasn't wasting any more time. When he tried running his hands through her hair, he discovered too many hairpins and too much hairspray. They took it down, but it was oddly stiff, so different from what he was used to. In short order, they were both naked, and he was pulling her on top of him. God, they fit so well together.

It was another hour before they got to his house. By that point, as much as he wanted to please her again, they were both exhausted, so they got into bed and fell asleep in each other's arms. He'd hoped to wake up in the middle of the night to enjoy her again and make the most of every minute they had together, but the travel and activity of the last few days caught up to him and the sun was shining into the room when he woke.

Alone.

Sitting up quickly, he listened for her and heard the shower. Deciding that was a perfect idea, he joined her.

"Knock, knock," he said as he opened the door and was hit in the face by a room of steam. "Are you in there? I can't see a thing."

He could, however, hear her laugh. "I am. I like my showers hot."

"So I'm noticing. Give me a second and I'll join you." He quickly used the toilet, hoped the flush wouldn't make the water scalding, then pulled back the curtain to find a wet and soapy Sheridan. "Come here, you slippery minx."

She wrapped herself around him and kissed him. "Sorry, I'm not good at sleeping in. And I had to get that stuff out of my hair," she said.

"Much better this way," he said, pulling on a curl. "Do we have time to..."

"Not really," she said with a wince. "We need to be at your—"

"Don't mention them while we're naked, please." He put a hand to her mouth, and she kissed his fingers. "I suppose it's just as well. I don't know if you've ever tried shower sex, but don't let the books and movies fool you. There's rarely enough room and most people don't, well, line up. It's usually a lot more work for a lot less pleasure."

"Another fantasy ruined," she said with a dramatic sigh. "I guess we'll have to wait."

She grabbed the soap and started lathering him, which made the idea of waiting less than appealing. But if they were late, there would be more questions and comments, and he'd rather not answer them, though the idea of getting on his knees and licking her to orgasm was tempting.

They got out, dried each other off, and got dressed. While Sheridan towel-dried her hair, Ryan made coffee for them. It was homey and comfortable, a perfect way to start the day.

As soon as they were ready, they stopped at the café to grab the muffins Sheridan promised she'd bring, then drove to his parents' place, arriving at the same time as Theo, Eden, and Harlow, Theo's dog and arson investigation partner. "Good morning," Eden said as a yawn overtook her. Ryan wondered if she and Theo had started the day similarly to the way he and Sheridan had.

Yeah, he was not going to think about his brother's sex life.

When they went inside, they were greeted first by Bowie, Mia's St. Berhusky, who ran to Harlow like they were old friends, which Ryan supposed they were. Guess that meant Cole and company had already arrived. If Nick and Dani brought their dogs, Ryan wondered if there would be enough room for the people.

Sheridan, holding the baked goods over her head so the dogs wouldn't go for them, went to the kitchen. He watched her adorable ass as she left the room.

"Dude, the way you look at her," Theo said under his breath. "What's going on?"

Shit. Why couldn't he hide things from his family? "Noth—" He stopped. He didn't want to lie, but he wasn't sure how much of the truth he wanted to share. "She's terrific. You know that."

"I do, but you two were supposed to have a *fake* relationship."

"We are. It is." Theo's brow went up. Ryan had always hated he couldn't do that little trick. Pulling Theo to the side, he said, "Fine, it's become a little more complicated than I planned, but it's still temporary. When I leave later this week, it's over."

Theo said nothing and didn't look convinced. Before Ryan could explain more, Nick and Dani's arrival was heralded with a cacophony of barking. Yup, they'd brought Otis and Lola. When he commented, Dani said, "Of course we did. We're going to be away for two weeks. I've never been apart from either of them that long." She bent down and gave them both hugs, her eyes bright with unshed tears.

When she stood, Nick kissed the side of her forehead and gave her a squeeze. "Try not to worry. They will be fine with Mom and Dad. And their uncles will come and take them out." Theo, Cole, and Dean had stepped up to walk the dogs at different times of the day. Otis had a great temperament, but everyone agreed he was too big for his parents to manage safely. It must be nice knowing everyone was around to help.

Shortly after Laurel and Hunter arrived, and his mother announced brunch was ready. People helped themselves from a buffet set up in the kitchen, then sat around the dining room table. Dani and Nick were toasted, and everyone discussed how wonderful the wedding was and asked about the European cruise they newlyweds were taking.

Throughout the meal, Ryan's thoughts kept bouncing between how Sheridan fit with his family as easily as Eden, Dani and Mia did, to how much he wanted to be alone with her again. In bed or out, he enjoyed his time with her. It was getting harder to accept that what had happened between them didn't mean anything. He reminded himself that their lives were in different places, on different tracks. That had been the case from the beginning and nothing had changed.

After waving Dani and Nick off a few hours later, he and Sheridan, along with Cole, Mia, and Dean, stayed to clean up and watch the Red Sox, who were flirting with a playoff spot that year. It was relaxed and easy, which would have made Ryan uncomfortable not long ago, but after the time he had getting here, and continually seeing the joy of the people he cared for the most, he could appreciate where calm and predictability had its place.

Of course, when they got back to Sheridan's place, calm went out the window and passion ruled, which was the perfect way to end the day.

On Monday, Sheridan had the day mostly off. She needed to go in and get food prepped for the week, so while she did that, he walked around town, taking pictures of the businesses. He stopped in to see Adam at The Bright Spot and heard about his new Sundae School program for teaching kids about ice cream making. Then he chatted for a while with Janelle at Tailor Thrift — and ended up getting a sweater he liked and picking up a band-T that went with one of Sheridan's father's records. He couldn't wait to see her face when he gave it to her.

After, he got lost for almost an hour in the Thousand Lives Bookstore and left with a heavier bag than he expected. By the time he was back to the Just Right, he was laden with purchases and starving.

Sheridan squealed and hugged him when she saw the shirt. "It's perfect! Thank you." She put it on over what she was wearing, and it went almost to her knees.

"Oops. Maybe not perfect," he said.

"Perfect for sleeping in," she said, and now all he could think of was her wearing it in bed. He was not going to get that image out of his head anytime soon. "So, what do you want to eat?"

You, he thought. "I know there are a lot of places here, but anywhere we go, we'll have to talk to other people, and I've hit my limit on socializing for the day. Any ideas?"

She went into the refrigerator and grabbed what she had. "How do you feel about grilled cheese and tomato soup?"

"Sounds perfect."

Tuesday morning, he woke long enough to give Sheridan a kiss before she went to the café, then fall back to sleep. When he got up, he checked his emails from the last several days. He'd almost completely forgotten about work and the real world. There was nothing needing his immediate attention in his inbox, so at nine he texted Theo and Cole, *Diner?*

They both sent thumbs up and thirty minutes later they were sitting at a table drinking coffee and talking about nothing more important than the fact that Rosie offered Cole a Moxie, making him and Theo gag. "More for me," Cole said.

Theo shuddered. "You can have it."

As Rosie headed to the kitchen with their orders, Millie came in. "Hello, boys. What a lovely surprise." She got hugs from them all, then made her way back to Rosie's table where Valerie Stewart was waiting.

"Tuesday breakfast club," Ryan said. "Almost forgot. I kinda love that she still does that." Millie had been getting together with her friends on Tuesday mornings for decades. Ryan assumed Leslie Franks would arrive shortly.

"If she ever stops, we'll know the world is about to end," Cole said.

"And now the next generation is doing it, too," Theo said. At Ryan's confused expression, he explained, "Eden, Janelle, Sheridan, Dani...anyone who's available meets at the Seven Brothers on Friday nights."

Interesting, Ryan thought. "Do you two have anything like that with Nick and the other guys?"

"Not yet," Cole said, "but it could be fun. I don't know if I'd want to be a regular at the Varnum, but we could probably find a place."

Theo nodded. "It's worth considering."

When Rosie served their meal, their focus changed. Ryan was glad he called them. He'd miss this place — and being able to get together with his brothers whenever he wanted— after he left. He was halfway through his pancakes when a phone ringing had all three of them looking at their devices. "It's mine," he said with concern when he saw the caller ID: *January.* She knew — or at least he thought she did — that he was with his family for the wedding, so this must be important.

Wondering if it was news about the Canillo job or a new gig, he stepped outside for privacy. "What's up?" he said.

"You did it," she said. "You fucking did it."

She didn't sound upset, but he couldn't tell what she was getting at. "That's great. What did I do?"

"You are one of the two finalists for the Canillo Group job. They are flying you and the other candidate to Malta on Thursday for interviews and more test shots. Looks like you'll be there for at least three days." His head was spinning.

"I was sure that after the problems we had with lighting in the Bahamas, I was out of the running."

"Quite the opposite. They were thrilled with your ability to think on your feet and come up with solutions." He'd have to thank Sheridan for her help with that. "And they were also impressed by the photos on your social media feed. I didn't know they'd check that, but they made a point of telling me they love the way you make things seem welcoming, inviting and...." She stopped, and he heard her shuffling pages. "Homey. That was the word they used. Seems odd to me, since these hotels are going to be a place for the ultra-rich, but I guess they think if the guests feel at home, they'll stay longer and come back sooner. Anyway, who cares about the why? You did it!"

Something she said hit him. "Did you say they're flying me to Malta on Thursday?"

"Yes, I already have your ticket from their people. First class out of LAX. And good thing because it's like a fifteen-hour flight."

He dropped his head into his hands. "I'm in New Hampshire, January. I wasn't supposed to fly back west until Thursday."

"Then change your plans. This is the job of a lifetime."

Yes, it was. This was the reason he kept his life flexible and open. Nothing to stop him, nothing to hold him back. They got off the phone, and he walked back into the diner in a daze. He stood by the end of the table and said nothing.

Cole finally asked, "Everything okay?"

That was the question, wasn't it? But he didn't have time to answer it. There were things to do. "I need to leave."

"What do you mean, leave? You just got here."

Wrong voice. He looked to where he'd been sitting and saw his mother in his spot. Shit. So much for having time to get his thoughts in order before springing this on her and his dad. He explained the job in brief detail and how he needed to get back to California immediately. "I'm sorry to take off so abruptly, but it can't be helped."

"It can if you tell them no," Millie said, crossing her arms over her chest. Oh, that was never a good sign.

In a voice as firm as his mother's, he said, "I can't, and I don't want to. This is the most incredible opportunity I've ever been offered, and I'm going for it."

"What about Sheridan?" He expected the question and expected his mother was not going to like the answer.

"She knew about this job. I don't think she'll be too surprised." Would she be as disappointed as he was that they had to cut things short? He'd been planning to take her to Cobblestones for a fancy dinner the night before he left to say thank you and give her a proper goodbye. And an improper one.

"But you two are dating."

His brothers suddenly got very interested in their food. Cole warned him that this would be his problem when the time came. "I know, Ma, but neither of us expected it to go beyond the weddings. It was meant to be fun while it lasted." Why did he feel a tightening in his heart when he said that? "I'm sure she'll be okay that I have to leave. I'm not that great a catch." That earned him a snort from Theo.

"But you can't... I mean, I thought that...." She blinked back tears and Ryan's heart broke. He knew what she wanted, but he couldn't give it to her. This wouldn't be easy, but it had to be done.

Pulling a chair from a nearby table, he sat in front of her and took one of her hands in his. "Mom, please. I need you to understand how important this is to me. You and Dad encouraged my love of photography, and now I get to do work I adore. I want to be as successful at it as I can. This job is a major step toward that. You always say that what you want most for us is to be happy."

"Of course it is, but—"

"Then that has to be our definition, not yours. You wouldn't have wanted Theo to stay if you didn't think he'd be happy here. You wouldn't have told Nick to leave New York or Cole to leave Emporium. It was something they chose when the time was right. *Because* the time was right. Please, be proud of me for getting this far, because I'm sure the competition is fierce, and know that someday I'll be ready to stop traveling and make different decisions."

Millie stared at him, took a deep breath, and gave his hand a squeeze. "But it's not the right time for you. Is that what you're telling me?" He nodded. "Then I don't have to love your decision to give you my support. I can be happy for you while being sad for me."

"Thank you, Mom." He stood and pulled her into a hug. As he held her close, he looked over her head to his brothers and took in the love and acceptance on their faces. And discovered he was also sad.

Chapter Thirty

Shortly after the lunch rush finished, Ryan came into the café, and, from the expression on his face, something was definitely wrong. "What happened? Is it Martin? Millie? Did something happen to Nick and Dani?" Her heart raced with worry.

"No, nothing like that. It's good news, but it's also not." He told her about being a finalist for the casino job.

"That's amazing, Ryan." She threw her arms around him and gave him a huge hug. "Of course they want you. Your photos are gorgeous. Why don't you look happy?"

He explained his change in travel plans and how he'd had to explain to Millie that not only was he leaving, but if he got this job, he would be gone for at least two years with little time to visit. "Honestly, it might be three years, but I couldn't bring myself to tell her that. Needless to say, she is furious with me. Oh, and worried that I'm breaking your heart."

Sheridan was proud of herself for keeping the smile on her face. This wasn't the time to admit she would miss him or worry about what might happen to her heart. No, she didn't want him to go, but she couldn't be anything but happy he had this opportunity. "I promise I'll convince her I'm fine. When do you head out?"

He brought her hands to his lips and kissed them. "A few hours. I need to run to Dani's house and pack, go to my parents' place, and say goodbye to my dad. Can I see you before I leave?"

"I'd be sorry if you didn't," she said. She was going to be sorry, anyway. He gave her a kiss and left. And for a second, she allowed herself to wallow in the unexpected punch of sadness. Apparently, it didn't matter that this break up was inevitable, or that she was going to be fine. She was sorry that their goodbye was imminent.

Two hours later, he was back. She had cinnamon rolls she hastily baked for him in a box. "You didn't have to do that."

"I wanted to." There was so much she wanted to say, but she didn't know how or if it would make things harder, so she stayed silent and kissed him, hoping that would speak for her. Hand in hand, they walked to his car as she tried to memorize everything about him. The wave in his hair, the dimple of his smile, the way he looked at her lips before he kissed her.

He leaned against the door, put his arms around her, and held her close. They kissed and lingered for as long as they could. More feelings than Sheridan had words for ran through her head — and heart — but she didn't voice any of them. She and Ryan had been barreling toward this moment from the beginning. And there was no stopping it now. The regrets she had about him leaving were small compared to the joy she'd found with him.

When he couldn't stay any longer, he gave her a soft kiss. So that's what goodbye tasted like. "I'm sorry for having to head out so abruptly. You've made coming to these weddings so much better," he said, then whispered in her ear as if it was too much to say out loud, "and that's not just about the time we spent in bed."

As they kissed one last time, Sheridan thought, *I love you*. Another feeling she kept safely to herself. All she said as she caressed his face was, "Safe travels and good luck."

As he drove away, his arm came out the window for a final wave. This time, she gave voice to her feelings. "I love you," she said, and even though no one heard it, she was glad to have said it. She wasn't sorry to have fallen for him and accepted the mixed emotions of the moment. As a cook, she understood the value of bittersweet.

The rest of the night she spent curled up under a blanket watching weepy movies and letting herself wallow. The next day, she was up bright and early, determined to focus on the café and the life she'd built. Fortunately, they were deep into tourist season and business had definitely picked up in the last few weeks, making her too busy to be distracted by thoughts of Ryan. Because as soon as she was home and alone, memories of him were never far.

He'd texted her when he got back to California and a few times over the next couple of days, but she did what she could to keep those conversations short and flirt-free. He was gone and if he got this job, he'd soon be on the other side of the world.

Which should, she hoped, give her plenty of time to get over him.

On Friday night, Sheridan got to the Seven Brothers early. Two nights alone had been enough. She needed to be with her friends. Before she ordered, Laurel sat down with two glasses of hard cider and handed her one. "What's wrong?"

Sheridan managed a small smile. She took a sip of her drink before saying, "How did you know?"

"Body language, facial expressions. I know you. Something is on your mind. Or is it someone?"

Yeah, Laurel knew her well. "Someone. I miss him." It felt good — and awful — to say it out loud, but once she started, she couldn't stop. "What Ryan and I shared was amazing, and so much more than I expected. I understand better what you and Dani have with the men in your lives. Finding someone who gets you is special. And for the first time, I can honestly say that I hope I find love again."

Laurel blinked hard and said, "Love? You love Ryan?" Her friend couldn't have looked more surprised if Sheridan announced she wanted to be an Olympic skier.

"I do." It was easy to say because it was true. "He's funny, smart, committed to his work and never made my commitments or my early mornings a problem. He's a good listener, a terrific lover." She paused as her face heated. Yeah, it was going to be a while before that didn't happen anymore. "Everything we shared was wonderful."

"But?"

"But nothing. This time was coming from the beginning. Yes, I miss him. But I'm not leaving Fable Notch, and he's off to conquer the world. Part of what I love about him is his passion for what he does. I'd never want him to change, even if it means we can't be together. Maybe it's because I knew nothing lasting could happen, I opened my heart. I can't regret that." She wasn't sure how much of this she believed and how much she was trying to convince herself it was the truth. Maybe a little of both. What she did know was she learned more about herself, what she wanted, and what she was worthy of. "You'll be happy to know I've changed my mind on one thing. Having a loving, sexual relationship *is* something I want. That's worth being happy about, don't you think?"

"It is," Laurel said, although she sounded concerned. Sheridan was okay if people didn't understand completely. She didn't either. "Given how you feel, I'm surprised you were willing to let Ryan go. Does he know how much you care?"

"I don't think so. I didn't tell him. And I didn't let him go. I just... didn't ask him to stay. There's a difference."

Wasn't there?

On Monday, Sheridan was going through her closet, deciding on what to wear, when she noticed the hanger with a certain white dress at the back. With all she'd been through in the past few months, it was time to let some things go. After doing prep work for the week at the café, she went to her house, pulled the wedding dress out and dropped it into a bag, hanger and all, then went to Tailor Thrift.

The bell jingled over the door as she walked in, and the soft scent of vanilla and cinnamon greeted her, the same scent that, according to friends — and Ryan — followed Sheridan around like a cloud. Her gaze was caught by a rack in the front with a sign that said, "You need an LBD," and she was drawn to a dress with cap sleeves, a deep neckline, and a skirt that flared out.

She pulled it from the rack and was holding it in front of her when Janelle came in from the back of the store. The designer was wearing a gorgeous light blue blouse that came to her knees, paired with leggings in a swirl of color. Sheridan suspected the shirt was from Ash's store, Fluid. The leggings were all Janelle. There was also a pencil in her ponytail.

"Ooh, you have a good eye. Classic lines, flattering silhouette. Not to mention it's a Royce." Royce was Ash's family's company. He remained on the board but stepped away to start a business that allowed him the creative freedom he wanted. And to be with Janelle. "That cut is perfect for you, and I'm pretty sure it's your size. Special occasion?"

Sheridan shook her head. "No, although I've been thinking I need to change things up. Add a bit of variety to my wardrobe." She told Janelle how she'd had to borrow something from Laurel for Eden's bachelorette party. "But my real reason for stopping by is wondering if you'd take this off my hands." She held up the bag she was carrying.

Janelle took the bag and peered inside. She looked at Sheridan, then back in the bag before grabbing the hanger and taking the dress out. She held it at arm's length and said, "I was right. You do have a good eye." She hung the dress on the rack they were standing next to and looked at it more closely. Turning to Sheridan she said, "This hasn't been worn."

Surprised by the comment, Sheridan said, "It has no tags." Sheridan had taken them off the moment she got the dress home. She'd been so foolish. Hopeful and naïve. Not any more. "How did you know?"

Janelle tipped her head from side to side. "A dress changes shape after it's been worn for any length of time, then more with each wearing. This is pristine. And lovely. Bias cut for flow, tasteful use of embellishments. This would look good on a lot of body types." Sheridan waited for Janelle to ask the obvious question. She should have known better. "Wanna trade?"

"Trade?"

"My black dress for your white one," Janelle said. Before Sheridan could answer, Janelle shooed her toward the dressing room. "Go, try it on. Let me see if it fits as well as I think it will. Then you can decide."

She did as Janelle said — as everyone, Sheridan assumed, did. Standing in the dressing room, she held the dress in front of her, unsure how it would look — or if she'd ever have a use for it — then realized if she didn't do as Janelle said, the woman might come in and undress her. She had a moment to wish she were wearing a better bra before taking off her casual clothes and zipped herself into the dress.

The transformation was immediate. When she stepped out and stood in front of the three-way mirror, she couldn't stop herself from twirling. The skirt flared around her knees, and she giggled unexpectedly. As her eyebrows went up in surprise at her own reaction, she covered her mouth with her hand. Meeting Janelle's eyes in the reflection, they both burst out laughing. "Does this happen a lot here?"

"People giggling in delight when they look in the mirror? As often as I can make it happen." Janelle gave a happy sigh. "I love when fashion and an unexpected choice takes a person by surprise. And I'm glad you had that reaction, because if you weren't sure, I was going to call over reinforcements to make sure you took the dress."

"It's not like anything I've ever worn. Which makes me wonder why I've never worn anything like it." She turned back to her reflection. She felt feminine. Beautiful. It was too bad Ryan would never see her in it. She had a feeling he'd appreciate it. But more importantly, she appreciated it. Her relationship with Ryan might have been short term, but the new knowledge and confidence she had in herself? That was going to last.

She didn't know how long she stood looking at herself before Janelle said, "So, what do you think?"

Still looking at her reflection, Sheridan said, "Wrap it up."

Chapter Thirty-One

Malta was gorgeous. Everything a tiny island destination should be. The Canillo Group had put Ryan up in a luxury hotel, although not one of theirs since that one wouldn't be open for another several months. The suite had more square footage than Sheridan's house. The food was exquisite, the views spectacular, the weather stunning. Every picture he took could be a postcard.

And after three days, he was ready to leave.

The interviews on his first day with the top executives had gone well. He liked the people involved in the project, the variety of the work they needed him to do — because every hotel was going to have unique features that needed to be highlighted — and how much creativity and freedom they were willing to give him.

Not to mention the first discussion of salary. January was right — this was the golden ticket. From what they were discussing, he'd make more than double his best year as a freelancer each year of the contract. Yes, he'd have to refer out his currently scheduled jobs to other photographers because they wanted him to start almost immediately, but it would be worth it.

And when he had the opportunity to work and show them what he could do, it was fantastic. The people on his team were attentive and knowledgeable. It was easy to get whatever he needed as soon as he needed it, and they went out of their way to anticipate what he might require.

But when he was back in his room for the night, memories kept slipping into his head. Try as he might, he couldn't stop his thoughts from drifting to Fable Notch. And the six-hour time difference between where he was and the east coast of the United States made it nearly impossible to do more than share a few texts and pictures back and forth.

His group text with his brothers got a lot of use. He sent images of beaches and cathedrals and received ones of dogs, mountains, and several from Nick and Dani on their honeymoon. Ironically, they were the closest to him geographically since their honeymoon had them in Paris for a week, followed by a seven-day Adriatic Sea cruise.

Fuck, he missed them all.

Part of it might be the abrupt way he'd had to leave. He'd been expecting to have another few days. More time with his folks, his brothers, and Sheridan, who he was hesitant to text. Being pulled away so suddenly had been rough on them all. He was going to have to go back this Christmas to make it up to his mother.

Once he thought of it, he decided it was the perfect solution. He'd fly out, spend the week from Christmas through New Year's with everyone, and use that time for the goodbyes that would help him get his focus back on what he wanted. Because this job was everything he'd ever wanted.

When he had his final meeting with the executives, he briefed them on what he'd done and spoke to them more about what he could do for their company. They loved his way of making viewers feel connected. The shots he liked best were their favorites as well, which told him that not only did they like his vision, but he'd be able to meet — exceed — their expectations.

He left several days later, proud of what he'd done. And as he boarded the plane for the nearly day long flights home, he knew the job was his.

Two days later, still not quite over the jet lag, he woke to a text from January. *Call. Now.*

She was always so effusive in her communication. Ryan decided on coffee first. Talking to January before he had any caffeine was not a good idea.

He padded barefoot to his kitchen and got a pot going. When he was halfway through his first cup, he checked the message again and saw January had sent it at six-thirty in the morning. Trying to decide if he'd had enough coffee to handle whatever she was about to tell him, he topped off the one he had and called her back.

"What took you so long?" she asked. He couldn't tell from her tone what her mood was other than impatient, which was how she sounded most of the time.

"Needed coffee. What's up?"

"You are." He didn't respond because the coffee hadn't kicked in, and it wasn't quite true. "You got it."

"That's nice," he said, not awake enough to process what she was saying.

There was an exasperated sigh on the other end. "The Canillo job. It's yours. They want you."

"Oh," he said. And then the news fully hit him. "Holy shit!"

"Exactly. You are going to be booked solid for nearly three years from what I can see in the initial contract, and after you'll be able to write your own ticket. Congratulations. You've made us both very happy." And by happy, she meant rich. This deal was lucrative for them both.

His head was reeling, trying to take in what all of this meant. Booked solid. For years.

He hadn't noticed he'd taken the phone away from his ear until he heard January's voice calling him and sounding far away. Picking it back up, he said, "Sorry. I'm still stunned. But thank you."

"You are more than welcome. I'll be getting the contracts later today or early tomorrow, so watch your email. Read them over, decide where you want to negotiate for more, and let me know."

"More? The offer isn't good?" That didn't sound like what he'd heard.

"Oh, it's great, but negotiating is always a good idea. Tells the client there are things they haven't considered and reminds them of how valuable you are. See if you want a bigger travel allowance, or more money to hire assistants. A driver to get you to wherever you need to be so you don't need to find your way around China. Ooh — how about a translator? That could be cool."

He tried to imagine the things she was suggesting. He'd stepped into another level of employment. "I'll take a look."

"Great, but don't take too long."

He texted the news to his brothers and Sheridan, who sent words of congratulations, 'knew you'd do it', and champagne and party face emojis. He called his folks, who were... pleased. "I know this is what you wanted, and I'm proud of you," Millie said. He accepted that was the best they could do. They could be happy for him and upset about the circumstances.

The contract arrived later that afternoon. It was huge. His eyes were bleary by the time he'd finished going through the pages, but one thing was clear. They needed him to start almost immediately, and it didn't look like he would be home for holidays any time soon. While he would have time off until they got close to the opening of the sites, once he signed the contract, his time would be theirs to dictate as long as he was working for them.

It was a lot to take in.

Feeling overwhelmed by what this commitment would mean, he closed the file with the contract and opened up the folders with the pictures from the weddings. He was still waiting for Theo and Cole to get back to him with the ones they wanted to put in an album so he could do additional editing on them. Instead, he reviewed the images to send to Nick and Dani so they'd have them when they got home from their trip.

Everything from their event was still in one folder, the wedding, as well as the photos people had sent to him from the events he'd missed, as well as the ones he'd done the day he wandered around town while Sheridan was working.

As he organized them, wave after wave of emotion hit him. He didn't realize how much of their lives he'd captured in those few days.

Theo and Nick laughing at something one of them said.

Cole and Dean talking, completely unaware of people around them, looking serious and connected.

His dad handing a plant to his mom, grown in the greenhouse he'd built for her.

He thought about what the Canillo executives had said — he had a knack for making things feel homey. But in this case, that wasn't necessary because it *was* home. Every shot reflected how he felt about Fable Notch and the people. He'd loved it there. The time with his brothers and their wives. Getting to see his parents whenever he wanted. Discovering new places, visiting familiar ones.

And over and over, picture after picture of Sheridan.

Working in the kitchen with Wesley at her side, hugging Dani and Laurel and playing with Otis. He missed her. Her smile, her voice, the scent of her skin next to him in the morning as he woke.

As he scrolled through the images, he noticed something missing. Him.

Other than the few Devon took during the ceremonies and an occasional formal shot, he was nowhere to be seen.

Then he came to the ones Sheridan had taken of him and his brothers. And then the ones Dani had taken of him with Sheridan. There was the first one of the two of them facing the camera, and Dani had been right. He looked stiff. He wasn't used to being the one in the pictures. No, he was the one who stood on the outside so everyone could see what he saw.

Then he scrolled to the next shot, the one with them facing each other. *There's a time and place for stiff, Sugar,* she'd said. God, she made him laugh. Remembering the moment, he smiled at the image of them looking at each other with....

Was that love?

He blinked hard, as if that could change what was there.

If anyone knew how much truth a picture could show, it was him, and Ryan couldn't ignore what he hadn't let himself focus on since the call that sent him halfway around the world.

He was in love with Sheridan.

And from what he could see, she felt the same way. Or at least, he hoped she did. He could be wrong. She'd let him go without any suggestion of continuing their relationship. She'd been thrilled for him when he told her the news about the Malta trip. And she didn't seem to have any regrets or concerns about him leaving.

But she wasn't the type of person who would hold someone back from their dreams. She, like him, wanted her choices to be accepted and wasn't going to allow anyone to take that from her.

You can write your own ticket, January said, about getting this job. And he could. But what hit him was understanding he could do that all along.

And he knew what he wanted.

He shut his laptop and groaned, glad that there was no one to see him. Oh, they were all going to laugh so much. The "I told-you-so's" were going to be deafening.

And every one of them would be worth it.

Chapter Thirty-Two

The days after Ryan left had been more of a roller-coaster than Sheridan expected, but for the first time, she didn't mind the ups and downs. Yes, there was sadness when someone asked about him, but that would stop as time went on. She enjoyed every thought of him and even had a good conversation with Millie. She was glad they hadn't had to tell Millie she and Ryan had been pretending, because while that may have been how it started, how it ended was real.

And special.

Laurel checked in, offering comfort and understanding which Sheridan appreciated, and when Dani came back from her honeymoon, they double teamed her, certain she was holding back because she didn't want them to worry. They definitely didn't believe the "I'm fine's" she offered, but as the days went on and there were no long crying gags or carb fests, they accepted that while she had fallen in love, she was managing.

That didn't mean there weren't times when she missed him. Times when she wanted to text him, send a picture, hear his voice. She held off from reaching out because it wouldn't do any good to keep the strings of connection. Not that she didn't want those on lonely nights where she wished he were in bed with her. She missed feeling him near, touching him, being touched. But she accepted the ache as a sign that she'd loved someone, and that was a good thing. And if getting over him was going to take time, at least time was something she had plenty of.

Almost three weeks after Ryan left, Sheridan stepped out of the café as a breeze blew in from the mountains, making her shiver. It might only be October, but she'd soon need more than a light jacket. Walking home, she was lost in thoughts of soups and new breads she wanted to try and didn't see the extra car in her driveway until she was almost at her door.

Then she saw the man leaning against the back bumper and froze.

When she locked eyes with Ryan, she couldn't stop her heart from leaping. He pushed off his car and ran the few remaining steps between them. When he got to her, he picked her up and swung her around, exactly as she'd once wondered if he'd do on the day she agreed to be his fake date. They were kissing before her feet were back on the ground. And, oh, how she'd missed the feeling of his mouth on hers. The way the tingles started in her stomach and radiated through her body.

When they stopped to catch their breath, Sheridan asked, "Why didn't you tell me you were coming? How long are you staying?"

"Interesting questions, but explanations later," he said cryptically. "Actions now. I missed you."

"I missed you too," she said, agreeing that any explanation could wait because the answers didn't matter. He was here now, and she was going to enjoy it.

Apparently, he felt the same way, because when they got to her bedroom, for the first time, they undressed each other slowly, tenderly. He pulled her hair out of its bun and ran fingers through her curls. She undid the buttons on his shirt before letting him pull her sweater over her head. As clothes were removed, she stroked every muscle in his arms, chest, and abdomen. He caressed her jaw, collarbone, and breasts. He gently sucked her nipples. She teased the shell of his ear, raked her nails down his back.

And they never stopped kissing. She thought her memories of how he felt were vivid, but they were nothing compared to the reality of him. She came alive under his touch and relished every sigh and moan that neither of them could control.

"Sheridan," he said, his voice a raspy whisper. "I've missed touching you, tasting you."

"I'm here," she said. "Take me."

Placing her in the center of the bed, he reached for her pussy as she wrapped her fingers around his cock. And as their need grew, they moved carefully, as if not wanting to rush through this moment. If this was to be her last time with him, she would make it last.

She spread her legs, and he settled between them. He kissed and nibbled his way down her body, licking at her belly button, grabbing her hips. When he got to her pussy, he used the flat of his tongue to lave her from bottom to top. She'd been wet from the moment he kissed her, but now a flood released. She heard him say,

"Fuck, yes," as her desire surged. His tongue continued to increase her pleasure. She ran her hands through his hair, pulling him to her as he pointed his tongue and slid first one, then two fingers inside her.

And slow became impossible.

She'd missed him too much, needed him too much. Her climax started, and she called out his name. "I can't... I'm going to... I have to... I want...."

As his fingers continued to please her, he said, "I want, too. Come for me, Sheridan."

It was like glass shattering and fireworks exploding and every perfect taste. She screamed, she clawed at the sheets, she tugged at his hair. She felt worshipped, adored. In love.

And he didn't stop. She thought she'd reached her peak, but he brought her to another that left her near tears with the overwhelming flood of bliss and love.

"I need you," she said when she could finally speak, and he kissed his way up her body, making her shiver. He found his pants, took out a condom, and was inside her before her breathing slowed. Her hips rose to meet his thrusts, taking him fully into her. Grabbing his ass, she pulled him closer, wanting him as deep as possible.

"Perfect," he said as they moved together. "You feel perfect. We feel..." He cried out as she tightened her pussy around him, wanting him as carried away as she had been. Hoping to give him as much pleasure as he'd given her, she wrapped her legs around him and reached around her thigh so she could caress his balls as he thrust into her. "Oh God," he growled and took her mouth in a punishing kiss. She loved his intensity, knowing he couldn't get enough of her.

He pulled out as far as he could and held himself there. She swiveled her hips, teasing him as he teased her, and he thrust back in deeply. Soon they moved in a pounding, relentless rhythm that had his climax crashing through him and left them both screaming and panting.

He collapsed on top of her, and she relished the weight of him, the confirmation that he was truly with her. "I can't believe you're here. That I'm not dreaming."

"You're not dreaming," he said and kissed her. Her lips felt swollen. All of her was going to be wonderfully sore in the morning. "I couldn't stay away."

"I'm glad." She was going to pay with a rebroken heart when he left again — and maybe this time she would need that carb fest — but she couldn't bring herself to care.

Eventually, Ryan rolled off of her, removed the condom, and pulled Sheridan into his arms. As they lay there, he caressed her back, loving how they were both sweaty and sated. He took a deep breath, beyond happy to take in the scent he'd missed so much since leaving.

It had taken three long days of driving to get here and was worth every minute. He sat up a bit, gazing at the woman next to him, who looked more than a little satisfied. Leaning over, he kissed her, loving the knowledge that if she felt the way he did, he could do this whenever he wanted. "God, it's good to be here," he said.

She brushed his hair from his forehead and said, "Not to ruin this wonderful dream with reality, but how long do I get to see you for? And are we telling anyone else you're in town, or will this be like when you came when I was sick?"

"I guess you don't follow me on Instagram," he said.

She looked puzzled. "Other than when we went viral, I never think to look at it. Why?"

"Because if you did, you would have seen I've been driving across the country for the last several days."

She sat up suddenly, and he liked that she didn't cover herself with the blanket. "You *drove* out here? Why?"

"It was the easiest way to get here with everything I own. Remember? It all fits in my car." It was time to say it out loud to the person he most wanted to tell. "I'm moving back."

She stared at him, surprise written on her features, but she didn't object, which he took as a good sign. "What about the Canillo job?"

"I couldn't accept it. The way the contract was written, I was looking at three years of being at their beck and call, maybe more. Almost no time for myself and forget visiting for holidays or other special occasions. I hated not knowing when I'd be able to hang out with Nick or Theo or Cole. I thought about what it would be like to hear my brothers were starting families and know I wouldn't see my nieces or nephews until they were walking and talking. I... couldn't do it. And I know I'm never going to hear the end of it, but I missed my parents. It was great to see them whenever I wanted."

"But this job is a huge opportunity. You said so yourself. All the doors it would have opened." He loved how worried she was for him.

"And it's still going to open some of them." Now that he knew what he wanted, and he was willing to do what it took to have it. "January told me to negotiate, so I did. I convinced them they would get more work from two photographers working together. That way, neither of us would get burned out, and we'd be able to support each other creatively. My agent wasn't happy about the reduced fee, but I told her it was that or I was turning it down completely."

She shook her head but smiled. "I can't believe it."

He had a feeling he was going to be hearing that a lot. "I've been my own boss for too long to completely turn over my professional life to someone else for such a long period. Besides, Ash wants me to do some work for Fluid, which I think will be fun. And I missed you. I missed you so very much, Sheridan."

She kissed him. "I missed you, too. And I feel foolish for asking this because I'm so happy, but are you sure?"

"Very." Now he needed her to believe it. "When I made it to the final round of the job, you didn't tell me not to go for it."

He loved that she looked surprised. "I'd never do that."

"You didn't tell me not to leave."

"I always accepted you would."

"That's the word — that's the feeling — that's made all the difference. Accepted." He caressed her face. "One of the reasons I never wanted to move back was because I believed I couldn't be myself here. Like I told you, I was always someone's son or someone's brother. But there were times when I was here that I got to be me. And it started with you." It was time to take that last step. "Do you love me, Sheridan?"

For a moment, she was silent. *Please*, he prayed silently, *don't let me be wrong.* "I do."

A knot in his chest he didn't know was there loosened, and he took her hands in his. "Even though I travel a lot, and am going to make a shit ton of mistakes because I'm new at this serious relationship thing, *and* have a lot of meddling family members?"

"Well, not compared to Laurel," she said with a chuckle. "But yes, even though."

"Do you want me to change?"

"Of course not." That she answered quickly and, if was possible, his heart opened more. "I like who you are, how you follow your passion, how you see the world."

"That's what I thought." He cupped her cheek in his hand, and she tipped her head to press into his palm. "I love you, too."

"Even though I haven't had many relationships at all, need to wake up before the crack of dawn, and be in bed early?"

"Even though. And there's nothing wrong with being in bed early." He wiggled his eyebrows.

Her eyes filled with tears. Not the response he wanted. "I'm afraid," she said, and he heard the honesty in her voice. "What if this doesn't work? Being here? Being with me? What if you feel trapped?"

"That's one of the many things I love about you. You'd never try to trap me. I know that." Before she could offer another objection, he said, "Maybe this will help. You're not the whole reason I'm moving back. These last few months, spending time with my brothers, my parents, and seeing old friends, made me realize all the things I love about this place. The support, the love. Not to mention the ability to get wherever I want in a few minutes — and always find parking." She smiled. "I know everyone thinks I left all those years ago without giving it a second thought, but it wasn't as easy as it looked. I was homesick a lot that first year, and when my dad had his heart attack, being on the other side of the country when I got the news was hell."

"But even that didn't make you move back," she reminded him.

"No, I hadn't grown up enough. I still needed to see myself as my own man. And my brothers weren't here, which makes a difference."

"So, you're not moving back for love." Worry had turned to teasing. Good.

"Not *just* for love." He kissed the tip of her nose. "But you're my gooey center. Everything else around it is wonderful, but it wouldn't be half as good without you." He pulled back and ran his hand through his hair. "But I'm making some pretty big assumptions. I should ask you if you want me around, if you're willing to see where this can go and what it can be for us both."

"You'd back off if I said I didn't want more than what we've already had?"

"I would. I might still ask you out and hope you'd come around, but if it's not what you want, I'll accept that."

"We haven't had a proper first date, have we?" she said with a smile he'd never tire of seeing.

"No, and my mother raised me to be a gentleman, so after I ravage you a few more times, and we tell everyone our plans, I'd be honored if you'd go out with me. I love you."

He didn't want to think of how his mother was going to react when he told her the news, but for now, he was going to lie here and enjoy being in the arms of the woman he adored.

"I love you, too," she said, kissing him softly. "Welcome home."

Epilogue

Seven months later

The last time Ryan celebrated Mother's Day with his family, he'd been in high school. Part of him still couldn't believe he was sitting in his parents' house with his brothers and their wives. Five couples, all living in Fable Notch. Not so long ago, no one in this room would have imagined an ending like this.

Because of the day, Sunday dinner had been changed to Sunday brunch. His "gift" to Millie was the official announcement that he and Sheridan were engaged. He'd proposed the night before, and he couldn't help but notice the diamond on her hand every time it caught the light. The proposal hadn't surprised her — it had been clear for a while this was where their relationship was headed — but the two rings were.

"What's this?" she'd asked when he presented her with a second box from Prince's Jewelers.

"You'll have to look to find out." He was jumping inside. He was glad she'd loved the traditional solitaire he'd chosen, but this one was special.

The hinge on the little black velvet box squeaked as she opened it. Inside was a slender gold band with a knot in the center. Nothing fancy, and that was the intention. "It's lovely, but I'm confused." He could see that from the two lines between her eyes.

"You work with your hands and with food all day long. I didn't want you to have to keep taking your ring off or worrying about misplacing it. This is for when you're at the café. I couldn't get something that looked like a cinnamon roll, so I chose a love knot instead." She was staring at the box again, her hand at her lips, this time her expression unreadable. Had he made a mistake? "Do you like it?"

She closed the box and threw herself into his arms. He caught her and held her tightly. "I adore it. And you. I can't believe you'd think of something like this." She'd kissed him passionately, and he'd carried upstairs to bed where they... celebrated all night long.

Getting up this morning for brunch hadn't been easy, but being with everyone was worth it. His mother had made more food than necessary, of course, and they'd be bringing home their usual leftovers.

When everyone was in the living room together – Ryan was almost surprised there was room for everyone, but he suspected that was why his parents had gotten the new larger sofa – Theo said, "Eden and I have a small gift for you, Mom."

"I told you, no gifts," Millie said with a wave of her hand.

"Yeah, way to make the rest of us look bad," Nick said.

Millie looked at all of them as she said, "My best gift is all of you here." Ryan knew she meant it. She'd been as shocked as anyone when he'd changed his work commitments and told her he was staying. He'd been enjoying settling back into life in Fable Notch, although he was still traveling regularly. Coming home to Sheridan was everything he'd hoped it would be. And more.

He put an arm around her and pulled her closer as Eden gave Millie a thin box with a bow on it. Theo was right. It was small. Ryan couldn't imagine what was inside. Millie took off the top, moved the tissue paper aside, and stared.

And then her eyes welled with tears that quickly spilled over.

"What the hell, Theo?" Cole said, sitting forward, looking anxious.

Millie pulled out the gift and showed it to everyone. A tiny bib with "I love my grandma" in yellow stitching. There was a quiet beat before a cacophony burst around them as everyone took in the news and responded.

"When did you find out?"

"I can't believe you didn't tell anyone?"

"How are you feeling?"

"This is wonderful."

"When are you due?"

Questions and congratulations rang out. With a hand on her stomach, Eden answered, "Thank you. I'm feeling pretty good. Morning sickness is almost gone. We're due in October."

Ryan waited his turn to hug his brother and sister-in-law, then returned to the couch to sit with Sheridan and watch his mother fawn over Eden. This was why he'd changed his life. To not miss moments like this. To share in the joy – and challenges – with his family.

To be there for the people he loved. This news was the icing on a perfect day, and as he kissed his future wife, Ryan reveled in the knowledge that this was only the beginning.

To find out about Elena's new releases, receive updates and fun freebies, join her newsletter at https://bit.ly/NewsFromElena

Which Fable Notch Books have you missed?

Once More With You (Eden and Theo)
Meant To Be His (Dani and Nick)
This Time for Us (Mia and Cole)
Can't Let You Go (Janelle and Ashton)
Bring Back Her Heart (Laurel and Hunter)
What You Wish For (Casey and Derek)
Just Right For Him (Sheridan and Ryan)

Acknowledgements

I cannot believe we have arrived at the final book in this Fable Notch series. It has been the most incredible experience writing these characters, seeing their love and passion come to life on the page and then sharing them with you. With every book, these people and their town become more real to me. Many thanks to everyone who has told me they wish they could visit.

I hope you found Sheridan's identification as demisexual believable and understandable. This wasn't done as a convenient plot device (I knew she identified this way several books ago), but it does play into her reasons for accepting Ryan's fake-dating proposal. I am grateful to my friends who identify as demi and were willing to give me feedback and share their challenges. In addition, the wonderful book *Ace Voices: What it Means to be Asexual, Aromantic, Demi or Grey-Ace* by Eris Young was a tremendous help. Their thoughtful work allowed me to better understand this spectrum, and the challenges faced by people who identify this way. I think knowing who we are, what we want and what we don't want—and being able to express that—is incredibly important. I hope you can always be you.

Writing is a roller coaster of a profession. One week the words and ideas flow and then... things will slow or stop. No warning, no understanding. Without the other writers in my life, it would be beyond difficult to keep going. I must send love to authors Sara Marks, Lisa Bouchard, and Laura Brown. Our weekly calls help me stay grounded, focused, and buckled in for the ride. To the Sunday Shenanigans – Paula, Misty, Win and Delia – thank you for the magic we create together. To be able to be myself, no matter how that looks, and to be there for you has been the most amazing gift. To the BFA Office Writers – thank you for being there, day in and day out. I love our top of the hour breaks, our NSFW conversations, and everyone's pets. I am a better and more consistent writer because of you. I have learned to trust my process and my voice because of the time we spend together.

To my husband and sons, boundless gratitude for believing in me and these books. Your encouragement, love, compassion and humor mean everything. Going after our dreams is rarely easy, but always worthwhile. Thank you for supporting me and mine. It is my pleasure to be there for yours.

And dearest reader, thank you for being on this journey with me. Every email, review, and social media comment reminds me that when I put these stories out into the world, someone is there to receive them. Don't worry – there are more Fable Notch stories to come.

Mugs up!

About the Author

Elena Markem writes emotionally rich contemporary romances about dreams, love, and taking a chance on both. Her stories reflect her belief that life is about the passions we pursue, the people who support us along the way, and never giving up on what we want.

She can't start work without coffee, fall asleep without reading, or listen to Broadway musicals without singing along (badly). She loves time to spend with her husband and sons, as well as weekends with girlfriends, rom-com and old movies, and anything that sparkles.

Feel free to join her on her ongoing quest for the perfect planner, the best diner breakfasts, and the gooiest chocolate chip cookies. In the meantime, she hopes you'll enjoy spending time in her sexy books where you'll find strong heroines, heroes who find them irresistible, and at least one scene involving comfort food.

Stay in touch by signing up for her newsletter at www.elenamarkem.com to get sneak peaks and free stories or follow her on Facebook, Instagram and Tiktok!

Made in the USA
Middletown, DE
13 April 2025

74042890R00217